THE SECRETARY

Also by **Deborah Lawrenson**:

Hot Gossip
Idol Chatter
The Moonbathers
The Art of Falling
Songs of Blue and Gold
The Lantern
The Sea Garden
300 Days of Sun

As Serena Kent (with Robert Rees)

Death in Provence
Death in Avignon

THE
SECRETARY

Deborah Lawrenson

Deborah Lawrenson

The
Book
Guild

First published in Great Britain in 2025 by
The Book Guild Ltd
Unit E2 Airfield Business Park,
Harrison Road, Market Harborough,
Leicestershire. LE16 7UL
Tel: 0116 2792299
www.bookguild.co.uk
Email: info@bookguild.co.uk
X: @bookguild

The manufacturer's authorised representative in the EU for product safety is Authorised
Rep Compliance Ltd,
71 Lower Baggot Street, Dublin D02 P593 Ireland (www.arccompliance.com)

This work is entirely fictitious and bears no resemblance to any persons living or dead.

Typeset in 10.5pt Adobe Garamond Pro

Printed and bound by CPI Group (UK) Ltd, Croydon, CR0 4YY

ISBN 978 1835741 436

British Library Cataloguing in Publication Data.
A catalogue record for this book is available from the British Library.

Secretary (n.)

late 14c., *secretarie*, "person entrusted with secrets or private and confidential matters" (obsolete); from Medieval Latin *secretarius*, noun use of an adjective meaning "private, secret, pertaining to private or secret matters".

LIST OF CHARACTERS

The British Embassy, Moscow

Lois Vale, personal assistant to the Minister, under deep MI6 special operations cover

Sonia Capell, a general office secretary

Nan Trusloe, a senior MI6 personal assistant

Roger Waller, the Minister, second in command to the Ambassador

Sir Duncan Mountbeech, the Ambassador

Hugh Burville, Head of Chancery

Tony Fielding, Head of MI6 station

Ellis Wachorne, MI6 officer, nominally political Third Secretary

Flora Wachorne, his wife

John Mowberry, a political Second Secretary, runs a weekly poker night

Bill Stoneley, academic Sovietologist and MI6 political researcher

Philip Vere Sinclair, a Second Secretary

John Linton, fast-tracked recent Oxford graduate, Private Secretary to the Ambassador

Eric, a cypher clerk

Rory Kendalmoor, administrative Third Secretary

Trudy, Frances, Valerie, Frank, Alistair, Eileen, Ann: junior administrative staff

Vera, KGB maid at Lois and Sonia's apartment

Kit Woodward, Administration Officer

Margaret Woodward, his wife

Goodrich, security officer

Beyond the embassy

Johann Dreschler, a German news journalist and MI6 "occasional"

Boyd Givens, diplomat at the Canadian Embassy, boyfriend of Sonia

Colonel Avrely Zhigunov (codename *Alexei*), a senior officer in the GRU, Soviet military intelligence

Nayland, a scientific expert sent to Moscow by the CIA

Pal, a veteran FBI counter-espionage agent, real name James Ingssen

Miss Harcourt, senior MI6 officer in London (special operations branch)

Mr Robinson, MI6 (special operations branch), organiser of Lois's deep cover mission

Mr Ellingwood, MI6 officer (special operations branch)

Real-life characters

Guy Burgess, British diplomat and Soviet agent, defected to Moscow in 1951

Donald Maclean, British diplomat and Soviet agent, defected to Moscow in 1951

Kim Philby (Russian codename *Sonny*), high-ranking MI6 officer and double agent for the Soviet Union, defected to Moscow in 1963

Yuri Modin, KGB agent, controller of Burgess, Maclean and Philby in London

John Vassall, clerical officer to the staff of the Naval Attaché at the British embassy in Moscow, 1952–54, arrested in London in 1962 and found guilty of treason

Prologue

The flame doesn't catch. She strikes another match. Ridiculously, her hand is trembling. Ordinarily, the paper and photographs should burn quickly enough. The negatives she snipped into fine shards ought to bubble and melt. But the more there is at stake, the longer it always seems to take to dispose of the evidence.

It wasn't always the case but these days the smoky sulphurous burst from spent matches signifies subterfuge and danger. It's the terror of discovery, of knowing she is on her own and has been since the beginning.

The front door down the hall rattles, breaking the too-loud silence. In the kitchen, leaning over the small, rusting tobacco tin, she blows on the flames, urging them on: ashes to ashes! Listens. It was nothing, something posted through the letter flap. She fumbles to light a cigarette. Throws in that match, too.

It can't be changed now. She is the one who has been changed. She has seen into the dark heart of a country where good people are destroyed for knowing the truth, where history is deleted and rewritten, and the more you know, the more risk you face. Not least from your own side. He's long gone now, but his warning rings in her head. 'We make mistakes not because we cannot see the truth but because we do not want to believe it.'

The scent of spent matches. The tiny fire.

This is truly a cold, cold place.

1

Wednesday, January 1, 1958

An auspicious year, I hope – it will bring my thirtieth birthday.

Filthy rain today. Went up to Charing Cross in the rain to meet Peter and had lunch at Piccadilly. An unsettling farewell and a final briefing at the Office. Then the business of packing again: was just getting down to it when Daph and Mrs Weston came most unexpectedly. It was certainly jolly decent of them to come. Then more panic when my clothes just wouldn't go in four cases; had to borrow my old black one back from Mum. Then a quick bath, and Ralph came to say goodbye – still raining – and we all went to bed early. Me thinking all the while, What am I doing going to Russia? and, Now I really must read War and Peace.

The woman behind the samovar was watching her.

Lois felt the stare skewer her back. Despite the intimidation, she stood a while longer in the train corridor and peered out through steamed-up windows. A desolate snow-covered landscape stretched to infinity; impossible to tell where iced grey wilderness ended and leaden clouds began. A cluster of rickety black shacks burst into view. Bent figures: women shovelling by the track, men hacking wood. A horse pulling a sledge. Then gone.

The Helsinki-Moscow express plunged on, faster now through this harsh monochrome world. Lois had a whole compartment with two sleeping berths to herself, a palace on wheels in comparison to those poor wooden shacks. The hammer and sickle insignia was embroidered on each headrest. Rocked through the intense black night of the East European Plain, she had slept surprisingly well. The heating vent choked up warm stuffiness, oppressive but better than being cold. She'd worried about that and in consequence was wearing rather too many layers. No restaurant car for breakfast, though, only tea from the far end of the carriage, where this stony-faced woman guarded a bubbling samovar set over charcoal and perhaps also the security of Mother Russia from dangerous foreigners like Lois.

Lois managed to buy her tea using sign language and a few small coins. A frugal breakfast indeed.

The man followed her as she returned to her compartment. She passed him in the corridor as he opened the door two away from hers in the carriage: a bulky individual in a black felt homburg hat pulled down low over his brow. Instead of turning to go to the samovar, he closed in behind her. He was so close he was able to stick his foot in the entrance to her compartment and push his way in. The manoeuvre was accomplished with shocking swiftness. No time to protest or cry out. He slid the door shut behind him, turned and stood stock-still, blocking her exit.

He was of medium build, in his worn-down late forties, but he possessed a quality of active stillness that left her in no doubt he would be capable of overpowering her quickly and silently. Steel-grey eyes locked hers.

'You will forgive if I not introduce myself,' he said in English. 'I am sure you understand why this not possible.'

His coat had curling lapels and an uneven hem. It looked as if it had been passed on several times through some charitable institution. Broad shoulders under the poor rough coat. A strong square chin. He was close enough for her to tell he had shaved carefully despite the jolting of the train. He did not release the steel gaze.

Lois waited, bluffing a worldly confidence she did not feel by offering no response. Travelling alone, the train from the Russian border to Moscow was the part of the journey when she was most exposed. She was prepared and vigilant, yet the reality of her defencelessness was a shock.

'I know who you are. Of course.'

It was a cultured voice, the English accent quite good but the cadences strangely musical. Russian, almost certainly. If anything, he was respectful. Regretful, even. Suddenly, the set of his features tightened, hinting at urgency. He went over to the table by the window and gestured for her to sit opposite. He did not remove the hat or coat, but the sense of menace eased.

'Please… forgive. Drink tea. You not have to speak if you do not want. For me, I must take chance to speak. There will be few opportunities in Moscow. Perhaps we meet, but we will not be able to converse frankly. I want you to know that nothing is what it seems. Very important that you know this, think about it carefully.'

Lois straightened her back. Hid her fear. Took a sip of tea that scalded her tongue.

'You know what "*pravda*" means, Miss Vale?'

She nodded.

'Truth. Official truth. And we must pretend to believe it. But that is difference between us. You are certain you can believe your press and your government. But you are wrong.'

She broke her silence. 'Of course we can.'

Uncomfortable heat rose, from the vent, from the extra cardigan and the hot tea. She felt anxiety simmer up and sheen her face and neck.

He shook his head slowly. 'No. Most terrible deception practised by enemy who pretend to be on your side.'

Through the weeping window the sky was turning an angry grey-ochre, threatening a heavy snowfall.

'We face same enemy. Most people in the West do not know it. Not yet. But you will see. In Moscow you will see.'

'I wish you would tell me what it is you want,' said Loïs, suddenly more impatient than scared, sensing some terrible need in him. Perhaps he would ask her to take a letter to a house or go to meet someone. Something that would compromise her right from the start. Ridiculous. As if she would fall for that.

A smile trespassed on his lips, then vanished like a figure in darkness. 'I want you remember my face. And to know that I am your friend. I can help you.'

He stared intently at her, as if watching for every reaction to what he was saying. The rails clattered and the carriage swayed.

'Burgess and Maclean now with us in Moscow. But the British know they are not the only traitors who worked for us. They look for more, but they do not find them.'

Lois remained very still, as expressionless as possible. The interior of the compartment took on a surreal quality. Beyond the misty window a black-and-white film of frozen wastes was playing.

The Russian stood up, nodded with a touch to the brim of his hat. A small gesture of respect. 'We will meet again, I hope. If I can…' But he did not finish. He slid the door open far enough to check the corridor, then stepped out quickly and quietly.

The rest of the sentence hung in the air. He had given no name, any name, by which she might know him.

Lois closed her eyes, running through exactly what he had said, pinning down the words. Fixing his face in her mind, concentrating to summon other images. Had she seen

4

him before, from a distance? She was almost sure of it. Not completely sure because she had been focused at the time on protecting her luggage from ransacking officials at the customs shed across the Russian border at Vyborg after having her passport stamped. A man in a homburg hat who ducked inside the doorway out of the wind to strike a match and have a smoke.

When she was sure she had it all straight, she made a few squiggles on a page at the back of her diary, using a personal version of the shorthand she used at work. She couldn't help feeling she had failed at some task while not knowing what that was. Had she blown the chance to make a contact? Or deflected an early attempt to compromise her? Some kind of test, then. Which kind, only time would tell. She lit a cigarette and leant back, exhaling deeply.

At Moscow central station, two women from the embassy were there to meet her. It was early afternoon and, judging from their attire, they had come straight from the standard Saturday morning at the office.

'Sonia Capell,' said one, holding out her hand. Petite, doll-like prettiness. Carefully made-up, just shy of too much. Neat navy suit under the open fur coat. 'You'll be sharing with me.'

'Nan Trusloe,' said the other. Older, stouter and plainer. No cosmetic camouflage of a red nose and cheeks. Tortoiseshell spectacle frames, round. Frizzy brown hair escaping from the mannish fur hat with ear flaps. Mud-green woollen suit. Tweedy country voice. 'How was your journey?'

Lois smiled. 'Not too bad at all.' Her seventh veil, that smile. It could be complicit and waiting for its recipient to catch on; it could be a signal that she was guarding her own thoughts. She had been told all this by others over the years who recognised it.

'All righty. Let's get you to your port in the storm, then!' Nan gestured to a driver who came over to direct the porter and between them they loaded her luggage into a large car.

The Meshchanskaya apartments were north of the Moskva River in an area known as the Garden Ring. Trees had been planted in an effort to soften the monolithic boulevards and dull blocks, but the overall effect remained intimidating. It was only three o'clock, but the sky was already dark slate. Lois shivered as she alighted from the car. It may not have been entirely down to the biting cold. The building was enclosed by a high concrete wall and the entrance was guarded by militiamen. They completed the signing-in procedure. The guard gave no smile or greeting.

The driver unloaded her luggage and spoke to the men in a terse Russian exchange before taking them to a lift. Lois didn't know whether she should offer a tip, but he left abruptly before she could even thank him.

Nan explained that she lived upstairs with another colleague, Valerie. There was quite a contingent of junior embassy staff in this apartment block.

'I expect you'd like a drink,' said Sonia, as soon as they were through the door. 'Tea – or vodka?' She grinned. 'Or ease yourself in with a gin and tonic? I expect you could do with one after the journey.'

Lois would have killed for a good cup of coffee. She stood, slightly stunned after the long journey, and focused on Sonia's expectant gleam. 'Yes, please. Gin, I think.'

The fourth-floor apartment was warm and fairly spacious. Definitely had possibilities. Two bedrooms, a sitting room, kitchen and bathroom. The armchairs looked quite comfortable and there was a dining table long enough to seat eight. Not bad at all. Lois had seen a lot worse, except for a patch in the wall of the sitting room where a hole had been roughly hacked. Wires hung out of the plaster and exposed brick.

'We had a little game of silly buggers before we came out to meet you,' said Sonia, noting Lois's reaction. 'So we can say what we like this evening, and it won't be overheard or recorded. When we get back from work on Monday, it will all be patched up, just like magic.'

'Goodness!'

'We can't do it too often. But on special occasions it's worth it.'

Nan reappeared after a cursory knock at the door. She strode in and fixed Lois with a direct stare, brown eyes magnified by the tortoiseshell glasses. Short sighted, most likely.

'I won't wish you every happiness in your new abode because that's hardly likely, but I've brought a casserole down. Here, do you want to keep it warm in the oven, Sonia, while we have a noggin?'

Nan was clearly used to taking charge. Tall and imposing, she fired off questions in a forceful burst, though she listened carefully.

'We look out for each other here,' she said. 'We don't want anyone coming off the rails. Being in Moscow is fascinating but no one finds it easy.'

Lois sipped her G&T. It was far too heavy on the Gordon's. Good call, though. The other two women visibly relaxed with the first drink. A toast was made to the start of the weekend, the whole evening and full day left of it.

A record player was put on. Lois listened politely as they chatted, feeling at one remove, but uncomfortably so, as if she were at the cinema watching a film from too close to the screen. Names and places that meant nothing as yet to her. Social events that had taken place and others on the horizon. Lois tuned in and out, suddenly tired to her bones. She declined an invitation to join them at a party. Best to leave it until she could think straight and make a good impression. The right kind of impression.

7

'Thanks, but not this time. I'd like to get my bearings and an early night if you don't mind.'

Sonia seemed to understand. 'I'll try to creep in quietly.'

Sunday passed, still and weighty. Lois cleaned drawers, wardrobe and shelves to get the measure of them. Unpacked with care. It always took longer than expected. Sonia was out most of the day then went for dinner with someone called Boyd. She was friendly enough, although there was something brittle about her. How much of that was Sonia's personality or the strain of life in Moscow remained to be seen. Her lipstick and powder were constantly retouched. She chattered to fill every silence. Clothes she'd tried on then rejected were discarded carelessly over the sitting room chairs. Lois itched to gather them up and return them to Sonia's room but held back.

Lois was glad to be alone with her thoughts, to have a good look around the flat and ascertain the geography of the block. The entrances and exits, in particular. She set "tells" over the whole apartment, not just her own room. A hair on the top of a drawer that would no longer be there if it was opened and closed. A tiny scrap of loose paper on the top of a door. There could be no let-up from the routine. No telling when it might be vital to know where and when the place had been disturbed.

Then she took herself off for a short walk around the icy surrounding streets, even finding a small snow-covered park, but felt jumpy and intimidated, had to tell herself to get a grip.

She couldn't get to sleep that night. First day nerves, she told herself firmly. It was always the same before going into a new office. But it was different this time. Miss Harcourt's words overran her defences. 'I don't want to understate how much you personally will be risking. If you are caught there will be no safety net… Should it go wrong, you will be branded a traitor to this country…'

Around one o'clock she heard voices outside on the landing. Lois caught "garden block" and "European air crew" and "still going strong". She shifted position, then again when she was no more comfortable. The bed was harder than she was used to. The room was overheated and the window taped up against the cold. Like the rest of the flat, it was functional rather than elegant. But from what she had seen and heard already, she wondered how much she would see of the apartment anyway, other than to eat and sleep. The social round sounded as gruelling as their working hours.

Lois sighed, sat up and switched on her bedside light. Moscow bulbs were dim but the flare of the lamp still made her blink. She reached for the handbag she had placed under the bed and extracted her new pocket diary, wondering whether she should have splashed out and bought a better, slightly larger one.

It was a little Pepys diary. She had bought it on her way back to Brockley, knowing it would remind her of home. Pepys Road was just around the corner – for some reason all the locals pronounced it "Peppies".

She began to write in careful, tiny script, recalling the events of the past few days. Her luggage strapped to Cousin Harold's car to get to the air terminal on Buckingham Palace Road at Victoria. The astounding cost of her excess baggage: £14 10/-! She made sure to note that outrage. Good job she'd had her chequebook handy. Mum couldn't keep her tears back as the coach was going. Not that Lois had been allowed to tell her anything beyond the obvious.

At the airport she didn't even have time for a coffee before the Copenhagen flight was called. It was a very pleasant flight, only her second time in an aeroplane, but no need to have felt squeamish about it. *Snow at Copenhagen; glad indeed of the fox-fur coat, new from Swan and Edgar, not real fur but still rather more than I'd wanted to spend*, she wrote. The fur was another strong recommendation from Miss Harcourt. *Not long to wait before the Helsinki plane took off; another smooth flight and lunch on board.*

At Helsinki she had been met by an embassy driver and taken to Gerald and Margery's apartment. She had never met them before, but they welcomed her as a valued old friend. The conversation continued until late, establishing connections and details that might prove crucial. They put her up for the night, making sure she had everything she needed. There was a genuine kindness and concern for her in their welcome that allowed Lois momentarily to relax. If she needed to leave Moscow in a hurry, they would provide safe harbour. *Overnight in Helsinki at G & M's lovely flat. Delicious dinner.*

On the Friday afternoon, January 3, her baggage was taken to the Moscow train. Then Gerald came for her in a taxi and put her in the right compartment. It was clearly a familiar routine. The train crossed the Russian border about nine o'clock that evening. In falling blotches of snow, an unsmiling Russian from Intourist had showed the way to the customs shed. Her trunk and five suitcases had been subjected to a close and thorough inspection, a rude introduction to the lack of privacy she could expect in Moscow.

She did not set down the encounter on the train that had first intrigued then shaken her, only a reminder of the circumstances that preceded it. *Slept til 8am – or was it 9am with the time change? Bit thirsty so I had some tea from the samovar and it wasn't too bad.*

2

Tuesday, April 12, 1955

Harcourt meeting 10.45. A smell of coal fires but meagre heat in the far reaches of cavernous rooms. A maze of corridors. Shown the way by another girl from the training section (office skills). The lady supervisor becomes agitated when one of her girls fails to find the right office. Presumably, a faulty sense of navigation augurs badly for future foreign assignment.

The first time they met after her preliminary interviews at Whitehall in 1955, Miss Harcourt looked her over with a strangely exacting disinterest.

'You won't be able to tell anyone what you do,' she said. 'And there's not the slightest bit of glory in it.'

Lois acknowledged this. She had known instinctively, it seemed, as soon as she saw the intriguingly worded advertisement in the *Times* and decided to see where it led. Miss Harcourt, gatekeeper of this shadowy and exciting world, continued her stringent appraisal commensurate with the grandeur of the setting: Carlton House Terrace with its endless confusing corridors and men waiting to dictate in high-ceilinged rooms, referring to themselves as "the F.O.", as if their employment by the Foreign Office conferred semi-regal status.

'Oh, you can say you work as a secretary, because you will be a secretary. You must always stick to as much truth as you can. Beyond that, if anyone asks, even your own family, you are simply a young woman who wants to see something of the world. You work, and you have friends, and you enjoy travelling and socialising, that's it.'

'I understand.'

'No boyfriend?'

'Several. But none who could detain me in London.'

Miss Harcourt actually smiled, a brief thaw before frost reformed. She must once have been attractive; undoubtedly, her appearance was carefully maintained in middle age.

'Why do you want to follow this path, Lois?'

A good question, and one to which Lois had no simple answer. Because she was so much the youngest in her family – a surprise second child for Charles and Lily Vale when their son Ralph was already eleven, and Lily nearly forty – she had watched her brother and his friend Edward and their many cousins put on uniforms to fight the war while she had still been a child. Even her girl cousins had gone into the Women's Royal Naval Service or the Women's Auxiliary Air Force while she had been able to do nothing. A couple of them, June and Mabel, had hinted that they had held vital positions that even now they could not discuss. As the years went by, she had seen them grow in self-confidence and enjoy Ralph's admiration. Because she was proud of them, and wanted something to be proud of in herself, too.

'I want to do my bit for the country, Miss Harcourt.'

Like Edward had. Ralph's best friend, son of the family next door in Tressillian Road. He used to lean over the garden fence and give her apples from their tree. He and Ralph had joined up and trained as RAF navigators together. Edward's plane went down over the Channel in 1944. The war had been over for ten years but was felt every day. The Vale house took a direct hit from a Luftwaffe bomb, but the family had survived. They managed to salvage a few meagre possessions from the smoking rubble, but essentially they lost everything. When Lois was permitted to return to London for a few days from her hated evacuation billet in Sussex, she walked in a daze by herself to the ruined house, saw men clearing the bomb site, and a bonfire burning. Watched in despair as what remained of her belongings was tossed into the flames but could not move, too shy to step up to ask them to stop. Later, ashamed of her lack of courage, she had vowed she would never allow anything like that to happen again.

There was another reason, though she was not about to say so. Top of the class at Grey Coat Hospital school for girls at Westminster, a scholarship girl with all fees paid, but no chance of going to university.

'There might be a bursary for a young woman of your calibre,' said the redoubtable headmistress. 'Let me see what I can do.'

'I have to start earning as soon as I can, Miss Chetham-Strode. My name's down for a secretarial and book-keeping course at the City of London College, just for a year.' Lois had to start contributing to the family finances. Money was tighter than ever. Any day, her father's job might go to a younger ex-serviceman. He was a conductor on the trams, having returned deaf from the First World War, but he was always so well turned-out off-duty that some in the neighbourhood thought he was a dandy.

'Times are changing, Lois. The war has brought us so many more opportunities.' The redoubtable headmistress meant for women. 'Don't do yourself down. Find a way to live up to your potential, for it is considerable.'

So Lois had discovered working as a secretary in London, as had the moderately talented men she had routinely saved from disaster, who fought to keep her when it was time to move on and who thought the looks she gave them were a green light to pounce when in fact they were the purest contempt. Was it hubris or hard-earned confidence that made her want to be recognised for the intelligent woman she was?

'I'd like to make a difference,' she told Miss Harcourt. 'And to live up to my potential.'

'You have made a good decision, Lois. We need girls like you, clever, independent thinkers, meticulous and somewhat... out of the usual recruitment lines. Now, shoulders back, head high. Dress as smartly as you can within your means. You have the qualities to be a credit to yourself and the service.'

It was her memory they wanted. Her phenomenally retentive memory, near photographic when it came to the printed word, and her ability to make fast connections. It came so naturally to her that she was sometimes astonished to find that other people could remember so little.

Her first assignment to the embassy in The Hague was supposed to have prepared her for this, an Iron Curtain posting. Russia! Not only a communist country, but the toughest of them all. She had wanted this, she reminded herself sternly as she lay awake in her Moscow bed. Excitement, independence, a chance to do something worthwhile. Well, now she had it.

In backwater offices in London and a country house in Shropshire they filled her head with their secret ways, tested her, engineered hypothetical situations she could never win, berated her, interrogated her, worked her all day and all night, left her in darkness and built her up again. Miss Harcourt had set it out plainly when she told Lois about her Moscow posting and sent her for further training in the countryside.

'It will require great strength of character, but you have been carefully chosen. This is an extremely delicate operation.

You will need to proceed with the utmost discretion and also ruthlessness.'

In the draughty old manor house somewhere near Ludlow, Lois only rarely mixed with the few other trainees. She was often kept busy during mealtimes in the beamed dining room and ate alone in her room. A sitting room set aside for evening relaxation was hardly used, and if she did find someone else there, usually a man, conversation was wary. Socialising was not encouraged. Only first names were permitted, and those were presumably false, like the one she used with them. Not that that bothered her overly. While she made friends easily and enjoyed a lively time as much as anyone, Lois was equally happy to be alone and her self-sufficiency was obviously one of the reasons she was there. Three weeks were spent learning vital details about Moscow and the embassy staff, being coached in how she should act in hypothetical situations, receiving critical notes for improvement, being kept up late and having to solve puzzles when she was dog-tired, even being questioned aggressively after being given too much alcohol one night. She was left in no doubt what living in Russia would be like.

She was introduced to physical tradecraft, real spy stuff. Not that anyone referred to themselves as a spy. Dead drops and code books, brush-past contacts and counter-surveillance techniques to ensure that she was not being followed: doubling back on oneself, taking random tube trains and buses, and rear exits of shops and hotels and apartment buildings. Definitely a step beyond her duties in The Hague which had been barely more than administrative and information gathering.

At Birmingham New Street railway station she was told: 'At ten o'clock, the man will stand under the clock for five minutes, checking his watch. He will look down at his shoes and realise that he needs to retie his shoelaces. He will be wearing green gloves. Take a good look at him. Make sure you will recognise him when you see him again. A small drama will take place which may or may not involve him. Commit what occurs to memory.'

'I understand.' She understood, too, not to ask questions, at least not yet, about the task she had been set.

The next morning, she went in to make her report. A youngish man called Ellingwood, pleasant Scottish accent and calm manner, noted down her observation of a young couple having a row over a missed train, giving nothing away.

'And now to these photographs, Miss Vale.' He dealt seven headshots on the table. 'Please point to the man under the clock.'

There were three possibilities, two close likenesses. She hesitated, then pointed to the fifth.

'This one.'

'Thank you.' No reaction to indicate whether or not she was correct. 'Who else was there also?'

Lois pointed to the third photograph.

'What was he doing?'

'He was observing, same as I was.'

'Where?'

'Behind me. At the news stand.'

The crux of the matter was that Donald Maclean and Guy Burgess had been gone nearly seven years, yet an active traitor, or traitors, remained at large. A distinct, galling possibility existed that this traitor was within the embassy in Moscow. The most recent confirmation had come from the other side, a Soviet diplomat who defected in Washington. Communications were being routinely leaked in Moscow. The Foreign Office faced very grave questions. The whole fragile system had been destabilised: they could no longer tell who was trustworthy and who was working for the other side out of ideological convictions. The settling of the dust after the great upheavals of two world wars had led to weaknesses and uncertainties. Not even the oldest loyalties could be counted on.

'There's still suspicion about Philby,' she was told by the man called Robinson in the house somewhere near Ludlow. 'Did well in Washington. MI6 station chief. One of ours – one of our best. Highly regarded, the rising star who crashed down in the fallout after Burgess and Maclean defected to Moscow. Did he tip them off that our net was closing in on their activities? We had to put Philby out to pasture for a few years, but now he's back in harness. Most of our people don't want to hear it, can't believe he's a traitor. Men have damaged their own careers by going against the tide. But we have to ask the questions.'

It wasn't the first time Lois had heard the name Philby, of course. Kim Philby, urbane and smooth-tongued, had made newspaper headlines three years before when questions were asked in parliament and he subsequently gave a press conference in his mother's flat in Kensington denying that he had ever been a spy, that he could possibly be the Third Man in the ring. Denying it with such confidence and aplomb that hard-nosed reporters fell under his spell and almost unanimously declared him innocent. The public now believed he had been unjustly accused as fervently as his old friends in MI6 did.

Robinson played her a news film of the event, stopping it and rewinding the tape spools to look closely at certain gestures and vocal mannerisms. Lois learnt new techniques to determine whether a person was lying. Lies were manifest in more than words. Lies were detectable in small movements of the eyes and posture; they could be heard in vocal inflections, in the twist of Philby's mouth as he declared, 'The last time I spoke to a communist, knowing him to be a communist, was some time in 1934.'

17

'He's not the only one we have doubts about, either. But all logic tells us it's more likely the most effective traitors are those we do not yet suspect.'

Living under deep cover in Moscow would require living a lie, just like they did. Living as – *being* – a liar by omission. Defending herself, when necessary, with lies. But for a good reason, she insisted to herself. Were liars born or made? Perhaps she no longer knew. She believed she was a good person; she believed in her country and was proud of those who had served so bravely in the war. She used to think the best of people, and in general she probably still did. It was her strong sense of logic and natural justice that had brought her this far.

'You need to cultivate a watchmaker's mind,' Robinson said. Owl glasses, tortoiseshell, magnified his mottled hazel eyes across the table. 'An ability to assess the connections between cogs and how movements are achieved. A steady hand. Delicate adjustments.' Oblique, but Lois saw at once what he meant. 'Learn to compartmentalise. From what I have seen, you have the ability to make a success of it. The gee-gees always come through.'

A racing man? Were they all gamblers? She supposed they were, in every sense that mattered.

'Gradually. Gently. The two "G"s that make for good intelligence work. And good intelligence comes in absolute silence.'

He made a steeple of his hands and assessed her dispassionately. 'Burgess and Maclean have caused much damage, not least to the British reputation with the Americans. Embarrassing and unproductive not to be a reliable partner. The FBI in particular has pointed the finger at senior British officers, who have been dragged through the mud only to be proved innocent. Unofficially, there can be no doubt that the KGB has other British agents. The most effective are those who know all the secrets, how all the wheels run. Could there be one in our Moscow embassy? That is the unfortunate question we face. Is anyone meeting Burgess and Maclean? Is there some channel to them in Moscow? Is there a Philby apologist in the embassy? Philby is currently in Beirut, ostensibly as a journalist but also, thanks to his faithful friends, he is back in the MI6 fold, feeding the greedy craw with information which may or may not be helpful from the Middle East.'

A brief rattle of cups and saucers from the tray on his desk. 'Here, take some tea. Earl Grey? I confess I cannot enjoy an afternoon without it.'

For a few minutes, life resumed a kind of normality. The room was what it had perhaps always been, a country house study, book-lined and a little musty. Robinson wore a tweed jacket and a familial air. He treated her with a lack of formality allied with respectful kindness that was calculated to instil confidence, as if she were a favoured niece. She was the chosen one, she alone the beneficiary of his life's work, charged with carrying it forward, though his lectures carried rueful warnings:

'Moscow is one of the most dangerous and treacherous cities in the world to be a Western foreigner. A branch of the Soviet Foreign Ministry provides embassies with interpreters, clerks, messengers, cleaners, cooks and drivers. Many of them are KGB informants or intelligence officers. Surveillance is constant, from shadowing outside the embassy buildings to secret listening devices and cameras, holes drilled in floors in the apartments and new battery-powered bugs that contain their own transmitters.

'Naturally, these Soviet staff are denied access to the areas of an embassy which contain classified material, but it is an unwelcome reality that they have plenty of opportunity to hide their devices and communicate with our people.

'On our side, there are no time-servers in the Moscow embassy. Every member of staff is there for a purpose and some personal quality. Never forget that. Every part of your task will be extremely delicate. It takes what the KGB calls a worm to catch a worm.'

She hadn't expected to be called in to see Miss Harcourt again before she left London. The lunch with Peter had already unsettled her. Piccadilly Circus. The grey rain outside. The expectation of an upbeat send-off dashed on the rocks of grim reality. Worse, the sense of a trap being sprung.

The Americans had turned up, were on the case in situ. A man named Stoneley, an Australian, unconventional, unpredictable and fiercely perceptive, had recently been seconded to the Moscow embassy from Foreign Office research. Both were unforeseen complications.

'I don't want to understate how much you personally will be risking.' Miss Harcourt stood with her back to the rain-lashed window, the shadows of middle-aged spinsterhood stark on her face under the electric lighting, even now evaluating Lois's reaction. 'This is a deep cover operation. If you get caught, there will be no safety net. This section is sacrosanct, secret even within MI6. Should it go wrong, you will be branded a traitor to this country, a Russian spy in our Moscow embassy.'

Breath solidified in her chest, but Lois nodded.

'No private glory, no part in history, only public ignominy. Hung out to dry. Let there be no doubt about that.'

'And if I decided I couldn't?'

'Too late, I'm afraid. The wheels, as they say, are in motion.'

Silence.

'But there *are* measures in place…?'

Miss Harcourt, businesslike as ever, offered no such reassurance. 'One more thing,' she had said. 'No paper notes, of course. Don't need to tell you that. But keep a diary, every day. Record ordinary, everyday things. Dull work at the embassy. Your occasional trips outside the capital. *Worked hard. Had lunch with so-and-so. Went to a party and met a nice man, wonder if he will call to see me again.* That kind of nonsense. Don't look at me like that, Miss Vale. It might be of the utmost importance to prove that you are romantically inclined, rather empty-headed, at times. But the details will act as prompts to the memory, help you pin down specific days if necessary. Develop your own private code. Stay in character at all times. Believe me, you will be worked hard enough. Only natural that you will want to play hard, too.'

3

Monday, January 6, 1958

*Taken to work by the office bus and met a lot of people whose
names I don't remember. Apart from the showpieces, Moscow is
shabby; people in the streets not smart though perfectly adequately
dressed, but faces are set to gloomy. Temp 25°F below today.*

*I'm to be the PA to the Minister, Mr Waller, who seems a
charming man.*

It was still dark when an embassy bus came to collect them
from Meshchanskaya. The armed guards at the gate remained
unsmiling as the British contingent trooped out. On board
the bus already were colleagues from other apartment blocks,
but, aside from a few desultory nods, they might have been
strangers on the Monday morning commute.

As the dawn lightened from charcoal to ash, wide streets
emerged, grander and even more intimidating than Lois had
anticipated: magnificent granite threats rising from banks of
snow. She caught her first sight of Red Square, vast and empty,
through a murky mist. St Basil's cathedral was a twisted sugar
confection, out of place in the austerity. The bus took a bridge
over the Moskva River, where ice sheets cracked and rode the
dark water in a slow-moving mosaic.

Moments later, they stopped at the gate of a grand mansion, all carved stone and roofline balustrades. Directly across the river glowered the fortress of the Kremlin with its watch-turrets and forbidding walls the colour of dried blood. The gold domes of the cathedrals and Ivan the Great's bell tower shone from within the stronghold like captured treasure.

A militiaman emerged from the sentry box and looked over the passengers in the bus. Lois sat up straight. Did he give her an especially hard appraising stare as a new face? After a minute or so, they got out and passed through into a forecourt.

The building was once a wealthy sugar merchant's residence, known as the Kharitonenko Mansion, a relic of pre-Revolution days. This much she knew from the briefings. The Soviet authorities had been doing their best to reclaim it, but thanks to the usual British deployment of cunning muddle and procrastination, it was still in use as the embassy and ambassador's residence.

Once inside, her fellow passengers relaxed a little. They gathered around in the grand entrance hall, introducing themselves far too quickly, but she caught most of them and filed them away in her mind. They all knew who she was, of course. She was to be personal assistant to the Minister, Roger Waller. As political head of the mission, he was second in command to the Ambassador, Sir Duncan Mountbeech. One of the men offered to take her upstairs to meet "the Min".

Deep red and gold and patterned wallpaper and heavily carved wooden furniture set a Gothic mood. A carved bird of prey on a staircase finial kept a savage eye on any movement. Lois's first impression was of a sumptuous Victorian hunting lodge in a novel by Trollope. She was led past dark panelling and up the polished wood staircase.

Beyond a heavily fortified door, Waller rose from his desk

to welcome her. Behind him, a large window framed a view of the river and the Kremlin.

'A daunting reminder, eh, Miss Vale?'

'Yes, sir.'

He was tall, with a slight stoop. A gentleman of the old school by all appearances. Grey hair fading to white, a bony face with kindly blue eyes. The dark suit was exquisitely tailored. A gold signet ring on the left little finger. He shook her hand and smiled as he spoke.

'Good to have you on board.'

The Minister reached around and flicked a switch on his desk. Lois jumped as music burst from an unseen amplifier, loud and stirring. Waller beckoned with a finger and walked over to a console table under an English landscape painting.

'Always best to take precautions,' said the Minister. 'KGB. Watchers and followers – and listeners. At all times. At the gate, noting who comes in and out. Perhaps more importantly, they prevent ordinary Russians who might hatch a plan to defect to the West from approaching the diplomatic mission. You are advised not to initiate friendships, or even conversations, with ordinary Russians. Dangerous for them and complicated for us. Any Russians you come into contact with will almost certainly be connected to their security services.

'If I could give you one piece of advice, it would be to pace yourself. This place runs on late nights and drinking.' As he spoke, he was writing on a single sheet of paper that rested on the glass-topped console table. He now turned it towards her. *Turn the wireless on loudly when you want to talk, or play records. Go into the bathroom and run the taps if you absolutely must talk about work. Try not to argue with other people. You never know what can be used against us all.*

She listened attentively, though she had already been well briefed on the set-up in Moscow. Chancery, as usual, was the hub of the embassy and dealt with political matters. There was a full complement of military, air and naval attachés and their staff. Apart from the Ambassador and the Minister, who were privy to all intelligence, the MI6 station comprised a First Secretary, an intelligence officer in the guise of a Third Secretary, a junior security officer and four personal assistants. The wildcard Stoneley was an Australian academic, an expert in Soviet political strategy and nominally attached to the embassy as an advisor. He was part of the research team jokingly named the Russian Secretariat. As far as "the funnies" were concerned, Lois would quietly be one of them in a purely secretarial capacity.

Burgess and Maclean could apparently be spotted now and then at the Bolshoi or in the park. Embassy staff were banned from approaching them or having any kind of contact. She wondered whether Waller would mention that.

He did not. The Minister put down his pen and ripped up the paper before throwing it on the fire. He had a stiff way of moving, as if his joints troubled him, but his aim was true.

'Too many mistakes in the past. We have to be very careful. I'm sure you understand.'

'Of course.'

'So you see, plenty of social life,' he said in a jauntier tone. 'America House is usually a safe bet for a lively evening, and you might even win something at bingo. Now, let's ease you in gently. I'm going to introduce you to Head of Chancery, and someone will show you around. It's really rather a splendid building.'

Her designated guide was one of the younger men. Lois progressed along the upstairs corridor, knocking on doors and shaking more hands.

'Cypher Room,' he whispered, pointing to himself. 'I'm Eric.'

This was a restricted area, where messages were encrypted and sent as telegrams. The safe inside contained the code pads to reset the cypher machines every morning.

Finally, they arrived at a reinforced door.

'Bug-proof room.'

They went through. Lois stared around her. The bug-proof room was a room-within-a-room, rather as if a large caravan had been parked in the mansion then raised up after being divested of its wheels. Inside, a long table gave it a curious boardroom air with the dead atmosphere of a bank vault.

'It does the job,' said Eric. 'The Americans have built one using a double layer of plexiglass, apparently. They call it the Tank.'

'Good heavens,' said Lois.

Eric made sure the door was shut tightly and grinned. He was around her own age, pale and eager in a hand-knitted sweater under his crumpled grey suit. His reddish hair was unruly despite his efforts with Brylcreem, and there was an angry rash on his neck where he had shaved.

'Where were you before?'

'The Hague.'

'I had a friend who was there for a while. Bowden – ever come across him?'

She shook her head.

'Must have been before your time. How did you like it?'

'Jolly hard work, but I made some good friends. Lots of Navy liaison, ships coming into Rotterdam and on-board parties. Those were often fun. I have a feeling it's going to feel a lot more closed in here.'

'You're not wrong there. But we all agreed to take on an Iron Curtain posting. We knew what we were getting into.'

'Yes, I suppose we did. Never really know what something is like until you see it for yourself though, do you?'

Eric laughed. 'Ain't that the truth.'

He seemed nice, chatting freely now about his childhood home in North Wales, asking her where she was from. If there was to be any sense of normality in Moscow, it would be crucial to keep on good terms with colleagues. There was not much chance of meeting anyone else. And you never knew when being friends with a cypher clerk might come in handy.

Eric opened the doors to the ballroom. It was all white and gilt opulence and polished parquet floor. The furniture was upholstered in brocaded gold satin. A ten-foot oil painting of the young Queen Elizabeth that captured her youth and beauty gazed down on a white baby grand piano.

'Used for important diplomatic receptions,' he said with pride.

Lois spun round with genuine girlish delight.

'You like dancing?' he asked, as if he might too.

'I love to dance.'

Lastly, he took her into the library. The books looked as if they had been bought by the yard, but the room had a soothing atmosphere and there was a bar on one corner.

'Doubles as a mess. Otherwise known as the British Club. Supposed to keep us and any stray compatriots out of trouble from more dubious establishments in the city.'

'And does it?'

He laughed. 'Must do a bit. It's full most nights. See you here later!'

She was deftly steered back to the Minister, who introduced her to a desk with a well-used typewriting machine in an anteroom to his own grand office with the daunting view.

Despite her fears, she was given an easy first day. Some telephoning for the Minister and a couple of short reports to type. In sharp contrast to the glories of the ballroom and the other graces of the old mansion, mundane rules were issued:

all files had to be signed out, and typewriter ribbons taken out of typewriters at the end of the day and locked away securely lest they release their secrets to the determined cryptologist who might break in during the night. Grand the house may have been, but it was freezing cold in all areas not reached by a hotchpotch network of fireplaces, electric heaters and hay-burning stoves. For most of the staff, fur-lined boots, even indoors, and many knitted layers under and over formal wear were the order of the day. Outside, temperatures of minus thirty and forty Fahrenheit were not unknown in winter.

Most people went home on the office bus for lunch, but Mr Waller invited her to eat with him and his wife at his splendid house ten minutes away by office car. All was thoroughly civilised and pleasant. Miriam Waller, tall and imposing, the seasoned diplomatic wife, greeted her with breezy professional goodwill. Conversation remained robustly impersonal: of ballet at the Bolshoi, opera at the Filial, the parks, and the country houses of Tolstoy and Tchaikovsky which were open to the public and could be visited by special permit.

At six o'clock, Lois had her first drink in the library mess. The junior members of staff all gathered around Lois, keeping her topped up with gin and orange. They seemed a normal enough bunch, though some were clearly going to prove more fun than others. All were curious about her; new blood was eagerly awaited in their closed social circle. What was running through their minds? Were some of them making rapid observations about her in the same way she had been trained to do?

Having shown her around earlier, Eric now took a leading role in kick-starting her social life. He whisked her through the room, bantering with the girls as well as the men. Sonia was in the thick of it, too. Lois chatted with a couple of secretaries, Trudy and Frances, with identical stiff perms set hard as helmets. They were from "Sad Sam", whoever or whatever that was. They treated her to a rundown of the quirks she could expect with the office equipment, some moans about the work and lack of appreciation for their efforts, and an invitation to see a film with them later in the week. Sad Sam, it transpired, was another walled and fortified apartment block like the one on Meshchanskaya, on Sadovo-Samotechnaya Street. The home perms had been administered there by Rita the previous night, and they weren't convinced she had followed the instructions to the letter.

It was an instantly sobering minus twenty-five degrees when they emerged and clattered down the flight of steps to the forecourt. Some of the men peeled off to the left towards "the Garden Block" that housed their apartments. Lois was asked if she wanted to continue the party with them, but by that time she was longing for something to eat and a few hours to herself.

She got on the bus home with Sonia. The front door to their apartment was unlocked when they arrived. Sonia was blithely unconcerned.

'It hardly matters. *They* come and go as they please.'

In the sitting room, the hacked walls where wires from listening devices had hung exposed over the weekend were now cleanly replastered and repainted. The paint was still damp, and an acrid chemical smell hung in the air. Lois checked the "tells" she had set in her bedroom: the single hair on the top of the door; the crumbs on the edge of each drawer; the tear of tissue paper in the wardrobe door. Not one of them remained in place.

Snow sugared the walls and spires and domes of the Kremlin and dredged the roofs and windowsills of monumental Communist Party buildings. Moscow had an undeniable beauty but could not provide much cheer. In the streets, small trudging figures in uniformly shabby dark coats passed beneath the stark enormity of the architecture. Blue and cream trolley buses trundled under overhead lines. Smoke belched from factories downriver and army lorries raced along with soil and rubble from the many building sites.

As Lois had been warned, work was relentless; it was a large, busy embassy. On her first "bag day" they raced to finish reports and correspondence to make the secure diplomatic bags collected weekly by Queen's Messengers and delivered to London. Mr Waller dictated a lengthy draft, but she managed it on time, though they were still at the office at eight o'clock. But the following morning brought the pleasure of post and parcels from home in the incoming bags.

The pressure of work had been bad enough in The Hague, but there at least they'd had some fun outside the office and the possibility of a private life. Here it was all seriousness and dread of missing a beat. She was feeling her way forward, trying to be amiable but unobtrusive. Remembering Robinson's briefing: *Take a little time to dig yourself in. Don't try to force anything, just take it steadily, naturally. Sometimes it takes years to set up a deep cover op, so this is a lot we're asking of you.* The saving grace was finding she actually enjoyed working for Roger Waller despite the fact that he pushed himself harder than any boss she'd ever had. She appreciated his gentlemanly graces and keen intelligence undercut with a hint of self-deprecating humour. Politeness was intrinsic to him, but his kindness seemed genuine.

She could have told him, yet she said nothing about the man on the train. She should have done so, right at the start. But no easy opportunity presented itself and each day that went by made reporting the incident harder without drawing unwelcome attention to herself. The fear grew that she had made a bad decision. She had compromised herself from the outset out of fear of making a worse mistake. *Stop this*, she ordered herself. She had made her decision. Perhaps there would still be a chance to reassess.

Lois was finally introduced to the Ambassador. His Excellency – universally abbreviated to H.E. – was a long, lean aesthete who looked as if he would be more at home in an Oxford library than a mansion fortress under siege on enemy soil. Sir Duncan Mountbeech had a set face, lined and carved as if by geological erosion, an impression enhanced by white hair that topped his head like snow on a crag. The confident rumour was that he had been involved in a secret code unit during the war and was widely supposed to have a brilliant mind and a fascination for Soviet affairs. When Lois was presented, he stood and picked up a paper from a desk with the intent swoop of a virtuoso violinist, and the same master's confidence. His friendliness in greeting her was professionalism at its finest but there was no doubting his enthusiasm when he tried to recruit her to the cause of amateur theatricals. He was proud, he vouchsafed, to believe the British did homemade entertainment better than any diplomatic mission in Moscow.

She was initiated into the mysteries of food orders from Gastronom. She went to the Garden Block, once the stables behind the Kharitonenko Mansion, and saw a film in the mess with Trudy and Frances. *The Bridge on the River Kwai*. She would have preferred something more cheerful, but she felt comfortable enough with them. They reminded her of the girls in The Hague: late twenties, early thirties, hard-working and loyal, attractive enough to have disasters with men, and sensible enough to know they were better off with no husband than a bad one. From certain words they dropped she recognised them as fellow members of the MI6 fraternity. As was Nan Trusloe; Lois had clocked that on the first taxi ride from the station. Not that anything was mentioned overtly.

Saturday mornings were normal working hours, the same as in London.

'We're all going swimming when we finish,' said Sonia at breakfast. She was more than usually perky after coming in very late after a date with the much-cited but so far unseen Boyd. 'Come with us. You do have a costume, don't you?'

Lois felt exhausted at the very thought. The raw reality of Moscow, the intensity of her mission (which currently seemed overwhelming and impossible) had drained her already. All she wanted to do was sleep.

'I love swimming,' she said. 'Yes, please – count me in.'

'You have a treat in store then. The pool is quite extraordinary.'

Lois had visions of a grand Victorian edifice, like the public baths at New Cross.

'It's an outdoor pool,' went on Sonia.

'In this weather? Please tell me you're joking.'

A shake of the head and a laugh. 'Not joking at all. It's all rather wonderful, actually.'

Lois hoped it would be, fervently.

At the Central Lenin Stadium, she, Sonia, Nan and her flatmate Valerie changed in a communal room from where a white-tiled channel led to the pool. One had to swim a yard or two to a glass barrier, then duck down underwater to get outside.

Lois emerged into a world of steam and snowflakes. Snow crusted the surround of a huge pool, like a pie that had sunk. The water was deliciously, almost unimaginably warm. She launched herself out with a cry of delight, floated on her back, face and mouth open to the falling white sky.

To be weightless was bliss. She forgot the heaviness of her eyes and the strain of smiling. She forgot the others. They were lost in the swirling white vapours. One long length, then another and another. On and on past grey structures painted with Cyrillic instructions. She might have been swimming alongside a surfacing submarine in the Arctic. A release. A relief. The ache in her neck and shoulders from the long hours at the typewriter eased in the sulphurous heat.

No one wanted to get out. They kicked around in a shallow corner letting themselves go and speaking freely.

'Head of Chancery has a wandering eye but he's too much of a stuffed shirt to do anything about it, at least not with one of us,' said Valerie. 'Frank's sweet, he lives upstairs with Rory. Eric's a puppy dog, rather a pouncer at parties, but harmless. Didn't he ask you to go to Kiev with him, Sonia?'

Sonia pulled a pretty little pout and adjusted her outrageously padded red swimsuit. 'I'm saying nothing. But everyone knows I didn't go.'

'This is a dreadful place for gossip. You'll soon see why,' said Nan gravely.

'Ann's been seen at America House with one of the Marines. Nice-looking chap, fair, brush-cut hair,' said Valerie, ploughing on. She was the chatterbox; a tall, thin woman with prematurely greying hair, stuck in a state of transformation between schoolgirl and career spinster. 'Joe Somebody. Has a fiancée back home but keeps it quiet.'

'Is he the one who cried on Eileen's shoulder about missing his girl in Nebraska?' asked Nan. 'Eileen's leaving soon. But if it is, before she goes she ought to let Ann know.'

'I'd leave Ann to it,' said Sonia. 'She needs some fun and she'll find out for herself soon enough.' Sonia lay back in the water, conical breasts pointing upwards like torpedoes. 'Eileen's getting married almost as soon as she gets back to London. Her fiancé's waited long enough, she says, and she can't wait to have to give up her job.'

'Shame,' said Nan tersely. 'She's a good'un. The F.O. can't afford to lose too many like her.'

Lois wondered whether the older woman had ever taken the career-ending risk of a romantic relationship. Sound logistical reasons for the Foreign Office not to keep women on after marriage there may have been, but even so, the system had always struck Lois as grossly unfair. Especially as the service made full use of married women as diplomatic wives – and paid them nothing. Women were allowed into the world of men only under strict rules of engagement.

'Sweet Frank's having a walk-out with a nanny working for one of the Spanish embassy families,' said Val. 'They were seen having dinner at the Metropol. That's pushing the boat out, so he must be serious.'

'Leave him alone,' said Nan. 'He's nice – and still very young. So's Rory.'

'Oh, Rory… how can a man be so attractive and yet not have a clue about anything? Have they just sent him out as bait for some treacherous Russian girl?' Sonia laughed. 'You see, Lois, it doesn't take long for us to get snapped up here. Far more single men than women!'

'She might not want to be snapped up,' Nan pointed out.

'Quite,' said Lois.

'Heard you were seeing someone, Val,' said Nan with a sly edge in her voice.

They live together, thought Lois. *Why would she choose to ask her in front of an audience?*

'I see lots of people all the time. Round and round goes the merry carousel. It's impossible to get off.'

'Tell us about you, Lois. We're longing for new blood,' said Sonia. 'What about your romances?'

'I was two and a half years in The Hague. The average Dutchman is of stolid Calvinist character. Not much to get excited about.'

'No one in the office?'

'Mostly married, I'm afraid. Oh dear, I can tell I'm a terrible disappointment already.' She would have to give something away. 'There was someone last summer, but that was in Austria.'

'Do tell!' urged Valerie, as keen on other people's stories as her own.

'Well, I've been going back to a little place in the Tyrol ever since I first went with my evening class from Goldsmiths' College. I feel as if I come alive in the mountains – it's the freshness, the intense green, the sense of being up in the air!'

That clearly wasn't what they wanted.

'He was quite the gentleman,' she went on, acknowledging this with a smile. 'I was walking down from Zellbergeben and I'd got a stone in my shoe. He stopped and asked if I needed any help, and we spoke for a while. Then the next evening I was at a dance in the Café Gredler and he asked me for a turn around the floor.'

'And?' asked Nan. 'You gave us more details about the mountains than the man!'

Sharp as a tack, thought Lois. 'Well, he was handsome, of course! With blue eyes and light brown hair, broad shoulders. He worked for a publishing company, on the sales side, I think. And he was light-hearted and amusing to be with, and… well, we had fun. And that was that. All over far too soon.'

Lois resisted the temptation to ask too many questions. There was no need. Sonia needed no encouragement to tell how she had been engaged back in London but had broken it off to come out to Moscow. Boyd was with the Canadian Embassy and since she'd started walking out with him and others, she'd realised there was a lot more single girl left in her than she'd thought.

'I must have known deep down that I wasn't ready to glide up to the altar of St Luke's. Though some days here in this dismal dump, I think marriage might be a good way out – an honourable discharge!'

Valerie launched into a saga about an unfaithful American when she'd been in Washington. Nan orchestrated the confessions but gave little away herself, listening intently and quashing talk of others who were not there to defend themselves.

Lois stretched in the hot water and let her mind wander to things best not confessed: that alongside her career-mindedness, she was a hopeless romantic who longed to find love, the strong, unreserved love that had sustained her parents through hardship as well as happy times. She had turned down many proposals, mostly from men who were attracted to her looks yet knew little of her inner life. She had wanted so much more than those suitors could offer: both love and self-fulfilment without sacrificing one for the other. But would it ever be possible to find real, true love on those terms?

As Lois allowed the memory of her Austrian interlude to expand, Valerie's complex entanglement with the duplicitous American melded into mountain paths and green meadows. The Gasthof Bräu and dancing at Gredler's on the warm summer nights. The kiss on the bridge over the Ziller, the river babbling over rocks beneath their feet. That was certainly not for sharing.

'America House is the best place for meeting eligible men here,' said Sonia, interjecting to bring Valerie back from the brink of righteous fury in Pennsylvania Avenue. She turned to Lois. 'It's quite the social centre, all the latest films and dances. All the diplomatic personnel and foreign press congregate there. There aren't nearly enough women to go round, so you'll be able to take your pick. On Thursday nights they have bingo games with prizes, open house to all the Western embassies, so it's all very cosmopolitan. The Swedes, the Finns, and the

Germans in particular really seem to enjoy it. We'll take you next time.'

She'd got off to a decent start with the women. Sonia clearly came from a very different background from Lois, though as yet Sonia had given no indication that she had noticed. So far, the atmosphere in the flat was the same as being billeted with other girls who had been evacuated, or perhaps a boarding school dormitory in Sonia's case. They were in this together and making the best of it.

The first rule was to behave naturally. Do only what a secretary from South London would be expected to do. That meant knowing her place with the diplomats and their wives, not pushing herself forward, simply being open and friendly and obliging. Cheerful too, if she could manage it. The men were going to prove much trickier. Eric was already showing all the signs of being too keen.

That night brought her introduction to formal social life at the embassy: a Saturday supper dance given in a plush but fading hotel by Philip Vere Sinclair, a youngish Second Secretary who surely had independent means, and his wife Diana, a saucer-eyed ex-debutante. There was a "livener-up" beforehand at a flat in the Garden Block of the embassy mansion before the junior staff were ferried to the party on the usual bus. Eric made sure to help Lois to a seat and claim the spot beside her. When they arrived, he took her coat and admired her blue dress, and then guided her into the fray. At his side, Lois met all the wives and security guards and several couples from the American and Canadian embassies, as well as Scandinavians and a smiling but hesitant Indian contingent. The party was another blur of names and faces.

But after another drink she found herself regaining her earlier relaxation. The economist knew a friend of hers from

The Hague, and the embassy doctor knew of others. His wife had worked with one of the girls in The Hague when they were in Madrid together. She was beginning to make connections, both with the recent past and with her new colleagues.

'Lois, have you met Anthony Fielding? He's one of our political analysts.' Nan had been sharing a joke with a tall, fit-looking man with an engaging smile. When she laughed, her wide, plain face lit up and she looked years younger.

He stuck out a hand. 'Tony. Glad to have you aboard.'

'Thank you.'

His handshake was firm. Close up, she saw his nose had been broken and a scar cut across his chin, but nothing marred his allure. The wounds only implied he was a man of enthusiastic action, and a lucky one at that.

'I say, are you keen on acting?' he asked.

She was momentarily taken aback.

'Do say you are. The Ambassador is frightfully keen on amateur theatricals. Apparently these relieve the oppressive atmosphere and allow the staff to focus on amusement as they all pull together.'

'Until artistic temperament exposes true natures and arguments ensue,' quipped Nan. 'But His Excellency can reliably be heard leading the laughter and applause.'

'I'm not very good at acting, I'm afraid. Never have been,' said Lois.

'Shame. You're so jolly pretty. I'd watch you in anything.'

Tony Fielding, professional charmer. Listed as political First Secretary, actually MI6 Head of Station. Comfortable in his velvet jacket and tie-less shirt, laughter lines fanning from his alert far-seeing eyes, ever the youthful wartime RAF pilot with the generic calculated insouciance. Hazardously attractive, notwithstanding the fact that his second wife had recently left him and decamped back to London.

Lois kicked herself for so flatly turning down the chance to join in with the shows. She might have gained some insights into the complex relationships within this artificial community. Perhaps she would offer to help behind the scenes later. She was saved from having to find a pretty answer to his outrageous compliment by the arrival at her elbow of Sonia and Valerie.

Tony flirted gallantly with them for a few minutes before being claimed for an earnest exchange in a corner of the room by a young man Lois had not yet met and who showed no sign of wanting to rectify that.

She had danced with Eric rather too often, Lois decided in retrospect. He was giving her puppy-dog eyes now whenever she moved from his side. Valerie's observation was spot on. But she had taken his kindness in taking her under his wing at face value and been grateful. She so enjoyed dancing under almost any circumstances. If nothing else, it was a rest from conversation and from overthinking. The art was to concentrate on the tiniest of details about every new person she met without seeming to think very much at all.

'Come skating with me tomorrow,' urged Eric. 'There's a pretty river path through Gorky Park, quite the winter scene.'

He still had his hand on her back.

'That's kind of you, but I was planning a quiet day to catch up with myself. I'm still unpacking. Letters to write—'

'Come on, Lois!' Out of nowhere Sonia materialised, pulled her round by the arm and waltzed her off towards a group by the balcony. 'Come and meet some people I think you'll like.'

Lois mouthed a "sorry" to Eric and allowed herself to be led away. 'Thanks,' she told Sonia.

'We girls have to stick together. And I'm sure we're going to be great friends, aren't we, Lois.'

Lois smiled, grateful for the timely intervention. 'I hope so,' she said.

Just as she had no intention of being "snapped up" by the first single man who fancied he was in with a chance, she found the best friendships evolved naturally over time. They were not dictated by simple expediency. Nonetheless, she allowed Sonia to introduce her to yet another batch of rowdy, slightly drunken strangers, and found a second wind to carry her into the fray.

4

Friday, January 17, 1958

Very busy today, the bag day which had been postponed day by day all week. Worked jolly hard – thankful for a meal cooked (terribly) by Vera the maid at lunchtime – Nan & I worked til eight. As usual there's one rule for one crowd and another for the other, though the Minister gave me a pep talk. I wish I could have spoken more with him. To bed as soon as poss tonight. Very late last night when I went with Sonia and Valerie to 'bingo' at America House. Quite good fun & danced afterwards, but too much drink around & difficult to get away. Met quite a lot of people though, including a pleasant German journalist.

As Western foreigners, they sampled all the glories that Moscow could offer but it was a superficial, artificial slice of Russia they were served. The ballet and the orchestral concerts were sublime. The exhibitions of scientific progress; the caviar and vodka; all was laid on for them. There was the ice skating in the parks, and performances by Cossack dancers. The most cosmopolitan restaurants did not serve particularly appetising food but almost always had tables for them, where they dined in close proximity to high-ranking Communist Party officials. But Lois was all too aware that beneath this vibrant surface was a suppurating stench far worse than the pervasive Moscow smell of diesel and cheap tobacco and sweat and boiled cabbage. It was the endless miserable queuing for basic goods, the pathetic bartering necessary to survive. The common knowledge, unprintable, of the secret police, the political prisoners, the labour camps and the millions dead, and the public submission all the same to the Politburo's relentless good news. Even the Western press corps was not immune to collusive reporting. Only four British newspapers were permitted access to Russia: the *Observer, Mail, Express* and *Telegraph*, and their reporters met at the *Reuters* office each morning to rework the standard agency copy in their own style, but only after agreeing between themselves a common story. All for one, and one for all.

And over it all hung the great darkness of the nuclear threat. The thought was there every morning when you woke that this might be the world's last day. The Soviet Union had already let off a test bomb this year, and January was not yet out. A destabilising power struggle in the Kremlin the previous year had given Nikita Khrushchev, First Secretary of the Communist Party, a chance to seize complete control. It could make you ill of depression if you dwelt too much on it. They had all been warned in London to be vigilant, to watch out for the signs of the "Moscow Dumps" or "Moscow Twitch" in themselves and others.

Everything was in high contrast. Bright sparkling days when the snow lay thick on the ground and the domes of the Kremlin flamed in the sun could raise the spirits like nowhere else she had ever experienced. Moscow was as breathtaking as the sub-zero temperatures when you walked outside. You could look up and be startled. You could believe for a few moments that you might be happy, then the sky would drop and you would feel the frozen weight of it, all beauty vanished.

Lois collated the papers and stood up from her typewriting machine in the side room. She smoothed the seat of her skirt. The door to the Minister's grand office was ajar so she gave a quick rap and went through.

She placed the typewritten pages before him and he reached for his pen to sign the letters before he had checked her work, which implied some kind of faith in its standard, she supposed. She had pushed herself to impress.

'How are you settling in?' he asked. The Minister had a gently charming voice to match his gently charming manner. It was like working for a slightly distrait bishop, Lois decided.

'All right, I think.'

'Rather a culture shock.'

'It certainly is, sir.'

Outside the picture window, the river hauled its slabs of ice. Slow and dark the water, jagged and lethal the ice.

'Try not to get too overwhelmed. Blow off a bit of steam with the others when you can.' The others on the junior staff, he meant.

'I'm being taken to America House for the first time tonight.' She gave him a wide smile, making sure it reached her eyes.

'That's the spirit, Miss Vale. Indeed, indeed.'

He reached for the switch. The sudden burst of strident music gave her a start, as it always did.

'There's a bar in the middle of town. Beer Hall No. 1, Pivnoi Zal Nomer Odin, not a bad sort of place – I mean, pretty grim, but they're all like that. Last year, a group of our chaps thought they'd go in and see what would happen. Well, a group of Russian students started chatting to them at the bar. Nothing underhand, in plain sight and sound. Talking about football teams, I believe. That was all. The next time they tried it, about a month later, one of the same students came towards them as soon as they came in and was very aggressive, telling them to go away. Barred them from getting any further in. He told them that the last time they just had a beer, they talked to three boys and one of them was now in a labour camp. Shocking. The result of thinking that life here is in any way normal.'

For a moment, his face held the same expression as the Russians in the streets, the darkness of heavy clouds and snow reflected on the faces. It was there in plain sight, the fear.

'I understand,' said Lois.

Nothing was said for a few seconds. The thought occurred that if she were going to report the incident with the man on the train, this was probably her last chance. Why hadn't she done so already? Though how secure was his office despite the blast of military marching band?

'Now, shall we gird our loins for my political report?'

Wordlessly, Lois fetched her shorthand notebook for dictation. The moment had passed and there was no going back. She would have to keep quiet about it from now on and live with the knowledge that she might already have made a big mistake.

Amerikanski Dom, the fabled America House, fronted the Moskva River very nearly opposite the entrance to Gorky Park and was home to the single male personnel, military and state, of the US Embassy, as well as the Marines who provided security. The Russian girls deployed as so-called maids to do the cleaning and serve in the cafeteria were extremely pretty, and that was surely no coincidence.

The building was a barn-like brick structure that had formerly been a morgue. Someone in the Soviet bureaucracy responsible for negotiating its use by the Americans had a biting sense of humour. The mess bar was spacious and considered the best spot in town, with dances and bingo nights and the most up-to-date records playing on the jukebox. There was even a house orchestra of embassy employees known as Joe Commode and his Four Flushers.

That Thursday night, conversation was noisy and becoming ever more so with beer and bourbon generously dispensed. In the crush, Sonia and Valerie struck up with a couple of Germans who were apparently regulars. Lois found herself chatting to a Swedish pilot, and they were able to make the acquaintance of a hearty Dane before they managed to get a drink. After the constraints of the outside world, the mêlée had an air of reckless abandon. Most of the junior staff from the office had turned out, glad to have different people to talk to.

The bingo games commenced. Lois relaxed, knowing she could take a breather from making conversation and look around without distraction. If she missed some numbers on her card, it hardly mattered. There were at least two men to every girl. Everyone was dressed smartly, and she was pleased she had made the effort with her forest green dress and pearl earrings. She was aware of admiring glances but held back from returning any of them. The time would come for flirting, no doubt, but not yet.

The games ended, and some excellent prizes were claimed: a watch; a wireless; a set of carving knives. A jukebox fired up. Couples started to dance. Some of them jived quite well to rock and roll tunes. But then there was a change of mood. A ballad about April love. Pat Boone. Lois had always liked Pat Boone. She didn't care much for musical fashions.

'Would you care to dance?'

Lois looked up. It was one of the Germans Sonia and Valerie had chatted to at the bar when they arrived. He was of medium height, with blue eyes and light brown hair, or maybe it was dark blond. A few years older than her. An open face and a ready smile. She got up from the table and allowed him to lead her onto the floor. *Ever the romantic*, she chided herself. She couldn't help it. She had a romantic nature. A romance might even be the key to surviving this cold, cold place.

'Are you enjoying the evening?' he asked.

'Very much.'

'Everyone turns up here sooner or later.'

'I'm sure they do,' said Lois.

A labrador gaze from Eric from the sidelines. She couldn't let that put her off her game. Several men had already asked her for a dance, but Eric hadn't. She hoped he was not going to be silly about her gentle turn-down after the party on Saturday.

The German had a reassuringly strong but gentle hold as he swayed her around the floor. Lois did so love to dance. All the more with a vigorous, handsome man who knew what he was doing.

'This reminds me of a certain café in Austria,' she said softly, in German. The dancing and music. The mountains and the river rushing past outside.

He picked up the pace and spun her around, reeling her in closer.

'You always did dance well, Johann,' she whispered.

'Burville,' he said into her hair. 'He's the one to watch.'

5

Friday, January 24, 1958

Could willingly have slept on this morning, but up and into the lion's den. H of Ch is not confidence-inducing. I wonder what makes him tick. Am going to have an afternoon walk in the park tomorrow with the German journalist. He seems nice and it looks like I am finding my feet here at last.

As Head of Chancery, Hugh Burville oversaw all cable traffic and security and most internal administration, monitoring all aspects of the embassy. After the elegant library calm of Waller's office, Chancery was a lion's den extending through an imposing suite of rooms on the raised ground floor. They commanded these spaces, these men, with their expansive arrogance and certainties. They imposed the traditions they had been brought up to inherit, Lois decided. Burville had created a facsimile Pall Mall gentleman's club that now and then slipped into farce. The rows of desks either side of a central aisle would occasionally become riotous, like a turbulent classroom: all cut-glass accents and combative public schoolboys. From a magisterial desk at the front, Burville, mid-forties, hair dark and plentiful, slim and sleek as an otter in a dark suit, ruled with the tender malice of the dedicated careerist.

In her relatively few dealings with him since the introduction on her first day, when his handshake had been no more than a limp touch, Lois instinctively felt he was a man on the up who was constantly trying to prove it, to himself as much as to others. He was exacting and critical, even in ostensibly friendly exchanges. He monitored every movement in his domain with narrowed eyes, and he was watching her now, his eyes wandering from a conversation as she crossed the wide floor with a document from the Minister.

She could either smile at Burville like a shop girl or pretend not to notice. He was recently divorced, not bad-looking, and probably fancied himself as a ladies' man, so she pretended not to notice. Lois had encountered his kind before: men who thought secretaries were barely more sentient than their machines and should know their place. Their place being nowhere near his places, which covered the usual ground between public school and the London clubs favoured by Whitehall mandarins. His old Oxford college tie flew like a pennant, the signal not intended for the likes of her. The Magdalen lily crest, as it happened. Lois had memorised the files. If intelligence work was all about recognising signs and patterns and making connections, she had to be able to spot the tarnished links.

Her heels clicked on the parquet floor. More conspicuous than she would have liked, she held herself tall, or as tall as five foot four could be, and aimed for dignity rather than display as she observed the occupants of the room. Moscow rules were tolerant of idiosyncratic office dress within the confines of the embassy. Colourful knitwear that would have raised eyebrows in Whitehall was the norm, essential for keeping warm, even indoors. A few of the men strode around in wartime greatcoats and the MI6 Chief Tony Fielding appeared regularly in a moth-eaten First World War sea captain's coat.

Valerie was at her typewriter, rolling in another paper with carbons. Eric came in from the cypher room and went over to the second secretary's desk. John Linton, Private Secretary to the Ambassador – she knew now that he was the man who cornered Tony Fielding at the party in the hotel – was in quiet discussion now with one of Fielding's intelligence officers, Ellis Wachorne, nominally Third Secretary, attired today in a garish striped sporting blazer. Wachorne was said to be under the heaviest surveillance of them all because he had arrived in Russia in the company of a Royal Navy lieutenant-commander on a ship from Helsinki to Leningrad harbour where they were clearly attempting to get the measure of the Soviet fleet. A fluent Russian speaker who had been sent to learn the language at Cambridge after national service, he had become the de facto daily press reader, giving daily summaries of all the important stories in the Soviet newspapers at the 9.30am Ambassador's meeting.

Lois delivered the Minister's document, receiving a curt nod in acknowledgement from Burville, and turned to go. If she could only spin it out a little longer, her careful timing would be spot on… she heard a distinct sound in the corridor, appeared to hesitate, and turned back as if to double check the pages she had brought. The arrival of the afternoon tea trolley, just as she had hoped, gave Lois her chance.

The staff gathered around, glad to take a break. It was only polite to accept the invitation to join them.

'I like your blazer,' she said to Wachorne casually.

'Cheers the place up, I feel.' He grinned.

'I've been told by the Minister to come to you if I need any translations,' she ventured. Although the Minister also spoke reasonable Russian, he was a Czech specialist, having served in Prague and Vienna immediately after the war.

'Righto. Be happy to help. How are you getting on?' His manner was friendly and curious. He gave the impression of a sporting man who also liked to read. Curly fair hair and alert brown eyes. She could imagine him lounging in cricket whites. Two crossed cricket bats were embroidered on his blazer pocket. On that imaginary pitch, he might have had a copy of Housman's poetry in his pocket. More to him than met the eye at first glance, at any rate. Though young, he was already married to a pretty, sociable wife called Flora.

'All right, I think. There's a lot to get used to, and no matter what you read about a place, in reality it's never quite what you expect.'

'Don't I know it! Every day we read *Pravda* and *Izvestiya*,' he told her, 'and every day it's a disappointment. Full of words but contains as much news as milk pudding. Articles invariably begin with trumpet blowing for the Soviet system and end by forecasting a magnificent future – you have to look in the middle for the "but" and try to deduce what the reality is. So you try any research publication you can lay your hands on looking for something to winkle out about how Soviet strategy is evolving. It's all detective work. Fascinating, of course, but frustrating, too.'

'It must be.'

'Well, come and find me with whatever you need deciphering.'

'Thanks.'

Burville was looking at her again, his expression not encouraging. Perhaps she was not expected to be so pushy, but Wachorne was the one doing most of the talking. There were clear divisions between the dips and the junior staff that she would be well advised to respect. The Head of Chancery's traditional responsibility for the smooth-running of the embassy included the morale and well-being of the junior and backroom staff but that was an aspect of the job conspicuously missing from Burville's demeanour.

'A cheerful face goes a long way,' as her mother always said. Lois stood her ground and smiled. No longer the young girl who watched, unable to step forward, as her well-loved books and wooden box of treasures burned on the bomb-site bonfire all the while Cousin May was driving an ambulance in the East End, and June and Mabel were helping to save the country in ways they were never allowed to speak about. A residual shyness remained, perhaps so deep in her nature it would never leave, but did not now hold her back; it had been transmuted into a calm self-effacement that more than one man had told her was mysteriously attractive.

So she carried on chatting to Wachorne. Nothing more than small talk, but he was amusing and pleasant, too. She stayed as long as she could without drawing undue attention to herself.

'You were getting on well with Johann Dreschler last night.'

Lois spun around. Eric had crept up on her in the corridor. Now he was blocking her way to the ladies' cloakroom.

'I beg your pardon?'

'That German reporter.'

'Is he? I didn't ask.'

'He works for the *Frankfurter Allgemeiner Zeitung*.'

'Well, good for him. Now, if you don't mind—'

'He goes through a lot of women. Quite the playboy.'

Lois gave an exasperated half-laugh. 'It was just a couple of dances.'

'Just so long as you know.'

His face reddened and his russet hair stuck up where it had escaped its Brylcreem hold. It was dreadful how sincere he looked.

'In that case, thank you. I will bear it in mind should he ever ask me to dance again.'

Winter dusk. On the steps of the Bolshoi Theatre, two men in dark coats spoke behind a pillar. One man, the larger, was an American, an old hand at this game. The other was Johann Dreschler.

Their conversation was deliberately ambiguous. Neither named the KGB officer who was being called back from London. The officer was Yuri Modin, strongly suspected of running an exceptional agent for more than a decade. But this agent was no longer at the heart of British and US intelligence operations; he was in Beirut, sending news stories and observations to Moscow as well as London that had no value, drinking heavily and gingering up his reports with speculation. The Russians knew him for decades as their man, Sonny.

'So Sonny's old friend is coming home,' said Johann. 'He is needed here now by his firm? Their Middle Eastern factory isn't working so well?'

'Production line keeps breaking down. Needs industrial quantities of alcohol.'

The American looked like a Cadillac dealer from Hicksville in his car coat with raccoon collar, his melted wax jowls and fat cigar. He might have come to Russia with a trade delegation. He was actually a veteran FBI special agent who had worked covertly for years with a very select band from MI5 counter-intelligence, the realists to the reckless showmen of MI6, to pin down the truth about the British traitors who were still active.

'You heard about our new guy?' he asked.

Johann nodded slowly but said nothing. They had known each other in the closed circle for a few years now. They trusted each other. Or did they?

'Gone missing. Not good at all. Any day now he's gonna turn up dead in a hotel room, even though the US embassy has given him his own apartment. Pickled and drowned in vodka when he only ever drinks bourbon.'

'Who else knows?'

'We're keeping it quiet. He was never here.'

Johann rubbed his hand over the lower part of his face as he finished telling Lois the story in vivid detail. The cold had reddened his nose and cheeks. It was Saturday afternoon and if anyone they knew happened to see them in Sokolniki Park, they could happily assume the outing was the start of a romance after their meeting at America House, warning from an interested party or not. Martial music reverberated from speakers at the entrance to the grounds as a grand boulevard of a path opened up before them, wide enough for a military parade. As they passed a couple of watchers in dark greatcoats, Johann made an expansive gesture and spoke clearly enough for them to hear.

'In summer, they have kiosks selling food all along here, and flowers and a circus and a funfair and a cinema.'

No trace of warmth and gaiety now. All was stark white and grey. Other walkers, rare as black swans on a vast cloudy lake, were distant dots.

'This park was laid out by the father of Peter the Great in order to pursue his favourite sports of hunting and falconry,' he went on, playing the tour guide, speaking English in his soft German accent. 'Now it is a People's Park of Culture and Leisure.'

Cotton-like puffs of ice and air swirled between them, and Lois was glad for the hundredth time that she had taken the advice to buy a fur coat and fur-lined boots.

'My regular tail is behind us, but he's all right. Sometimes we actually like each other. He'll stay well back. I took the liberty of telling him I'm hoping for a new romance. I hope you don't mind.'

'If needs must.' She met his eyes. They shone bluer than

ever in the wide, white expanse all around them. Lois thought, once again, most inconveniently, that she might rather welcome a real romance with Johann.

He smiled and offered his arm. She took it.

'The new guy who's gone missing is a complication,' he said. 'His name is Nayland.'

No wonder Miss Harcourt had decided to warn her. First the FBI man arriving in Moscow and now this other American had turned up and run into trouble. All very interesting, but a risky complication.

They turned down a side path hemmed by snow-laden trees. Lois sensed rather than saw their tail do the same.

'As the old handler of a once-powerful foreign asset, Yuri Modin is a man of importance in the KGB,' said Johann. 'The question is, do they want him here to liaise with another agent – another big fish?'

'Indeed.'

'No sign of anything yet?'

'No. I'm looking hard but—'

'Ach, this was always going to take some time.'

They walked on in silence for a few minutes. A path led across a lawn or meadow into a wilderness of pines and spruces, birches and oaks. Lacy clumps of snowflakes played chase in the air against the dark evergreens as the wind whipped up.

'To look on the bright side,' she said. 'It means that if this intel is right, and Modin does have another asset inside our embassy, his arrival will be the catalyst that shakes things out.'

Johann had been in Moscow for a year already when they met in Austria. Whatever she had expected after her initial briefing with Robinson and Ellingwood in London the previous September, Johann was a very pleasant surprise.

He had dealt deftly with the stone in her shoe as she sat on the grass. He paused, put a hand up to shade his eyes and looked down the valley. The yellow church far below in Zell seemed to glow in the sun. A cooling breeze pulsed through the steep green meadows below. Clumps of wildflowers bobbed their heads in clover.

'Infinite shades of green,' he said. 'Ivy and sage, and moss and spring willow.'

'Forest and glade,' she supplied in response.

'I am happy to meet you, Lois.'

'And I you, Johann.'

He offered to walk along the path awhile with her. It was perfectly natural: she was alone; he was alone. Two young people in the Tyrol who both enjoyed hiking.

He was tall without being noteworthy, with a face she thought of as quietly handsome; it was not until she spent some time talking to him and noticing how his eyes were lit with clever perceptions, and that his teeth were white, even when he laughed, and his nose a noble form, that he became more than he seemed at first glance. He had worked with the Allies after the war in Berlin, and he was Austrian not German. Afterwards, he had gone to Frankfurt and built himself up as a journalist. He was a good one, too. His grasp of detail and his instincts for the story within a bigger picture were second to none. For some years he had been quietly re-employed as an "occasional", an ultra-secret British asset.

After Johann arrived, the days passed in a state of excitement. Lois had an intense feeling that she was doing something important. There was also the entirely unexpected pleasure she experienced in Johann Dreschler's company. He was six years older than her, courteous in a way that seemed sincere yet relaxed, cultured and moved by music and poetry; he asked gentle questions and seemed genuinely interested in her answers. He was highly experienced in the duplicitous world she was entering, yet he seemed to care only that she should be aware of his fundamental honesty.

'There must be no secrets between us,' he told her.

Their task was to build an understanding before she was posted to Moscow. They had to get on the same wavelength, evolve a way of communicating in public and in private, learn to trust each other implicitly, and how to use each other. There would be no one in the embassy she could turn to. They had a week to establish a working relationship. So much was dependent on events outside their control. Flexibility and incisive reaction would be key.

'We'll have to wait and see,' he said more than once in answer to her questions.

Miss Harcourt had assured her that Johann Dreschler was absolutely trustworthy.

'A very safe pair of hands indeed. If you have any pressing concerns on the spot, you can go to him.'

'Who else will know who he is?'

'No one.'

'Not even Head of Station?'

'Absolutely not.'

By the second day, on a walk high above the Ziller Valley, where birds wheeled and called, she thought they would work very well together.

By the third evening, they were dancing at the Gredler.

On the evening before he left, he gave her an edelweiss flower he had picked and kissed her. She did not pull away. Afterwards, she looked at him quizzically.

'I just wanted to know if it might be possible for us to put on the show of a romance between us. It would give us the perfect excuse to spend time together.'

The river babbled at their feet. A Schuhplattler band was

playing nearby, and the sound carried of dancers stomping and clapping.

'And what is your conclusion?' she asked at last.

He smiled. 'From my point of view, it would certainly be an option.'

'I see.'

She turned away. Stared up past the onion dome atop the tower of the lemon-yellow church, up to the darkening greens of the mountains where they had walked that afternoon. A private smile on her lips.

He turned too, his back against the railings.

The fact that she liked him very much as a person was an unexpected bonus. They could openly and genuinely enjoy one another's company without more complications than there already were.

'We'll have to wait and see, won't we,' she said.

Edelweiss for truth, courage and hope.

There must be no secrets between us.

In the Russian winter, a flat white carpet of snow stretched before them, dull silence in the freezing air. Trees shivered. The KGB watcher trailed behind at a distance as they marched on, arm in arm.

'A funny thing happened on the train from Helsinki,' she said.

He listened intently to her account of the man in the homburg hat. Made her describe him in as much detail as she could remember. Then asked her to do so again. Fixated on the steel-grey gaze and the exhausted overcoat.

'He called you by your name, you're certain?'

'I'm certain.'

'Did he seem agitated, as if he was taking a risk speaking to you?'

'He was very composed.'

'He was in complete control of the situation?'

'So it seemed.'

'What did you think he wanted?'

'I assumed he wanted to compromise me before I'd even got to Moscow.'

'His voice. The tone, the accent. Any inflections?'

'Good English but not perfect.'

Johann stopped and faced her. 'Someone who has learnt to converse with native speakers? It's in the vowels, always the vowels. English or American markers?'

'No Americanisms. Do you have any idea who he might be?'

'I wish I did.'

'I didn't report it. I could have done – should have done – anytime until the other day with Waller. I don't know quite why I didn't.'

Johann was silent.

'Training, you know. But I have a horrible feeling it would have been better to—'

'There's no evidence you encountered him, no note he passed or you wrote. Not even afterwards?'

'None.'

'So, it is done now.'

There was nothing more to be said.

On Sunday afternoon, Sonia went out to a play rehearsal. There were always play rehearsals, it seemed, with the Ambassador's enthusiastic blessing. After which, her flatmate had a date with an American doctor.

'Don't let on to Boyd, will you?' she warned Lois airily as she left.

Lois winked at her and resisted asking about either man. 'Have fun!'

Sonia blew her a kiss from the doorway. She whirled out and a sense of calm returned to the apartment. A red dress dripped over the back of one armchair and a matching pair of shoes lay drunkenly under the coffee table. Lois still wasn't sure quite what she felt about Sonia. It wasn't that they weren't on friendly terms, they absolutely were, but there was something about her that Lois found oddly resistible. Undoubtedly, it was the forced nature of their apparent friendship due to proximity and necessity that Lois didn't feel comfortable with. In The Hague she had had her own little flat. But she couldn't fault Sonia's willingness to be friends. The clear social divide between them was never mentioned. When Sonia talked of dances, they were debutante balls on Park Lane and nightclubs frequented by the wealthy West London set; when Lois spoke of dancing, she thought of the Palais de Dance at New Cross. It was all still dancing and good and bad partners, though. Perhaps the issue of class was Lois's problem, not hers. Was she being too sensitive? Or perhaps it was simply Lois's nature to proceed cautiously in friendships, only slowly letting her guard down as new points of connection were established. Whereas Sonia simply seemed to declare friendship into existence.

Half an hour later, Lois signed out with the Meshchanskaya guards and hurried out on foot. She went a circuitous route, ascertaining at every corner and in every reflecting window that she was not being followed. Only when she was sure she was not, that it was true that secretaries did not warrant routine surveillance, did she make her way to St Philipp's church.

The church sat forgotten in straggly trees, as Johann had described. A mangy cat assessed her warily. Grey stucco, once white, was cratered and decaying, and only a trace of gold paint remained on its three mosaic icons prominent on its rotunda. The great door was heavy with winter damp, open only in the sense that the lock was broken. There was no sign of life or any recent service, though someone had roughly scraped the path of snow so her footprints would not show. She joined the quiet flock who would not deny their faith: the old and the ill-educated whose observances were tolerated, but only barely, by the State.

Inside, an empty vaulted chill. But the air held a memory of extinguished wicks. On the Eastern Orthodox altar stood a defiant army of candles, tips soft to the touch. To the right, on a low wooden cupboard, an iron construction held thin votive wands. Lois knelt in front of it, said a silent prayer, then reached around to the back of the cupboard. The loose panel at the back came out easily; nothing behind it, only rougher wood. It would hold a message on a slip of paper. Nothing there this time. Nothing expected. But it was always a good idea to familiarise oneself with a hiding place, to prepare the ground, set the precedent that this was a church she went into sometimes for her own private, inviolable worship, in case they needed to make use of it as a dead drop.

Back at the flat, she unzipped her leather writing case, unclipped the pen and simply dated the page. No address, only the safe signal: *Moscow, midnight* in the top-right corner. *Dear Elsie*, she wrote. *I'm not going to write much, just a quick line to let you know all is well. My second week is over, and I seem to be getting the hang of it all. So far, so good, as they say, though very cold. I went to America House on Thursday and met some nice people, including a handsome German journalist, so I'm feeling optimistic that there's going to be some life outside the office. I hope Peter is well. Give him my love, and to you as always, L xx.*

She folded it into an envelope and addressed it to Miss Elsie Glover, 16 Heathview Court, London SE3. It would go in the forward tray for the bag in the morning. Miss Harcourt had impressed on her the wisdom of sending brief updates in letters to a third party, in this case to a friend with whom Lois had worked in The Hague, who could be relied on to forward it discreetly.

6

Friday, January 31, 1958

Arctic temperatures. Didn't think it could get much colder. A swine of a day, including a dreadful scene down by the river. Waller as shocked as I was. He is a gentleman – genuine, I feel. Still a few people at the embassy I haven't come across yet but I'm sure they will come out of the woodwork eventually. Unexpected visitors.

By the end of January, Moscow was savagely downcast. On the nineteenth, the Soviets had tested another nuclear bomb, a high-altitude rocket, in Kazakhstan, devastation estimated "total" over a radius of a hundred miles. Blackened snow lay piled at the sides of the roads. A smile was unthinkable. The tension took hold of you, day by day. Being on your guard at all times meant unwelcome physical reactions in the body. A tautness in the neck, in the arms, the knees. Low-level fear became normal, or, rather, what getting through every new day with a veneer of normality entailed. Like white breath ballooning in the freezing air, everything was on show.

Work rose to gigantic proportions. Though they partied by night to mask the ugliness and try to forget, the embassy was a place of critically serious endeavour and the demands were relentless. Lois's in-tray rose with urgent reports and letters for the bag. Each slogging day followed the last, reprieved only by the delay of the Queen's Messenger by snowstorm and mechanical difficulties on a plane. First for twenty-four hours, and then another day. But so great was the mountain of reports and letters that it was no hiatus, merely a breathing space to make sure everything would be done on time.

A couple of the other secretaries were off with the flu, and it was all hands to the pump. By lunchtime, everyone was starving hungry and bussed back to the flats for whatever meal the maids could provide, some days better than others and the absolute worst being watery potato pancakes with an over-boiled egg. Lois began Russian lessons. A Madame Popakova came every Thursday evening to teach her and Sonia.

When John Linton, the ambitious young Private Sec to the Ambassador, made a passing derogatory comment about Germans in Moscow within her earshot at a party, Lois was prepared to dislike him until he mentioned Johann.

'A good newsman, fine piece last week about Bulganin,' she heard him say. Perhaps he wasn't so bad after all, just an arrogant boy not long out of Oxford with an excellent command of the Russian language.

The closed circle in Moscow was very closed indeed, though she still had not met Goodrich, the young MI6 security officer. In fact, there didn't seem to be anyone of that name at the embassy. She thought it best not to ask anyone straight out.

'Look at that,' said the Minister.

It was ten in the morning, still not quite light. Lois joined him at the window. Down on the embankment, a group of men had gathered in the chilling smoke-grimed mist. The men seemed to be arguing. One caught hold of something using a long wooden pole with a hook on the end. They tried several ways to haul something out of the brown river through a crack in the ice.

'Or perhaps best not to look. Sorry,' he said.

A body was being hauled out of the water. Dark clothes, dark trousers. Dark worms of hair. The face and hands white-grey, as if they had turned to marble. An icy marble man caught in a dark, dripping net.

She couldn't look away.

'Poor soul. Wouldn't have stood a chance if he went in last night, with these temperatures,' said Waller. 'Though at least his family won't have long to wonder where he is. Sometimes, in spring, they bring them out and find they were last seen alive in November.'

Still Lois did not avert her eyes from the scene. Duty over rising nausea.

'An accident – or deliberate?'

'Suicides in this way are not unknown. But it could equally well be foul play. Also not unknown.'

A small crowd was forming on the embankment. Far above them all on the other side of the river, the Kremlin's high walls and towers remained a suggestion of smudged towers in the gloom.

The body was laid out on the frosted stone. Someone delved into the inside of the sodden coat, presumably to see if it contained any means of identification. Exhausted by their efforts, the other salvagers turned away, giving a fuller view of the corpse on the hard white sheets of the riverbank, staring up blankly into the mist.

Waller took out a small pair of binoculars from his desk drawer. After a long look, he took a deep breath. He fumbled with his cigarette box and offered her one.

She accepted gratefully, heard the snap of his lighter and turned to lean into the flame. His hand shook slightly but she judged it inappropriate for her to ask if he was all right. He was the embodiment of calm establishment order, steady and disciplined in his three-piece charcoal pin-striped suit and pearl tiepin. Only a tic under one bloodshot eye gave away his unease. So they inhaled in silence, facing the window.

His exhalation was so long, so clearly a sigh of relief, that it seemed to surprise him as much as her.

Lois turned instinctively.

'For a moment there, I thought it might have been someone I once knew,' he said.

They continued watching. A black van drew up. A stretcher was produced from the back doors and the body lifted onto it.

'It wasn't him, though,' said Lois.

'No.'

The Minister picked up some handwritten pages from his desk. 'I suggest we both have a cup of tea, and then you can get on with this. No tearing hurry.'

Lois hesitated as she turned from the window. 'Will we ever find out who he was, do you think?'

'I shouldn't think so. It's a cruel place.'

She caught his eye and held his gaze. Neither spoke but he seemed to be making an evaluation. She had the wild thought that this might be the turning point, an end already to her charade. A hint that he knew exactly what she was?

He looked away as someone knocked softly on his way in. 'Ah, Hugh. Good timing. If you don't mind, Lois...'

Waller handed her the sheaf of paper. She nodded to Burville on her way out and left them to it.

Two days later, the students came to the embassy gate.

If it hadn't been for thinking about the dead body, she might have missed them. The Minister had slipped out of the room for a moment, but Lois was at his desk by the wide window. Had every reason to be there, too, as she was about to place some papers in the tray for his approval and signature. Was he making her job easier, knowing he had nothing to hide? It was disconcerting to suspect her mission was not as completely confidential as she had been told. Either that, or she was suffering the early effects of "Moscow Twitch". She took the chance to glance over the documents and files on the Minister's desk without disturbing them. A review of Khrushchev's visits to the Ukraine. A report from the military attaché apparently detailing troop movements in the Black Sea region. Another report from the Ukraine, this one from Bill Stoneley, the Foreign Office Research Department's academic in residence. Waller liked to work on a clear desk. They were all advised to do so, though not everyone was capable of complying.

Below on the embankment, the spot where the corpse had been dragged out bore no trace of the drama. Snow had slurried and refrozen on the grey stones, wiping away all evidence. Nor had the macabre episode drawn comment from others at the embassy that she thought it might. A couple of the girls had mentioned it with a shiver, but no one had made much of it. Was that odd, or a facet of knowing that too many terrible things happened here?

She was looking out, therefore, thoughts elsewhere, as two young men stopped on the pavement outside the embassy and exchanged words. One, the taller, approached the guard at the gate. There seemed to be some difficulty in communication, but the young men did not walk on. They stood and waited in their striped college scarves and duffel coats. British-looking, not Russians. They stamped their feet and clapped their arms across themselves.

The guard must have telephoned up to the duty officer. A few minutes later, a figure emerged from beneath her vantage point and walked down the entrance steps towards the gate.

It was Ellis Wachorne. A short exchange ensued, and the gate opened. The two young men were granted admission but only as far as the entrance steps. They spoke briefly to Wachorne. One of them reached into his coat and passed over an envelope. They all walked back to the gate and the visitors exited.

Lois closed her eyes and concentrated on committing the scene and a description of the strangers to memory. It might be nothing, of course. Good practice, if nothing else.

'Nothing better to do than linger and dream, Miss Vale?'

She started.

Hugh Burville had soundlessly entered the room. Elegant as ever, though on the small side, he stood like a storm ready to break as he surveyed every aspect of her and possessed the space.

'Just waiting for the Min. I mean, Mr Waller,' said Lois, sounding too daft by half. She cautioned herself against overdoing it. 'He had to pop out, said he would only be a minute.'

Burville's gaze moved over her to the desk, to the closed drawers and the bookcases.

'If you were looking for him, he should only be a—'

His face was noticeably hollowed, sinewy almost in its lack of spare flesh. His shoulders were too small for the chalk-striped suit, as if he had lost weight.

'I'll find him.' He left without an ounce of normal politeness.

Was that an odd encounter, or his usual curtness when dealing with junior staff, especially the women?

Lois waited until the Minister returned so as not to leave the papers unattended, informed him that Head of Chancery was hoping to see him, then took some papers down the corridor to be filed in Registry. With any luck, it would be nice timing for the tea trolley.

Eric was in high good humour, which grew the more gin cocktails he knocked back. He was clearly getting keen on her, which was unfortunate but might be useful in the short term – the very short term.

The Garden Block party was frenetic. A record player was at full volume, pumping out a series of new rock and roll tunes acquired through the American Embassy. Conversations rose to shouts, and there was laughter and the occasional breaking glass. Lois already understood very clearly the mandatory quality of the gaiety. Pulling together, the bulwark against despondency.

She had been out of luck at the tea trolley. She'd been hoping to find the amenable Ellis Wachorne there, or else someone from the Russian secretariat. She'd missed it though, and couldn't loiter too long between Chancery and Registry without drawing attention to herself. The rest of the afternoon was spent attacking a draft report on Soviet policy, or as much as could be detected, concerning relations between East and West Europe. All the time wondering: who were the two young men who had come to the embassy gate? What had they handed over? Why had they come?

Lois poured herself another tonic water at the help-yourself bar – a sideboard covered in bottles – and talked inconsequently to Rory Kendalmoor. Valerie, jaunty in slacks and a pink sweater, told a long, though quite amusing, story about a French diplomat, his dog and a tin of caviar.

The carpet was rolled back. Lois had attempted to jive with Eric, but there wasn't enough space, and he was terrible dancer. For him, it was all about letting off steam rather than reacting to the music with practised steps. Defeated by their jerky skirmish on the parquet floor, he flopped back on a couch next to Rory, pulling her along with him. He pulled his tie loose and undid the top button of his shirt. Sweat was gleaming on his forehead.

'I found out, by the way,' he said.

'Oh, yes?' Rory didn't sound that interested. He didn't look at Lois, either.

Lois perched on the armrest next to Eric, listening.

'Neither of them known,' said Eric. 'History undergrads, not languages. The tour checks out. London University.'

'Any use?'

'Who knows?'

'What's this?' asked Lois brightly.

'Interesting visit the other day,' whispered Eric hoarsely. 'Two young chaps from the UK, students, presented themselves at the gate. Said they had something important to tell us.' He was already drunk and slurring his words.

'And was it – important, I mean?'

'Well, that's the thing. It might be. Or it might not. Whole thing could be a bloody set-up. Who knows?'

'But you heard them out?'

'I didn't but Wachorne rather had to. I mean, s'probably undergraduate japes-sh, but you can't necessarily assume that. Burgessh 'n' Maclean have rather set us up for thish kind of thing. Bastards!'

His garbled words were increasingly hard to understand. Lois wanted to ask more but it was hopeless.

'Come on, Lois, my turn for a dance!'

She jerked her head up to find Frank holding a hand out to her, thinking he was rescuing her perhaps. She had no choice but to be towed into the jumping, heaving, foot-trampling centre of the room to rock around the clock for the third time that evening.

They drank more, danced more, shouted more. Some people seemed to be having fun, while others were simply in a state of smiling anaesthesia. Eric was flying on gin, his hair sticking out in all directions. Despite volunteering to do so, he did not seem capable of organising their departure in a taxi. Lois seized the chance to suggest that they walked back to Meshchanskaya. The freezing night air would sober him up and give her a chance to speak to him before that process was complete.

He was delighted, of course.

Streetlamps shone like Belle Époque baubles, and vehicle lights painted streaks of red and white along the dark military avenues. She grabbed his arm not only to steady him but provide a visual lie for any watcher that this was nothing more than a romantic stroll after a decadent Western gathering. After a few minutes, they reached Moskvoretsky Bridge. It was guarded by militiamen, two at one end, two at the other. The domes of the Kremlin gleamed above white trees.

'Thass where the man approached them. In the middle, out of sight of the guards.'

Lois had no idea what he was talking about. 'Does that seem likely?' she asked neutrally.

They walked out on to the bridge. The water was silent and black below. Gas lamps glowed rather than cast light. Lois looked to the ends of the bridge. It was true that the sentries were not visible.

'Thass what they said. Or what the message to London said they said.'

The students?

'A Russian. Assked them if they would take a package. They wun take it. But he did give them a letter. They took that. Decided to bring it to us.'

'The young fellows who came by the embassy gates?'

He nodded.

'What was in the letter?'

'Shouldn't tell you that.' He pulled himself up taller. 'But as you're so lovely…' He looked all around. There was no one near. They might have been alone on the bridge.

'Might have a defector on our hands.'

'No!' She hated the way she sounded when she played dumb. 'A Russian coming over to us?'

Eric nodded emphatically. He really was very drunk.

'Oh well,' said Lois. 'I expect we'll find out. All in good time.' She was angry now. How had the vetting process been so lax as to allow an inexperienced young lad like Eric access to sensitive information through the cypher room? Surely messages like this should have been encrypted and sent by specialists with top security clearance.

He put a hand on her shoulder. Moved for an opportunistic kiss. She turned away smartly, bending down to pick up the handkerchief she had purposely dropped. Just in time to allow him to save face by pretending she hadn't noticed.

They set off again, walking across to the north bank. Straight ahead was the cathedral built by Ivan the Terrible, sinister as a fairytale with its byzantine radish domes. Few vehicles ventured onto the bridge, even fewer pedestrians. It seemed there had to be a compelling reason to be on foot at night in the depths of winter. Eric stumbled, then moved in to try to kiss her again as she reacted to save him from falling. She dodged him easily, then put her arm under his.

'Maybe trying to walk back isn't such a good idea after all,' she said firmly.

At the nearest taxi rank she gave the address and helped him in. He was asleep with his head on her shoulder when they arrived back at the apartments. She delivered Eric to the second floor – his roommate Alistair, another cypher clerk, was less than pleased at the state of him – and went on up to the fourth with a small sense of achievement.

7

Thursday, February 6, 1958

The great Stoneley! Every bit the whirlwind I'd been expecting but quite special. I enjoyed our coffee break. Had been feeling rather out of my depth but he was very sympathetic, especially about my journey out. Not going to take anything for granted but between him and Johann, life is looking up.

The Minister departed on a scheduled trip to Kiev. Intourist and Burobin finally came through with the tickets and permits, though it had taken several attempts; no sooner was everything agreed than the Russians found someone to raise an objection and the whole palaver had to be started again. In the event, Waller had been cleared to travel only hours before his plane took off, leaving Lois a full in-tray, instructions to take work from whoever requested her services, and an entirely misplaced early optimism that she might have a slightly easier time of it and an opportunity to concentrate on other matters. Chance would be a fine thing.

The telephone didn't stop, some of it important, some of it utterly trivial. Mrs Waller was in a quandary about a burst pipe; how utterly infuriating, it *would* be the week Roger was away – and what did Lois think about numbers for her At Home on the twelfth? Would it be too much to ask that Lois might telephone those who hadn't replied? The order had to go into Gastronom with plenty of time. Lois worked through lunch.

Two o'clock brought a new face into the anteroom where her typewriting machine exercised its tyrannical hold.

'Looking for the Min,' said Bill Stoneley without introduction or preamble. He had a broad Australian accent.

'He got off to Kiev at last.'

'Ah… of course. *Reve ta stohne Dnipr shyrokyi* – "*The mighty Dnieper roars and bellows!*"'

She smiled, apologetically uncomprehending.

'Taras Shevchenko. "The Mighty Dnieper". The great river that flows from Smolensk through Belarus and Ukraine to the Black Sea. Lifeblood of Kiev.'

He was a big man, shoulders as broad as his smile, which gave the impression he was continuously amused, as indeed he might have been. Bill Stoneley was emphatically not a spy, or so he said.

'I am a curator of rumour,' he would announce to the inquisitive before they could make fools of themselves. 'I may be our Russian secretariat's idea of a joke, but my opposite number over at the US Embassy is called Vlad Prokofiev. Look him up, it's true!'

Even in his small, panelled office, a room that might once have been the butler's pantry, he dressed as a caricature of an Englishman: tweed jackets, checked shirt of the kind favoured by off-duty army officers. Sometimes a deerstalker hat. His native Australian accent was a jarring inconsistency, though one, it was supposed, would be unlikely to reach the Russian ear.

He had known other foreign cities where espionage was as close and vicious as a knife fight, notably in Istanbul during the war, that great supposedly neutral bunker between East and West where it was no more unlikely that a beautiful belly dancer would reveal her Yorkshire origins in a torrent of gutter language than that the British Ambassador's valet was a Russian spy and his chauffeur a German informant, and none of these as unlikely as a corrupt Turkish policeman who was working solely for one foreign power. Istanbul, hot sweaty den of adult games involving pimps and peccadillos, gun runners and carpet baggers, turncoats, gamblers and unlikely winners. Stoneley had fought his own battles there using his native wit and disregard for orders. Guile over gun warfare. He had a useful air of distraction. Too many esoteric thoughts were apparently occupying him to listen carefully or to be much good to anyone.

It would have been a grave mistake to underestimate Bill Stoneley. Lois knew that much from her briefing back in London.

He lived alone with the housekeeper and cook kindly supplied by the KGB and appeared to delight in practising his ever-improving command of Russian on them. They were not to know that he had a degree in Russian language and politics from London University and specialised in open-source intelligence and threat analysis. Nor that his bumbling, affable persona hid a mind that could slice to the heart of an issue before his unknowing conversational adversary had realised they were being pumped for details. The untidiness of his flat, and his propensity to lose silly items, gave entirely the wrong idea about his general hopelessness. He was always kind, to everyone. Never a raised voice or sharp tone. Gratitude for all that was done for him. It was most disarming.

'Is there anything I can help you with?' Lois hoped it wasn't a mammoth report to be typed before she had made nearly enough progress with the Minister's in-tray.

'Well, I *was* answering a call from Waller to discuss my views on how Soviet thought is evolving but as I haven't got sense out of the Soviet Foreign Ministry since the last time and they don't know much themselves because the inner circle of the Party handles all the important business, there wasn't much new to say.'

'Tricky.'

'I'd like to talk to someone in the inner circle, of course, but for some reason they don't seem keen to speak to me.'

'Most inconsiderate of them.'

Stoneley laughed, a rich rumble. 'I was also hoping to have a little chat about the body that came out of the river. Rather annoyingly, I didn't see it myself, but I want to build up an exact picture. Reckon Waller had the best view but looks like that will have to wait.'

'He's back on Monday. But…' She took a risk. 'I was standing at the window with him.'

He considered this. 'Hope you weren't too shaken up?'

'A bit.'

'Only natural.'

'What do you think?' asked Lois, keen to keep him talking. 'Are bodies pulled out of the river here usually suicides?' She was intrigued. Not so much by what he was asking, but why now, more than a week later?

'On balance, yes. Tell you what, I'm going to chat up the tea lady, get her to put some hot water in my thermos flask, and we're going to take coffee and biscuits out in the fresh air for a bit. There's a glimmer of sun come out to torture us during working hours, but we will not be outdone.' He tapped his bulbous nose.

They took a turn around the garden of the mansion, Stoneley swathed in an ankle-length fur coat that moulted and smelled like an ancient cat.

'One of the yardmen laughs and tells me this style went out with the ark, but it's the warmest coat I've ever worn. Found it in one of the attics upstairs,' he confided. 'Now, you were going to tell me more about that river incident.'

She told him everything she could recall. He was avid for detail. What age, what height, what shade of hair? The shape of the head, the length of the hands? Any obvious wound? Then he began asking, subtly, about the Minister's reactions.

He indicated a wooden bench overlooking the frozen tennis court. It was hidden by a group of bushy fir trees from the windows at the back of the building that included the Ambassador's office and residential quarters. They sat. A tin of slightly stale digestive biscuits appeared along with the thermos flask from the capacious depths of his coat.

'Wasn't there quite a group watching the scene from the Chancery window?'

Bill looked over the rim of his cup through steam and the caramel aroma of Camp Coffee. She could see him making an instant calculation and kicked herself for coming across too stridently. Was it normal for him to give coffee in the embassy grounds to other people's PAs?

'Yep. There was.'

'Have I been any help, told you anything you didn't already know?'

Discrepancies were dangerous. They could reveal a great deal, usually detrimentally. But she had to know.

'What you've told me pretty much tallies. No one else noticed the guy reaching into the coat to look for identification, assuming that was what it was for. One funny thing. Apparently Burville went white, and you know what his first reaction was? "Bloody hell, that's Maclean!" It wasn't, of course. You could see it wasn't when the body was flat out on the bank. But the height and the long Western-style coat... I suppose that was what made him think it.'

Was that who the Minister thought it might be, too?

'It would have been a terrible coincidence for him to have washed up right outside the British Embassy,' said Lois.

'Too right! No coincidence at all, then. Don't be shy, have another.' He indicated the biscuit tin and took one himself, chewing with evident relish.

'Thank you. Do you ever see Burgess and Maclean out and about?'

'Spotted Burgess a few times shambling along the street. Maclean only once, at the Bolshoi with some Soviet bigwigs.'

'You didn't approach either of them?'

'It was tempting, but no. Best to leave well alone.'

Lois took another sip of coffee. Outside in the cold, as an unexpected treat, it was utterly delicious.

'Maclean's still a very sore point,' he went on. 'Struth, all the mandarins in Whitehall, all the higher-ups at the Washington embassy and in Cairo, none of them could countenance the truth that the traitor could be "one of us". They had known him and his family for a long time. They liked him. They had a whole network of old friends in common. Abroad, they covered for him out of loyalty. He might have been getting blind drunk and argumentative and sleeping out on park benches, a sorry sight in the mornings, but no one ever sent word to London that something was wrong with him.'

He paused and took something else out of his pocket. 'Actually, someone did try to stop the rot. Security officer in Cairo. Army, non-commissioned, had come up through the ranks. He did the right thing, sent a discreet letter to London about Maclean. And what happened?' He wiped his mouth with a mauve handkerchief the size of a tea towel. 'Nothing. Maclean had too many people back in London to vouch for what a jolly good chap he was, how intelligent, how efficient and hard-working.

'While Maclean was in Cairo, the Americans found evidence of years of leaks from the British Embassy in Washington. They

77

told London with similar results. The Brits investigated all the cypher clerks and secretaries, especially those who had foreign blood, and didn't even look at the likes of Donald Maclean with all his establishment connections. They just couldn't imagine it, you see, that someone with all the advantages in British society could possibly not appreciate how lucky they were and want to defend that.'

'Dreadful,' said Lois carefully. Was there any possibility that he was telling her that he knew exactly why she had been sent out to Moscow?

'And then bloody Burgess, too. No. You spot either of the wretches, you give them a wide berth. Do not approach under any circumstances. If they're on fire, you let 'em burn.'

She gave him a sharp sideways look.

He met her gaze with a nod. 'I'm not joking. I know... I *knew* good people who disappeared thanks to them. Disappeared, almost certainly dead. In the most appalling circumstances. If most people only knew how much damage those men did... I'm sorry to set this out so bluntly, Lois. May I call you Lois?'

'Of course.'

'And you call me Bill. First name terms for those who dare join me *al freezo*.'

They sipped in silence for a minute or two.

'Macmillan called the Maclean and Burgess affair a "personal wound" and he was right, you know,' he resumed. 'Struck right at the heart of the family. Did us no good at all with our American friends, who tried to tell us. But the betrayal from one of our own in all senses... it was very hard to bear.

'My job is all about making connections. Seeing links when others assumed they were accidental, tangential, coincidental. There certainly is such a thing as coincidence, but not very often. Lucky breaks are rare. Usually coincidences show the way to the bigger picture. But the Russians enjoy their deception operations, almost as much as we do. It's a game of bluff and double bluff. The importance of hiding the object in plain sight.'

'But the body wasn't Maclean.'

'No.'

'Any idea whose it might be?'

'I have heard a little rumour that it was... American.'

Lois had an uncomfortable intimation that she was both receiving an oblique message and being tested.

'Goodness! Is that... likely?'

'It's possible. Keep your ears and eyes open, eh? If you hear anything – anything at all – or remember anything more, I'll be interested.'

Definitely a test. How much did he know? Or did he simply assume from her position as Waller's PA that she was MI6-cleared? If anyone at the embassy knew her true mission, it would surely be the estimable, unconventional Bill Stoneley.

'Of course. If there's anything in it, I'm sure someone will be talking about it at America House next time I'm there.'

'By the way,' he said, too casually. 'I heard a whisper from another embassy that you were approached on your journey in.'

'Really? How odd. Approached in what way?'

'On the Moscow Express. Classic Russian playbook, of course.'

Don't avoid his stare. Lois looked him squarely in the eye and shook her head. 'I can't think where that would have come from.'

'One of the Canadians was on the same train. Noticed you as you left your compartment on arrival in Moscow.' Stoneley paused to gauge her reaction. 'Said he was surprised to see a young Western woman coming out. Thing is, his couchette was in the same carriage, and earlier he'd seen a Russian closing your door behind him.'

She pulled a puzzled frown. 'What, leaving my couchette?'

'So the story goes.'

'I'm not that kind of girl, Mr Stoneley!' Lois managed to produce a light laugh. 'Besides, I don't think my flannel nightie would cut the mustard for a modern day Mata Hari.' Luckily that amused him. She calmed herself. The best lies were almost entirely true, and much more plausible than flat-out denial. 'Though, come to think of it, there was a small misunderstanding at breakfast time. A man opened my door and came in before he realised he'd let himself into the wrong compartment. He thought at first I was in *his* compartment. We had a few words while we sorted it out. He was embarrassed and he left.'

'I see. Something and nothing, then.'

'So it would seem.'

'It's getting too cold to linger. Shall we?'

She took the shaggy fur arm he offered. Impossible not to be drawn to Bill Stoneley, but dangerous.

That evening she did her best to reset her hair, dressed carefully in a red dress with flowing skirt and used slightly more eyeshadow than normal, all the while trying to brush away Sonia's imperious curiosity about where Lois was going and with whom. Her flatmate's inquisitiveness was unrelenting.

'Come on, Lois, do say!'

'You know, I think I'll keep everyone guessing. Provide at least enough intrigue for a whole evening of delicious speculation and a welcome new topic of conversation!'

'Is it someone new? Tell me!'

Lois laughed lightly. 'Allow me some secrets!'

'Oh, you are too *brutally* annoying, dear Lois! Friends tell each other everything.'

'I'm teasing. It's only Johann.'

Sonia seemed relieved. Lois sensed that for the sake of equilibrium she should not enjoy a more exciting social life than her flatmate. Better to give in quickly than to show she could keep secrets, even inconsequential ones.

As Lois brushed her eyebrows lightly with her tiny flat mascara brush, she wondered why exactly she had decided to make a special effort. She wanted Johann to notice, she decided. There had been nothing between them so far since that moment in Austria. Was there ever going to be? It seemed important to know. Or was it simply that she wanted to make the best impression possible on the first evening that she had information to share?

Johann's apartment on Yaroslavshoye was pleasant enough. Smaller than most of the diplomatic accommodation, but deliciously unshared. She felt she could breathe again; it was so hard to relax with so many people around her at Meshchanskaya. Johann took her coat and complimented her on the red dress.

He put the record player on, some discordant jazz. Not even the offer of a drink before he led her straight into the bathroom. He opened the taps and, as water gushed into both the basin and the bath, handed her a notepad and pencil. He was all business.

Body in the river might have been an American, Lois wrote on a notepad, still standing. 'Just a rumour or have you heard anything similar? *Nayland*?' she mouthed.

'Maybe. Who told you?'

Bill Stoneley, she wrote.

A cloud of steam was already starting to rise above the bath. So much for bothering about her hair before coming over; it would start to frizz soon. Johann sat down and reached over to adjust the hot tap. She joined him on the rim of the tub.

Johann took the notepad and pencil. *If the Americans know, they aren't saying. Nayland here on special operation – he's deniable from start to finish.*

'But thanks. That's useful,' he said. He pulled out the pages they had used, balled them individually and tossed them into a metal bin by the basin. He took out his cigarette lighter and set the crumpled paper alight.

She watched the flames licking. What any of it might tell them about a traitor in their midst was hard to tell. Nothing, probably. An American problem, and for once nothing the British could be blamed for.

'It may or may not have any bearing for us,' said Johann, apparently also having some of the same thoughts. 'By the way, while we're here. Someone should...' He took up the pencil again and wrote, *give a warning to one of your third secretaries.*

Lois felt herself getting uncomfortably hot. 'Tell me.'

I know about your two student visitors. 'Maybe others do, too. You know how tiny matters are blown out of all proportion here.'

'How did you hear?'

'I overheard.' *In America House. Maybe he was lucky, and I was the only one who did. And that he wasn't at a restaurant next to a table of Soviet officials. But he gets drunk, and he seems to need to prove his worth. Dark red hair.*

'Eric,' she mouthed.

'He talks too much.'

'Yes, he does. Though sometimes that's useful.'

'Not when it makes him an idiot.'

Lois said nothing. Then she took the notepad and scribbled an account of the rest of her conversation with Stoneley. Best to mention the whisper from the Canadian Embassy and her response, just in case.

Johann seemed to accept she had done her best to limit the damage. He gave himself the final word by ripping out those pages and setting them alight. Then he turned the taps off and opened the bathroom door to let out the steam.

They went for dinner at the Praga. Their table for two – tiny glasses of vodka and a long wait for the inevitable beef stroganoff – would no doubt fuel the diplomatic gossip mill.

Johann talked rapidly. The craft of foreign reporting. The selective editing of events. The power of the unseen, the unreported. A world without windows. He was an idealist, she realised.

Sometimes Lois felt this was the most important thing she would ever do in her life. From this, all else hinged. But that night, her thoughts wandered as Johann got into his stride. She had always known this job would be a kind of loneliness in the midst of the crowd. It was always a question of trust, an all too precious a commodity in this nervy atmosphere. Moscow extorted a price. They all lived on their nerves, suspicious of everyone and everything. Was that why she had felt the urge to dress up and make a special effort to look attractive – because she needed more than just words of comfort from him?

She was glad when Johann offered to take her home in a taxi.

Outside, there was barely a soul in sight. All was muffled and closed in by new snow, a bitter night in a strange and hostile city. In the rolling barge of the ZIS limousine, he finally stopped talking and put his hand over hers, but it was nothing more than a comforting gesture. He had given no indication he had noticed anything different about her at all.

They rode in blessed silence for a while.

As the car turned into Meshchanskaya Street, he said, 'You are a very beautiful listener.'

She tilted her head to him in acknowledgement. He moved closer and kissed her. It was so unexpected; she was taken aback but did not rebuff him. The kiss went on for a long time, gentle yet exciting.

At last the driver tapped impatiently on the glass partition with a coin. They parted with laughter, and Lois signed in with a lightness of heart she had not felt for many months.

8

Friday, February 7, 1958

Lunchtime walk on embankment with Ellis W. Very pleasant but the conversation a little dark. Probably a timely reminder.

Lois was asked to pitch in with Chancery work. Defeat of the Minister's in-tray was still not assured, but it was a chance to observe Hugh Burville more closely. Prejudices aside, he possessed an effortless intellect coupled with confidence that he was valued by his peers in Whitehall. There was no doubting his skill at rattling off memos and summaries of complex situations for her to transcribe, all the while continuing to look through her, not a crack in his aloof and inscrutable veneer.

She also had some friendly exchanges with John Mowberry, Second Secretary (Political) who spent his days at his desk analysing Soviet internal policy by trying to match their stated aims to actions. As far as Lois was aware, Mowberry worked under no kind of cover. He was a popular member of the large embassy staff and apparently the most lethally effective player at the weekly poker evenings held at his apartment. For that reason alone, he ought to be one to watch.

The change of routine also brought her into closer

proximity to the mercurial young MI6 officer Ellis Wachorne. Wachorne was impressed by the speed of Lois's work, and even more so by her astute questioning of a small error he had made. By the time they had corrected it, reasoning that it was best done straightaway, they had missed the bus home for lunch. He suggested good hot beef stew in a Ukrainian café he favoured, followed by a brisk walk along the embankment.

'It can send you crazy, being under constant observation,' he said as they marched along afterwards, full to the gunwales. A biting wind was doing its best to clear the clouds, now and then unveiling a pale, exhausted sun. 'I hope you don't mind… it doesn't hurt to have a bit of fun with them sometimes. Draw the Russians out by doing something that gives them an idea, then wait to see who does what with it.'

'What do you—? Oh, I see.'

'They know I'm married, so to be out walking with a new and attractive young woman, apparently carelessly…'

A nice boost, that throwaway compliment, even if it didn't mean anything except gratitude that she was willing to go along with the ploy.

'All this cat and mouse business,' she said guilelessly. 'It's not until you get here you realise how bad it is.'

'You single girls are jolly brave to come out here.'

'Or jolly silly.'

He laughed. 'Is it worse than you thought?'

'It is, rather. But I'm getting used to it. I suppose you can get used to anything after a while.'

'That's the spirit.'

'Or one starts to see only what one wants to see. I say, I heard some people thought the poor soul who came out of the river was Maclean!'

She waited but he did not oblige with a comeback. Fresh snow squeaked under their galoshes. Rare shafts of sun lit them a glittering path. It seemed like weeks since they had seen the sun.

'It was rather morbid. But rather horribly fascinating, too,' she ploughed on. 'What do you think – suicide, accident... murder?'

'My first instinct was suicide.'

'For what reason?'

'He didn't look like a down and out. He didn't look as if he would have toppled into the river by accident. If he had problems they were likely bigger, more complex than lack of control or drunken stupidity. There didn't seem to be a wound that would indicate murder. So... suicide. It's rather an unpleasant reality in Moscow... and afterwards. Young clerical officer in the Naval Attaché's office a few years back. Bit of a loner, probably queer, got himself into a state but seemed to be keeping it together until the end of his posting. Then he tried to top himself. Another jumped in front of a train three months after returning to London.'

'Oh, my.'

'Sorry, sorry, Lois – what am I saying! I don't mean to upset you. Forgive me.'

'It's all right. We're told to look out for those who might need help, aren't we. Best to be aware.'

'Absolutely. Best to be aware,' went on Wachorne. 'This atmosphere unnerves people. The single, more junior staff are at particular risk, you see, because the Russians know that they were likely to be more vulnerable as well as more susceptible to being corrupted. I saw one young chap go downhill last year. But you'll already have been warned about this, don't mean to give offence.'

'None taken.'

'Gosh, what a terrible subject for a walk.'

'You're right.' A pause. 'It wasn't Galton, was it, who went downhill?' It wouldn't be because she had only that moment plucked the name from the air. She braced for him to tell her it was the mysterious Goodrich.

'No… not him…' He made a backwards gesture with his head. 'You've noticed we have company, I presume?'

He stopped, so she did. They were facing each other. Out of the corner of her eye, Lois saw a man walk over to a tree and light a cigarette, absorbed in his own business.

'Yes. I was aware of him as we crossed the bridge, and then as we came into the park.'

'Good. Anything else?'

She looked him in the eye, but he gave nothing away. She turned very slightly, looking to the side but not down as she opened her handbag and reached in for a handkerchief. Another figure, further in the distance, strolled over to a bench to sit down.

Lois dabbed her nose delicately. She wanted Ellis Wachorne's respect, but not to give away her training.

'Looks like they put two men on the job.'

'They can't hear us out in the open, by the way. We thought they might be able to, but it seems not. So you see, walking is an excellent activity. I enjoy it very much, and sometimes a breath of fresh air at lunchtime is just what is needed to say a few things that need to be heard only by the right ears.'

'I understand,' said Lois.

Again, just as she had with Bill Stoneley, she felt she was both being given a message and being tested. They continued along the embankment. The faint sun sheened the remaining ice on the river and imparted a surprisingly serene and lyrical mood. The watchers bustled after them.

'It would be a shame if we tired them out, wouldn't it?' He grinned. 'I suspect they get much less pleasure from these promenades than I do. Especially if they haven't tucked into as decent a lunch as we have!'

Lois felt another sudden surge of light-heartedness. She had seen Johann two evenings that week and romance was definitely on the cards. She had begged him to ditch the discordant jazz at his flat and put on something they could dance to. They'd waltzed around the sitting room like mad things, then she'd kicked off her shoes and flopped back on the sofa, laughing. Real laughter, releasing all her pent-up nervous tension, feeling safe for the first time since leaving Helsinki. Or perhaps it was just the sun and Wachorne's irreverence. Finally, she was making some headway into the tricky network of relationships and expedient temporary friendships that was the currency of any embassy.

This was underscored by Wachorne's invitation to come over one evening for a casual supper with him and his wife.

'I think you and Flora might get along. Don't want to jinx it by saying so but do come and see. Goes without saying she'll rustle up something delicious to eat. She really is marvellous, especially when you consider how limited options are here. Though not as bad as for the ordinary Soviet, of course. Count our blessings!'

Kind of him, and she said so. He did seem a more than usually thoughtful young man.

9

Sunday, February 9, 1958

"Moscow Nights". Quite the iceberg. The cigarette box.

Eric asked her again to go skating on Sunday with a crowd of junior staff.

'We're going to Gorky Park. It's not much fun on our stuff at the moment,' he said. A makeshift rink was made every winter on the tennis court in the embassy grounds, but the ice was bumpy, packed hard.

It had been years since she had skated, and even then she hadn't been very good, but Lois accepted. She had to know how much he remembered of their conversation and what had happened since. Valerie provided her with some skates, old but comfortably well-worn, that were handed down the transient ranks each winter, and a padded jacket, possibly from the same source. Lois dressed carefully in her black slacks and Fair Isle jumper. Nothing too alluring, the last thing she needed was to give him the wrong idea. Girl next door, all the way.

Sonia went on ahead, collected for lunch by her Canadian admirer. Was he aware of the gossip about her and the Russian on the train – could he be the Canadian witness? Had Sonia picked up anything? Surely she would say if she had. It was impossible not to be consumed by suspicions.

It was another leaden afternoon, cold as Siberia, but Gorky Park put on a glorious winter show. Paths along the river had been prepared and frozen into a snaking rink through snow-capped trees. Above the treeline soared Stalin's modern gothic Ukraina Hotel, a monument to power designed to impress and intimidate. Below, sweet Frank Patterson, one of the Registry clerks, a slight, bespectacled lad from Liverpool, wobbled precariously on skates that were too big for him, earnestly aided by his flatmate and fellow Northerner Rory Kendalmoor.

Lois laced up the skates and allowed Eric to take her hand as she nervously approached the ice. Gratefully she caught sight of Nan and Valerie gliding towards them. She tentatively put one blade down and felt it slide. Sure enough, with both feet on the ice, she found her balance, trying to remember the movements needed. She pushed herself forward with a jolt. She decided she wouldn't be daunted, couldn't be defeated. Not by something so much in her power to control. Mind over matter.

One wobbly slide, then another. Then again.

She was away.

How far away she was. It seemed a hundred years since the train to Moscow. The hot, bitter tea from the samovar in the corridor. The stranger in her compartment. It was as if the journey through the night had brought her through a hole into a different world where blackness prevailed despite the white covering of snow. She felt an unexpected surge of excitement at her own daring.

Russian men and swarms of children hissed past on long speed blades. Nan was moving sedately as Valerie prattled as ever. Soon they were catching up with the others. Eric was hanging on to her hand, but he was almost holding her back now. She dropped Eric's hand, but he caught her mitten again.

'You're doing very well. Quite the iceberg, aren't you, Miss Vale?'

'I shall take that as a compliment.'

'You do like me, though, don't you? You made sure I got home after that party. Not something you'd do for someone you didn't care for.'

'I was being kind,' said Lois. 'You were kind to me when I arrived, so—'

'She likes someone else,' said Sonia, barging up. 'Don't you, Lois.'

How long had she been behind them?

'I like plenty of people.'

'Including the German chap?'

'Maybe.'

She pushed off again, wobbled but managed to save herself.

It was dark by four o'clock. Lights began to twinkle in the trees along the route. They skated on for what felt like glorious miles. Delightful strains of music floated above the winter scene – *Tchaikovsky*, she thought. Bursts of *The Nutcracker* filtered through the trees. As they flew along to the end of the lap, Lois spotted Johann waving to her at last. Though she was beginning to tire, the sight of him perked her up. He gave her a show of his proficiency on the ice in a few flashily confident movements and apologised for his lateness. She took the hand he offered, and they glided off.

She forgot her annoyance at his keeping her waiting and worry about the reason for it. They did a lap of the park alone, Lois serene with the strength of his hand in hers. The music changed. A song poured out that seemed to encapsulate all the sadness and loss in Russia, not in the words she could not understand, but in the yearning, stirring melody. Johann sang along pleasantly until it faded on a mournful minor key.

'Is that a traditional air?' she asked.

'No, a popular record of a few years ago. It's called "Moscow Nights". Muscovites have taken it to their hearts.'

'It sounds as if it might have been sung for two hundred years.'

She wanted to tell him about the walk with Ellis Wachorne but judged it unwise. Sonia, or anyone else, might slide up close enough to overhear again. The others were gathering by a hut selling hot drinks.

'We can't talk,' she said under her breath when he bent over to help her take her skates off. 'We'll have to chat with the others. Eric's here, too.'

She made the introductions. Sonia and Valerie he already knew from America House. Sonia sparkled with a sharp flirtatious edge; Valerie was clearly delighted to have a new audience for stories already familiar to the others; Nan was calmly welcoming. Eric, Frank and Rory shook hands with him, Eric visibly annoyed and downcast, Rory with his usual diffidence. Frank alone was openly friendly, comical in his Russian fur hat with ear flaps. It seemed to sit too high and square on his head, at odds with his thin, English face and intense stare mitigated by round metal glasses.

Warming hands around mugs of hot sweet coffee, chapped faces bright in the steam, they stood and discussed the press corps, the diplomatic community, pulling out people they knew in common, gauging reactions.

Johann outlined his survival plan: 'Go to the ballet, go to the opera, go to concerts. The music is the best in the world. They have to give the masses something good, and by God, this is it.'

Lois laughed, mostly in relief that he hadn't focused on the many negatives like everyone else. They talked for a while of Tchaikovsky and Rachmaninov, who was a particular favourite of his. He was all openness and sociability. A gregarious man who enjoyed speaking to strangers and finding out about them and accepted the curiosity of others in return. The Cold War as a winter scene, she thought, stasis as World War Three was put on hold for an afternoon. Terror of atom bombs and columns of marching men could be forgotten as the music played and skates scratched ribbons on the ice.

'How did you get into journalism?' asked Rory. He was all at sea with Russian composers.

The war had disrupted his studies in Heidelberg, Johann replied, but that experience was far more use to him than a diploma. He had ended up in Frankfurt and a training post on a newspaper. No, not the famous *Allgemeiner Zeitung*. That was a privilege, an honour, he had had to earn.

Lois had asked him the same question in Zell. 'So, you are a bona fide journalist, then?'

'You couldn't train an agent to be a doctor or scientist or a businessman, sooner or later they would give themselves away,' Johann had told her then.

But you could train one of them to be an agent after they had established their professional credentials. Journalists and photographers were obvious covers, and there had always been plenty of crossover there. You had to be able to remember fine details. From a usual drink to the kind of cigarettes a man smoked, to the state of his fingernails, to where he said he was born. Nor could you write any of that down; for the most part, the only safe vault was the memory. It was the smallest quirks that offered the biggest clues. Finally, when you come to write a report, let it be complete and factual whether or not it makes complete sense. Do not omit what you do not understand, or decided might be misleading. There is no place for personal judgement or interpretation. You only know what you can see and hear. Let those who see the bigger picture make the assessment.

Rory seemed so very young and awkward in comparison as he listened. Valerie trapped Frank in the web of a complex tale about her uncle in Norfolk. Lois caught Eric watching her, his nose clearly out of joint.

Back at Meshchanskaya, Lois was still a block of ice, slowly thawing from the outside in with tingling sensations. An iceberg, Eric had called her. And so she was. She curled up on the sofa, still huddled in her Fair Isle jumper.

'I was watching you,' said Sonia slyly.

'I'm sure my skating was most amusing.'

'At America House. It didn't look as if you had only just met him.'

Lois fought to conceal her annoyance – with Sonia, but mostly with herself.

'Whatever makes you say that?'

Sonia shrugged. 'You seemed, I don't know, very comfortable when you were dancing with him.'

She was no fool. Lois realised she had underestimated her.

'That's because he actually seemed to know how to dance unlike some of the clodhoppers who've been dragging me onto the floor.'

'I've made you go red,' crowed Sonia. 'You really like this German, don't you!'

'So what if I do?'

'Does he know?'

Best to give her the upper hand on this, to let her feel she had something of little importance over her than anything else.

'Please don't tell him, whatever you do, Sonia!'

Actually, it might be useful if Sonia gossiped about her and Johann. It didn't really matter either way, but best to let Sonia think it did. Lois went into her room. Nothing had been disturbed.

Sonia followed her in. Lois immediately felt uneasy. So far there had been an unspoken agreement that their bedrooms were sacrosanct private spaces. Sonia made a show of casting a searching look all around.

'Where is it?' asked Sonia flatly.

'Where's what?'

'My enamelled cigarette box.'

'It was on the coffee table last time I saw it.'

The cigarette box was always there, in front of the couch. An enamelled thing, not particularly pretty. Vera the maid filled up the box each morning from the carton in the pantry. She probably only did it in order to steal some. It hardly mattered, they bought Rothmans so cheaply from the commissariat two hundred at a time. Lois kept her preferred menthol cigarettes (Consulate, the brand name made her smile) separate. But most people preferred plain tobacco and putting the cigarettes in the box allowed visitors to help themselves.

'Well, it's not there now.'

'Did you put it somewhere?' Lois asked mildly.

'Why would I take my own box and put it somewhere?'

'Put it *down*, I meant.'

'Have you taken it?'

'No. Why would I do that? Vera must have moved it. Look in the pantry, perhaps she was filling it and got distracted.'

Sonia stomped off to the kitchen. When she returned with the box, she glared hard at Lois.

'You knew it was there, didn't you? You think you can play tricks on me!'

'Sonia, I knew nothing of the sort. It was a logical suggestion.'

But Sonia would not leave it. It was over nothing, but she got herself all worked up and did her best to involve Lois in the drama. Lois's innate reserve and patience, perfect qualities for the job, as well as their imposed friendship, now seemed to be an irritant to Sonia.

'You're a dark horse, aren't you,' she said, making it into an accusation.

Tread carefully, Lois. Don't react too much.

'Word is, you go out walking with Ellis Wachorne.'

'I did go on a walk with him, as a matter of fact.'

'He's married, you know.'

'Very happily so. I am well aware.'

'It's a fine line, getting too friendly with the dips,' said Sonia, trying another tack. 'Especially for a girl like you.'

Lois felt a jolt of anger but managed to control herself. 'What do you mean by that?'

'You know what I mean.'

Let it go, she thought. *This is her problem, not mine.*

'It was his suggestion. We'd had to finish a job, and then we'd missed the bus. The sun was out, and we decided not to miss it. It was a pleasant saunter, no more, no less.'

'I came home for lunch on my own.'

Silence.

'You'd better be careful the Min. doesn't find out,' Sonia went on.

'Oh? Why's that?'

'He doesn't like loose talk in the office. He's had two PAs in the past year. The first was transferred early. Your predecessor only lasted six months.'

'Oh? Why was that?'

'Couldn't cope with the pressure. Or so it seemed.'

'What do you mean by that?' Lois wiggled her tingling fingers, then stopped when she saw Sonia's expression. It was dreadful how she had to be aware of every little word or gesture with Sonia. She needed constant attention and turned unpleasant if it was withheld.

'Why do you think you're so much better than you are, Lois?'

'I – I don't. I'm just trying to do my best. Why do—?'

'As a matter of fact, I don't like that German. He's…' she seemed to be searching for a reason not to like him, 'arrogant. Too cocky by half.'

Johann hadn't reacted to her charm offensive.

'He's press. They all act like they know everything.'

Sonia shook her head. For some reason her eyes were teary.

'Look, why don't you come and meet Johann properly? He actually enjoys cooking and he's having some friends along to his place. I'm sure you'd be welcome.'

'Can't, sorry. Full schedule what with the play, Boyd and a rather dashing Dane I've met.'

'Get you!' Lois's attempt to lighten the mood was blocked with a black scowl.

On St Valentine's night, America House was decorated with huge red hearts made of cardboard. Battalions of bottles stood behind the bar, and candles flickered. By ten, it was packed.

All the junior staff seemed to be there. Frank was with a pretty girl, young and plump, and had eyes for no one else.

'His Spanish nanny,' Valerie explained.

Eric ignored Lois, and so did Sonia. But Lois was danced off her feet: by Johann, by the British contingent, guards and US Marines, and several tall, broad Finns who pushed through the throng to ask her. The atmosphere was rumbustious, like the Christmas dances at Goldsmiths' College. Hard liquor flowed. Joe Commode and his Flushers worked themselves into a frenzy until they were relieved by the latest American records played through loudspeakers.

It turned into one of those nights fired by the intention to forget unpleasant truths. Eric got drunk again and forgot he was ignoring her. He claimed Lois for as many turns on the floor as he could, vying with a Canadian called Irving, all dimples and a good smile, who knew what he was doing with a jive. Lois drank only tonic water dressed up with ice and lemon and listened carefully to what he said. He gave no hint he knew anything about her. She walked between tables and swayed among the couples on the dance floor. Nothing of interest was to be picked up, despite the reputation of America House for indiscretion.

Flirtations simmered between other people's wives and husbands and escalated in the darker corners. Blind eyes were turned. It was the pressure, the effect of living in a closed society. A natural reaction to the Moscow blues. What passed in America House stayed in America House. If she'd thought she'd ever catch careless talk of the recovery of the body in the river or speculation about the dead man who had never been in Moscow, she was clutching at straws. The music and shouted conversations grew ever louder, until it was too hard to have any kind of conversation. It was 4.45am before she got home.

Sonia was in an odd mood the next morning, the worse for wear no doubt. First she didn't want the coffee Lois made too strong, nor to eat a late breakfast at twelve, and then she did. Loaded silences were interrupted by aggressive little sallies about Lois's clothes, and the way she cleared the kitchen too soon, and, worse, Lois's apparently irritating calmness in the face of provocation.

'What's that peculiar look you give me?'
'What do you mean?'

'You're doing it now.'

'I'm really not.'

'Of course you are. You know exactly what you're doing. You really do think a lot of yourself, don't you!'

'I don't want to argue, Sonia. What's this all about?'

'You know what you've done.'

'I really don't.'

'I'm talking about Irving. Last night.'

'We had a couple of dances, what of it?'

'You knew that he's Boyd's friend.'

'I can assure you I did not. And that I did nothing that can possibly interfere with your ambitions in that direction.'

'Ambitions? Is that what you think? What a thing to say!'

'Calm down – please, Sonia.' Lois was starting to feel uneasy about where this could lead. 'Keep your voice down,' she whispered urgently. 'I'm sorry, that was a silly thing to say, just the first that came into my head. I didn't mean anything by it.'

'And you've already got Eric and that German mooning over you. You don't need anyone else, especially not Boyd's friend. It's all right for you, you don't suffer with your nerves,' said Sonia.

Lois was baffled. Until now there had been no evidence that her flatmate did either, though the current unwelcome scene was more evidence that she would jump on any little perceived slight and make a drama of it. She was going to have to be even more careful from now on, as well as try not to be resentful at the sapping of her energy and resources.

'You just retreat into your own little world and leave me to it.' Sonia's face was reddening, and her eyes were wet. 'It's not easy to cope here.' The pretty little face screwed up like a pug's. In her craving for attention, she seemed to have forgotten that she was the Moscow veteran, not Lois.

It was true, though, that Lois had the mental capacity to close herself off. She had always possessed it. She would have to find a way to impart some wisdom to Sonia without patronising her – for both their sakes.

'I've always been a bit of a daydreamer, if that's what you mean. You're not the first to notice.'

'I want to shake you out of it!' shouted Sonia, returning to the attack.

'But why? I'm not doing you any harm, am I?'

Sonia was full of moans. Frances didn't like her. Nan had been rude and ungrateful. The Head of Chancery was a swine.

'I was talking about it with Sergei. He thinks you are clearly not a team player.'

Lois resisted the temptation to react in the way she was supposed to. She walked into the kitchen and filled the kettle. She left the cold tap fully open so that the water hit the sink noisily. Sonia followed her, seeming to relish the prospect of an argument.

'Who's Sergei?' asked Lois.

'Just a guy at America House.'

'You know him well?'

'Well enough. He gives me lifts home now and again. He likes me, and I know I can rely on that. What's it to you?'

'You brought him up. Is he Russian, with a name like Sergei?'

'He's a Yank. Well, he sounds like a Yank.' Had Sonia realised she'd said too much?

'He's with their embassy, one of the Marines?'

An awkward pause.

'So, do you often discuss our set-up here with this Sergei?'

'He's a friend of mine. But what's all this? You're awfully keen to deflect from the subject. I hate the way you're all out for yourself!'

Lois made herself another cup of coffee, fighting to keep calm. 'On the contrary, I'm trying to look out for you.'

Sonia wanted a full-blown row, but Lois pleaded a fictitious headache after the exertions of the previous evening and went and lay down on her bed. Without a date to go walking in the park or skating with, there was just nothing else to do. Sonia worried her, though. First she came on too strong seeking – needing? – Lois's friendship, now she was needlessly argumentative. How could a girl with such a lack of inner resources have been sent out here? It made no sense, or rather pointed to a continuing lack of perception in London. Was Sonia the embassy's weak link? It seemed unlikely given that she was only a normal secretary without clearance for confidential comms and would have no access to sensitive material. There was also the possibility, one that Lois had not wanted to consider seriously until now, that Sonia was the intruder who was most often disturbing the "tells" in Lois's room.

10

Monday, February 17, 1958

Tired with muzzy head but work was fairly under control today. Sonia rather depressed, I think, but it really doesn't help to keep on about it.

Met Johann at the Metropol early tonight & we had a delicious dinner before going to the Bolshoi to see Jeanne d'Arc *– kitchen sink modern! The final adagio performed by Eleonora Vlasova and Yuri Grigoriev of the Moscow Stanislavsky Ballet was beautiful. Sergei Someone also stood out. Enjoyed it but was very tired at the end. Then went back to Johann's and read poetry! Not to bed before 1am again.*

Neither Eric nor Frank knew a Sergei at America House.

'More likely to be one of the Russian militiamen with a name like that,' said Frank, stating the obvious.

It was Johann who provided the answer. Sergei Hawkins was a translator at the US Embassy. Some said he was the son of an émigré White Russian mother, others that his father had been a high-ranking military officer before he was forced to flee; it was unclear whether any of it was true.

'He's bilingual, clever… unpredictable. Useful on several levels but not universally trusted by his own side.' Johann drew deeply on his cigarette, leaving his wine unsipped. He always seemed to prefer smoking to drinking. They were at the Metropol hotel where he had a favourite table to the left of the bar with a full view of the door. He had tipped up the base of the table lamp on a cigarette lighter so that shadows fell across their faces. Not even the most talented operative could have read their lips.

Lois didn't want to speculate out loud about Sonia's naivety, for that was what her instincts told her it was, but at the same time she knew she had to make a disclosure of sorts.

'Sonia seemed a little unsure of him, where exactly he fitted in with the Americans. He has been giving her lifts home.'

'I see.'

'It might be nothing, of course.'

Another deep inhalation and tangible pleasure in releasing the smoke. 'You were right to mention it.'

What Lois was keeping to herself, at least for now, were Sonia's remarks about her self-containment. '*You just retreat into your own little world.*' Neither did she like it when Lois enjoyed a flirtation with too many different men, another aspect of her true personality. Sonia was perceptive enough to add another layer of jeopardy to the mission. And she was indiscreet, always wanting to show how much she knew and keen to angle for more disclosure. Sonia had a brain, and she was bored – a potentially lethal combination, whatever her motives.

They went through to the cavernous glass-roofed restaurant. It was always full, though the service was often dilatory and rude. Lois hoped they would get something to eat, and swiftly. Johann had wangled seats at the Bolshoi for a performance of a new ballet, *Jeanne d'Arc*, and she had been so looking forward to it. Her first glimpse inside the famous theatre, first sight of the vaulting perfection of Soviet dance.

'I was at the Café Lyra the other day,' said Johann, glancing around from his new seat against the wall with a view of the room and the entrance. He had tipped the concierge well to get it. 'They serve a good stroganoff – meat unspecified, but what is life without risk? Very reasonable Georgian champagne. I sent a bottle of champagne and a glass with my compliments to the KGB man who normally follows me around most evenings. But the fellow just left. I didn't mean for him to go. I hoped he might enjoy the champagne, that it was a way of thanking him for his discretion, but he wouldn't take it. Ach, swell, there he is again, over there, standing against the pillar.' Johann shook his head in amusement. 'There's one American you should meet.'

Lois wondered how much time he had been spending with the Americans. She was picking up all kinds of US inflections and phrases in his speech.

'If you think so,' she said. 'Cousin?'

A "cousin" was the term MI6 used for members of the CIA.

'Of sorts.'

A party of doughy Soviet officials was shown to a table nearby. Johann began to talk about poetry.

On the Bolshoi Theatre's classical pediment, Apollo wore a cloak of fresh snow to drive a chariot drawn by four rearing horses, though the city had been sunless for what seemed like months. Lit by the blazing entrance, white puffs of snow danced like tiny ballerinas in the darkness. Johann saw her catch one on a finger and laughed.

Jeanne d'Arc was starkly modern in setting. The final adagio performed by Eleonora Vlasova and Yuri Grigoriev of the Moscow Stanislavsky Ballet was soul-stirring against the totalitarian flag swirled on the backdrop. For a few hours, Lois was weightless in the music.

The music rang in her ears as Johann offered his arm and they walked part of the way back to his apartment on Yaroslavshoye. Snow had fallen more heavily again while they were in the theatre, muffling the night outside. Their galoshes crunched on the uncleared pavement. Now was the time to speak urgently, if they were going to.

'What news about the letter brought by the students?'

'There doesn't seem to be any movement. You were telling me about your American cousin,' said Lois. 'Before we were rudely interrupted by Party officials.'

Johann laughed. He seemed to enjoy her gentle irreverence.

'The two matters may not be unconnected. The cousin tells me that a similar approach might have been made to the US Embassy at the end of last year.'

That stopped her light-hearted mood. 'Might have been?'

'An approach on a bridge. Dismissed as a hoax.'

'So our situation is probably a hoax, too.'

'Not necessarily. The approach was made to a couple of US scientists here for an international conference, but they wouldn't take a letter from the Russian. They only reported the approach to the embassy. They were able to give a description. If it tallies with the description of the man the British chaps saw…'

'But in that case, the British friends will already be liaising with the relevant people in the American Embassy, no?'

Exhausted suddenly, Lois couldn't see or know anything apart from how raw and cold and leaden Moscow was, how grim the grey faces. The hacking coughs in the streets, the graceless sniffing and spitting. She heard coarse, drunken laughter from a side street, and it pierced the icy night air.

'My cousin is worried about sharing information right now, for obvious reasons,' said Johann.

'But you could get the description from him?'

'I have it. A middle-aged man. Hat pulled down. Powerful shoulders. Cloth coat. Could be half the men in Russia. Could also be a classic dangle.'

The dangle, a complex bluff of enticement and double dealing. A grub on the end of a fishing line. A bite could lead to a ton of trouble from the counter-espionage team offering up a potential spy for the West who was loyal to the Soviet Union all along. If you fell for it, the KGB would know what you wanted to know and know what you didn't. You could all too easily be fed misleading information. If it was genuine, though, you had an asset worth his weight in gold.

Johann began telling her about the site of the old cathedral. The Moscow authorities were planning a huge outdoor swimming pool where once another stunning gold-domed cathedral had stood. The Cathedral of Christ the Saviour had been demolished in the 1930s to make way for a magnificent edifice to be known as The Palace of the Soviets. Conceived by Stalin as the ultimate emblem of the triumph of communism, this building was to be the tallest on earth, topped by a monstrous hundred-metre tall statue of Lenin.

Lois listened in silence as they walked on, arm-in-arm, twenty yards ahead, now only ten yards ahead of their Russian watcher.

'Construction began in the late 1930s, then stopped when Hitler invaded Russia. The steel frame they had begun to build was pulled down to be used for the city's fortifications. Building never resumed, even though after the war the architect included a victory theme for the interior. But they've finally just decided to scrap the whole idea in favour of using the circular foundations to make the biggest swimming pool in the Soviet Union and probably the world. It was Khrushchev's suggestion, or so they say. Twenty thousand people will be able to get in at once!'

At his apartment, he kissed her and gave her a gift. A slim volume of poems by Rilke.

'For code,' he mouthed. 'A visionary poet of the soul. He came to Russia, you know.'

Then he picked up another volume. It was Palgrave's *Golden Treasury of English Songs and Lyrics*. She had a copy of her own, back in London. It had been one of the first books she had bought when she left college and started earning her own money, a replacement for the copy she'd loved as a child and lost when they were bombed out. At Johann's urging, she read some Tennyson and Matthew Arnold aloud, and he asked – in writing on a notepad – if she would record her English voice speaking them for him.

He produced a tape recorder and placed the microphone in front of her on a table. When she said she felt self-conscious, he poured her a glass of sweet red Russian wine.

Hours later, they had filled the spool of magnetic tape. He had other tapes, on which – he explained, again in writing – he had the sound of a small cocktail party, and a large dinner party that ended in playing records. He would cut and splice these tapes. He could even insert her readings into them, entirely appropriately, of course. He could make them say whatever he wanted, more or less. There might come a time when they would be very useful. He sometimes used them to give the impression he was at home when he was not – he had made tapes of himself cooking, humming to himself, listening to a record, spending a quiet evening alone. He even used tapes of a noisy party to cover conversations. It was much more effective than running water.

Johann used the machine with deft assurance. His broad capable hands spun the reel of magnetic tape and placed it in a box that purported to contain a Dvorak symphony and stowed it with other musical recordings.

Then he turned and opened his arms to her. They were truly complicit, his mischievous expression said, standing firm against oppression, equals to the joyless atmosphere of threat and suspicion. For the first time, their mission seemed exciting, just as an adventure in espionage was supposed to be. She was alive with the thrill of secrecy and higher purpose.

11

Wednesday, February 19, 1958

Was going to stay in tonight but came the opportunity to go to Tchaikovsky Hall & see the Cossack dancers who are going to England. Was going with Nan & ended up with free tickets given to the Ambassador & in his Rolls, complete with flag! Male dancers absolutely stupendous – but didn't go much on the shiny satin. Man next to me developed hiccoughs, perhaps in sympathy. Afterwards, we wandered round outside looking for the car with all the Russians thinking we were mad.

Met Johann later and went to the Hotel Ukraina. Fascinating evening, rich in detail, including spotting HB.

Snow flurries attacked in stinging swarms. Clumps the size of coins exploded on exposed skin. It lay pristine for a few hours, then froze hard again in the sunless canyons of faceless Soviet buildings. More snow fell, lay, was trodden, blackened, refrozen. Winter gripped ever tighter.

Everyday work mounted with little respite. Lois more than pulled her weight. She was helpful to all. She noted everything, cultivated friendly relations with her colleagues and was constantly vigilant. A hunter in the hide, waiting for something to happen.

Johann said no more about the American cousin. Lois allowed Sonia to win insignificant battles in the flat and made grinding efforts to try harder with her until it became clear that any concessions only made Sonia more demanding. She persevered with the Russian lessons, even when she could hardly keep her eyes open, and tried out her new phrases in the famous GUM department store on Red Square. With its airy walkways of shops it was like a roofed-in street with bridges spanning the upper floor. A large fountain of greenish water plashed. It looked elegant and impressive, but the food displays were made of plaster and wax. Women on the tills used the abacus to tot up bills, and under slogans reading *Workers of the world unite!* glum customers waited in endless lines for food, once to hand over their money in exchange for a receipt, once more at the counter to collect what they had paid for, though there was rarely anything decent to buy. The arcane system was replicated in all parts of the store. The only speciality was disappointment.

She spent more time with Johann and did not correct the girls when they started to refer to him as her boyfriend. Eric barely spoke to her. With Johann as her guide, she learnt more about the city where no one was safe and told him what she had observed at the embassy, down to the smallest, most useless detail, none of which, in another of his Americanisms, added up to a hill of beans. One night at a party at the Danish Embassy, a man she knew vaguely from The Hague came up to her and introduced himself with a completely new name. Sonia's Boyd turned out to be a balding bore from a good family, whatever that meant, and to have an interest in exotic butterflies.

She found nothing at the embassy on which to peg a suspicion.

'So you find nothing,' said Johann, shrugging. 'The truth is that the best outcome is finding nothing. That means there is no leak.'

'No leak that we know of. If there is, and I still have no clue to it, I will have failed.'

The longer you were in Moscow, the more you knew, the more intimidating it became. It was the front line of an existential war between two world systems: one in which the individual was free to choose and make mistakes; the other where the state chose everything and mistakes did not officially exist. Five red stars on the domes of the Kremlin palaces mocked her from the Minister's window. Lenin and Stalin lay in state in Red Square and queues of country workers in their felt boots and padded jackets waited every day to pay their respects.

One evening, Johann met her after a Cossack dance performance concert at Tchaikovsky Hall, and they dropped in for a drink at the Hotel Ukraina. Lois had not yet been inside this spired giant that seemed to insinuate itself into every view. Up close, she could see the hammer and sickle motifs carved into the building's exterior. The cavernous lobby was like a grand railway station without the train departure boards, overseen by a ceiling fresco in the Socialist-realist style entitled "Labour and Harvest Day in hospitable Ukraine". Bronze statues, including "Queen of the Fields" and "Mother", stood watch. It was one of those places where all kinds of people turned up, Johann told her, and he was right as usual.

Lois spotted Hugh Burville and a rough-looking man in the bar. The Head of Chancery did not look up, far less acknowledge her. He was sucking his pipe, apparently still unlit, and using it to make gestures in emphasis of his point. She nudged Johann, who did not react.

When she turned to him, she saw his face had drained of colour.

'Johann?'

He pulled her in front of him, keeping his back to the bar, as if he did not want to be recognised.

'Go. Quietly slip away.'

'What—?'

'Just do it. Now.'

The urgency with which he pushed her back overrode her need to know what was going on. She obeyed.

Johann was in the foyer when she returned from the cloakroom having collected her coat, pulling intensely on a cigarette. Without a word, he escorted her out.

'Was it the man with Burville?' she asked as they slushed along the dismal pavement. His arm over hers was both taut as a cable and jittering. His shock, now he had left the scene, was more, not less, palpable.

'The man with Burville? No – of course not.'

'Why "of course not"?'

They marched in silence.

'Talk to me, Johann. Who was Burville with?'

'No one.'

'Well, clearly not "no one".' What was wrong with him?

'No one important. A friend of his at the French Embassy with marital and vodka problems.'

'So why on earth—?'

Johann stopped, pulling her roughly around to face him. They were between streetlamps and more in darkness than in light.

'This has nothing to do with Burville, OK? It was someone else. Better you never saw him. Better you never know his name.'

Silence, a mutually obstinate one.

'He's one of those men who don't exist.'

'Now you are starting to make me cross, Johann.'

'One who pulls the strings. The Swiss Banker.'

'Go on.'

'The man who bought the West.'

'What do you mean "bought"?'

'Don't be naïve, Lois.'

She bridled.

'He financed the bomb,' said Johann. 'The hydrogen bomb.'

'That's different.'

'Is it?'

'The Swiss are neutral, anyway, aren't they?' Even as she said it, Lois felt stupid. Where *did* the Swiss stand in the Cold War?

'Oh, this is far beyond nation states.' Johann seemed to have recovered his composure. 'The Banker and his associates are on the side of money – and control. In a cold world of competing global interests, they are the only ones who win every time.'

They started to walk again.

'When you say *control*—'

'The ultimate power.'

'In Russia, too? So...' She was finding it hard even to imagine what he was telling her. 'So that's good, no?'

He shook his head impatiently. 'They don't want peace between nations and ideologies! It's quite the opposite!'

She was silenced for a minute or two.

'How do you know who he is?' she asked finally.

'Because I saw him quite often in Berlin just after the war had ended. And before you say anything, it's the story that can never be reported,' said Johann. 'Though, for our own satisfaction and safety,' he added tightly, 'I sincerely hope one of the photographs I took over your shoulder with the camera in my tiepin actually comes out.'

Another evening, a man in a dark cloth overcoat brushed rudely past them in the foyer of the Leningradskaya Hotel. Johann cursed him aloud for his bad manners, then said under his breath, as the man walked away, 'That's our American cousin. Pal.'

Ten minutes later, Johann left her at their table and recovered something the American left in a lavatory cistern. They lingered for another half an hour over their drinks, and then left.

'Where are we going?' asked Lois.

'Back to my flat, as quickly as we can.'

A few minutes later they were heading there in a taxi.

The package was bound in plastic. Johann cut it open carefully and released two grainy black-and-white photographs of a man. One was a full-length capture of him in a coat and hat as he looked around at the door of a building. The other was a headshot.

'Photographs of photographs. The best that can be done sometimes. Ever seen him before?' Johann whispered. It was hard even for her to hear above the aria from a noisy opera that trilled and roared from the record player. Over that, the tape recorder was broadcasting their own voices declaiming Rilke and Tennyson too loudly.

Lois looked closely, hesitated. She closed her eyes for a few seconds, then put a finger over the forehead of the headshot.

'I think I might have. If this one was in colour I would know, but... can't be absolutely sure.'

'First impression, gut reaction. Yes or no, have you seen him before?'

She nodded.

'Good. Now, tell me where you saw him.'

He didn't want to lead her, she understood that. But questions crowded in, bringing terrible self-doubt. She had to be right about this.

She mouthed rather than spoke the words, as if to a lip reader. 'The man on the train from Helsinki.'

Johann visibly relaxed. 'Well done.'

'Who is he?'

Johann took a small notebook from his pocket, ripped out a fresh page and lined up matches and a large ashtray before he wrote on it. *Avrely Zhigunov. Colonel. GRU.*

So many things Lois wanted to say and ask but did not dare, despite the cacophony in Johann's sitting room. That would make sense of the upright bearing, broad shoulders, the direct gaze, the short haircut. Maybe even the mean coat – some kind of disguise? Johann was already burning the paper.

Cousin Pal… he's the FBI man? scribbled Lois.

Johann nodded.

How did Pal get photos? she wrote again.

Col tried to contact the US Embassy last year. US thought Col was fake.

But Americans kept files anyway?

A nod from Johann. The page went into the ashtray. The scent of burning. The loud, busy music. Their own recorded voices echoed like madness.

More scribbling. *Nayland, missing now presumed dead, was also here to check out Z story.* 'By the way, thanks to your roommate, we nearly didn't get this,' he mouthed. 'She told her friend Sergei that you weren't to be trusted – and by implication, neither was I.'

'What?'

Johann nodded slowly, watching her reaction. 'Pal wanted to see who you were. Apparently Sergei is as indiscreet as she is. I assured him you were the sane one.'

'Good God.' Lois felt sick. What was Sonia playing at? And what was Johann thinking? Had he just blown her deep cover in order to persuade this Pal to continue trusting him?

The American remained a man without a name, without a face, and now he had seen her, she remonstrated.

He did at least seem to recognise the anguish he had caused her.

'It's OK, *Schatzi*. All OK.'

Schatzi, little treasure. A sweet endearment.

Johann smiled, shaking his head. *The British Embassy is full of spies. So is the United States Embassy. So is the Press Corps. Everywhere you look, it is a hall of mirrors, and everyone knows it,* his expression seemed to say. *Calm down and compartmentalise, protect yourself from what you cannot deal with at any one time.*

He gave her a glass of wine.

Schatzi. She liked that. She reached out for him.

'It's frightening sometimes, Johann. Already it's likely a man's dead over this and—'

'It's the way it is,' he whispered. 'Anyone can kill if they have to.'

She was about to dispute that when he put a finger on her lips. His eyes sent a brutal reminder that this was no game.

'Anyone,' he said.

It was not until Saturday afternoon that they were able to meet for a walk and speak properly. The weather had brightened, thank God. These exchanges would be so much easier when the winter had passed.

They stood close, gazing up in awe at the Kudrinskaya Square Building, another of Stalin's monumental skyscrapers known as the Seven Sisters. It soared into a blue sky, all brute strength topped by what looked like a stolen church spire. Or was it supposed to reference a rocket? The sought-after apartments it contained were said to be home to test pilots, rocket scientists and other stars of the aviation industry. A prevalent rumour had it there was a bomb shelter in the

117

basement to preserve these titans of the Soviet cause if the Cold War suddenly turned hot.

Pal was not a true cousin, Johann reminded her. He had been sent out on secondment from the FBI, and it was that service, not the CIA, that had worked doggedly on the Burgess case in Washington in 1951 in alliance with MI5. Pal's cover was that he was a member of the Commercial section at the American Embassy who was drumming up business with Soviet industry with the occasional help of a director of an electronic components firm in Maryland, name of Nayland. Yes, it was complicated. Yep, wheels within wheels. Of course, Pal knew about oscillators and capacitors. He had worked on making new intercept machines and decoders for long enough. Good ones, too; computing machines that had mined the truth about Burgess in DC.

'So the Americans *are* taking Zhigunov seriously?'

'Seriously enough for the CIA to send Nayland, one of their specialist "occasionals" with the necessary scientific knowledge. Zhigunov – though let us call him... Alexei from now on – is a GRU man. Military intelligence. Like our own rival agencies, sometimes they fight each other. He doesn't agree with KGB tactics, which is useful. Alexei has a cover story as a member of the State Scientific Technical Committee. He organises exchange visits of foreign delegations with scientific and trade interests, and this provides plausible opportunities for espionage on behalf of the GRU. He was returning from a meeting in Helsinki when he made his approach to you.'

'But the Americans didn't fall for him last year.'

'No, they dismissed him as a "dangle".'

'So what's changed?' asked Lois. And what was happening with his approaches to the British? She felt sheepish that she did not know, almost as bad as not doing better with him on the train.

'Certain sections of the American intelligence machine are as suspicious as we are about what's going on out here.'

'And that's where Pal comes in.'

'About the size of it. He's gone through the files and done his research. He thinks... Alexei could be the real deal. Pal was the one who manoeuvred to get Nayland out here for a closer look. But look, if we were the ones to investigate further, it would save face both for the Americans and the British. Keep it below the surface.'

She did not like the sound of that one bit. Hard to forget what might have happened to Nayland. *Anyone can kill if they have to.* She would do well to remember that.

'That's not what we're here for, Johann.'

'Isn't it? But who knows where this leads, eh? A negative tells you as much as a positive. Does the man who turns down information do so because he knows it would expose him? Would some unfortunate associations be exposed? Pal thinks we should try to meet Alexei.'

Lois got the point. How were they going to manage to do that, though, without giving rise to suspicion that she was far too interested in matters that did not concern her?

They walked on.

'Look,' said Johann, almost as if he had read her thoughts. 'We go to Vienna together. In May.'

'Vienna?'

'There's a conference at the Atomic Energy Agency,' said Johann. He was striding energetically now, as if propelled by excitement. 'The usual deceptions, naturally. "The main objective of the Agency is to accelerate the contribution of atomic energy to peace, health and prosperity throughout the world by fostering the exchange of scientific and technical information on the peaceful uses of atomic energy."' He made a short derisive sound in his throat. 'I can plausibly cover it for the newspaper. He – Alexei – is going to be there. Do you think you can get leave to come?'

'Let me think about it.'

Later, as he took her home, he pressed her. 'People are always going off here, there and everywhere. Not always a holiday, either, as I'm sure Intourist knows.'

'Should we go together, though?'

'It would be better, much more natural, for us to go together,' he said. 'By the way.' He reached into his inside pocket and brought out a packet of postcards depicting Moscow scenes. 'Tucked in with these is a copy of the best negative I got of our Swiss friend at the Ukraina. Keep it safe in case anything happens to my photo album.'

That is going to be harder than he knows, thought Lois grimly. It was alarming how easily things went missing in the apartment. The most concerning was the brooch she had been searching for everywhere for days.

12

Saturday, March 8, 1958

Sonia left at 6 for the show Harlequinade *& I relaxed in a long bath. Concerned about her. She's been friendly and I can get on with her, but she blows hot and cold, all too much. But she'll enjoy the attention the play brings. A born actress. She likes the sparkle.*

Chatted to Fielding afterwards. He is trying to translate a German story and wondered if I could help.

The embassy ballroom had become a theatre. Critical tendencies were softened in the library mess before the spectacle of colleagues tripping through Terence Rattigan's satirical farce *Harlequinade*. Lois found herself laughing and thoroughly enjoyed all the silly antics. The backdrop wobbled, a chair creaked and then collapsed, taking John Mowberry with it. He lay on his back, legs wiggling in the air, milking the audience's mirth. Sonia was charming as a long-lost daughter who provides a pivotal plot twist. For a couple of hours, they could have been anywhere.

Lois felt a pang when she realised Sonia would no longer be spending lunchtimes and evenings rehearsing but would be in their flat, constantly wanting chat, irritable if attention was withheld. It was an extra strain Lois could do without. After much inner anguish, she had decided not to say anything about her loose talk to Sergei. It would open too big a can of worms.

After the final curtain, everyone swarmed in good humour to the library bar again. Tony Fielding materialised and thrust a powerfully strong gin and tonic into her hand.

'I told you you should have been up there on the stage.'

Lois smiled politely. 'And I still wouldn't have been able to act, but cheers.'

'I've had some interesting lines of inquiry from Bill Stoneley lately, and I believe I have you to thank.'

'Oh, yes?'

Fielding gave her a lewd wink. Though his voice was smooth as ever, too many drinks had taken the edge off his man-of-action appeal; for the first time, she saw the reckless lout in him.

'The information was apparently given to him by someone I believe you know.'

Too many *believes*. In his standard diplomatic phrasing crouched a tiger. It sprang.

'Johann Dreschler. He's a very interesting character.'

'I'm glad it was helpful.'

'Seeing him anytime soon?'

'Not tonight.'

'I'd like to meet him properly, drill down into the Berlin situation. Would you come to dinner with me, the two of you?'

Alarm bells ringing in her head, she had no choice but to lie. 'That would be lovely, thank you.'

Fielding started telling her, not altogether coherently, about a Soviet writer who had recently been released from a labour camp, but the crowd jostled and interrupted and began to move as a body on to America House for more excess of drink.

'Come on, Lois, the night is young!' Fielding had her by the elbow, steering her not with force but with determination.

'Or are you angling to go straight back to my place? Either way, I think I'd like to get to know you better. You are very lovely.'

Why had she told him she wasn't seeing Johann that night?

'I'm so sorry, but I can't.'

'Why not?'

'That... is for me to know... and you to find out.' She smiled with as much flirtatiousness as she could falsely muster. How had she ever thought he was attractive? He was a lecherous roué.

As he was carried away on a tide of mass boisterousness, Lois left her drink barely tasted on a bookshelf and gratefully went back to Meshchanskaya with Nan, who was always cheerful and full of common sense. She could relax with her and wished she could also confide in the older woman, but of course that was impossible.

Was she paranoid to question Fielding's motive in mentioning Johann? What was his drunken proposition in aid of? Could she really go to Vienna with Johann? She would have to use her precious leave. Should she, in any case, be following a path dictated by the Americans, instead of concentrating on what she had been assigned to do within the Moscow Embassy? It was true that anything she helped uncover would broaden the picture and might provide an answer. What would be the consequences of discovery? If Fielding and the top brass at the embassy found out what she was involved in, they would be appalled.

She had a cup of Bournvita with Nan, then went downstairs for a blissfully early night. Her final thought before falling into a long dreamless sleep was that if Johann was all for Vienna, she had to trust him. She had no choice.

Sonia had not forgiven her, it seemed. She huffed and sighed around the flat the next morning, then sulked when Lois asked her what was wrong. What exactly was to be forgiven was anyone's guess. Far more worrying was the fact that the brooch was still missing.

Lois had been in the habit of checking every few days that it was in its safe place. The last time was after work on Friday, when it had gone. The pocket in her spare sponge bag was still soft, still lined with the cotton wool, but it was now smooth to the touch. The hard relief had gone. Her first thought was Vera, of course. The maid supplied by the KGB, not nearly as hopeless as she made out, though there was no disguising the awfulness of her lunchtime cooking. The question was, would she ask her directly? The danger was that if Vera were not the culprit, the enquiry would alert her to the fact that Lois did not trust Sonia, and where that might lead did not bear thinking about. Oh, it was too bad, the way everything had to be thought out and then rethought, nothing ever certain.

And here was Sonia again, delicate mouth set to argumentative. She stood in the doorframe as Lois went about tidying her room.

'You're very particular, aren't you.'

Lois went on folding her clothes. Taking them carefully from the clothes horse where they had been drying overnight.

'It's very… suburban. This care you take of your clothes. All the washing and ironing. Why don't you send them out?'

Ignore the implied slur. Lois thought of tree-lined Tressillian Road in Brockley, the neat Victorian houses, the larger ones divided into flats. Not wealthy people. Honest, working people who kept the great city of London moving and safe and clean and repaired and supplied with food.

'The laundry here ruins things, as you know.'

Lois took the heather and green twill dress from the hanger on the doorframe. She had made it herself from a Vogue pattern. It had turned out well.

'Very unusual dress,' said Sonia.

'So you've said.'

Lois smoothed the seams of the lightweight woollen twill. It wouldn't need ironing. Good woollen fabric never did. She had gone short the week she bought it in order to buy quality that would last.

'Where did you get it? Is there a smart label inside?'

Sonia had looked. She knew there was no maker's label. The woman was bent on riling her. *Don't rise to it*, Lois told herself.

'It was made for me,' she said. Well, it wasn't a lie.

Lois waited until Sonia went out. There was dust on the windowsills and dust mixed with sooty grime on the skirting boards. The coffee table needed polishing. A spot of cleaning, that was the way to go. Calming, too, if inexorably, scorn-inducingly suburban. But useful.

She finished putting away her clothes and stepped out of her room, closing the door behind her. In the dull, slightly grimy kitchen, she got out the basics from behind the curtain beneath the sink, ran some hot water in the bucket with some soap flakes and damped a sad, brown cloth. Ran it along the windowsill leaving a comet trail of tiny bubbles. The grime lifted but not her spirits. She checked in every corner, every hidden crevasse, knowing her covert search was in vain. She had taken the brooch off carefully, put it in the pocket of the sponge bag as she always did. She was not careless with it. She wore it now and then to establish its normality, trying hard not to be too self-conscious when it glittered from her lapel. It had not disappeared by accident.

That evening, Sonia was going to a party.

'With the Great Dane,' she told Lois loftily, though Lois had not asked. 'Keep Boyd on his toes.'

Sonia had on her black velvet dress, a close-fitted garment that most likely bore a very smart label indeed. She was slightly flushed but very pretty in her doll-like way, her blue eyes surprised by black mascara and her pert, red mouth enamelled with shiny lipstick. She swung her hips as she walked over to where Lois was sitting reading on the sofa, turned her shoulders and bent to fill her cigarette case from the box on the coffee table.

She was wearing the brooch.

Lois was so shocked she couldn't think what to say. Her head span. To say nothing would hand power to the wretched woman. To let her go out wearing it would run the risk of her losing it. To make too much would highlight the importance of the piece. Sonia wasn't stupid. Had she already worked out what it was?

'Hey,' she came out with as Sonia clicked her cigarette case shut. 'I've been looking for that.' Don't accuse. Act normally. It's what anyone would say in the circumstances.

'Sorry?' It wasn't an apology.

'My brooch.'

Sonia hesitated, crinkled her forehead in apparent confusion, then put a hand over it.

'Oh, this. I didn't think you'd mind. Flatmates share and share alike, don't they?'

'Actually, Sonia, I do mind. It's special to me.' Don't ask where she got it from and make her lie about finding it between the cushions on the sofa or in the bathroom. 'May I take it, please?'

'Really? You couldn't spare it just for an evening?' The stare was accusatory, then wounded.

'It's special. I'm sure you can understand.'

Sonia blew out her cheeks as if signalling to an invisible audience that she was about to do something she didn't agree with but would go through with it to keep the peace. An agonising pause. Then she gave a forced laugh.

'Oh, go on then, Miss Prissy. If it means so much to you.'

At last she handed it over. Lois smothered her relief. Sonia flounced towards the door, raising a hand, half saying goodbye, half showing she didn't care. A waft of Jolie Madame lingered in the air.

Lois was going to have to have a word with her about pinching her perfume, too.

It was a pretty brooch, a spray of sparkling heather.

'Silver and paste,' said Miss Harcourt, as if there could have been any doubt about that. The paste gems were slightly discoloured, some uneven in their metal fittings. A secretary from South London wearing diamonds would have drawn too much attention.

It had a minuscule battery behind it and a wireless frequency. A microphone on her lapel.

'It's experimental,' said Miss Harcourt. By which she meant that it might not work, assumed Lois. It had a range of only fifty feet, which meant she would need any accomplice to be in a nearby room with a receiver and tape recorder. It had worked during training, but sadly not when she and Johann had tried it out in his flat. It was hard to know if it would ever be of any use, but he had promised to work on it if he could source a better microphone.

If Sonia had rifled through her belongings, she had probably found the diary, too. Lois couldn't imagine the woman would stop there. Like as not, Sonia was reading it. Did she do it out of boredom or jealousy – or for a darker reason? Lois snatched up a pen and quickly caught up to date, planting a few seeds of disinformation to see where they surfaced.

13

Monday, April 14, 1958

Burville told a tale over the Chancery tea trolley about his passion for circuses, especially the lady acrobats. Wachorne said he'd take him to the Moscow State Circus and they could hang around backstage.

An astonishing piano performance at the International Tchaikovsky Competition – more "Moscow Nights".

Tony Fielding is jolly attractive despite the risk-taker's swagger. So far he hasn't said anything more about going to dinner with him, with or without me bringing a friend. He seems to have lost interest.

At last winter was loosening its grip. Crowds gathered on the bridges to watch the ice break up and the floes race. Icicles sheared off from rooftops and people died. Flags hung sodden and dripping, blood-red against the blackened snow still piled in the streets.

Word filtered out to the diplomatic community that no less than ten nuclear test bombs had been exploded in the space of nine days that March, in Kazakhstan and in the Arctic Ocean archipelago region of Arkhangelsk Oblast. The Kremlin's internal struggle came to an official end. On

March 27, 1958, the Supreme Soviet –the legislature of the USSR – voted unanimously to give even more power to First Secretary Khrushchev and make him also Soviet Premier. He was now undisputed leader of the Soviet Union and quick to consolidate this control by establishing a USSR Defence Council led by himself, effectively making him commander in chief. Khrushchev was now the unassailable force. His only redeeming factor for the West was that he had spoken out against the murderous repression of the Stalin era.

Lois's radio set stopped receiving clearly, and the World Service crackled with interference. Rory offered to come down from the flat upstairs to look at it, adjusted the aerial connections and fixed it in minutes. The least she could do was offer him a beer.

On his own, he was much easier to talk to, not so diffident. He had a sweet smile and a self-mocking sense of humour. He hadn't bothered to take off the glasses he wore in the office, but they did not detract from his good looks: the high cheekbones and grey eyes and hazelnut brown hair with a quiff that he pushed back nervously. His sweater was not hand-knitted, but his shirt and trousers were neat and tidy and unremarkable, as if all his sartorial effort had gone into finding the right clothes to blend in without making a mistake. He missed playing football, he told her, and did the pools every week because it reminded him of Saturday teatimes at home in Lancashire. Manchester United, he supposed, though he wasn't a fanatic for any team, they all had their good points. Any team in the North, that was. He couldn't support any southern team, obviously.

'I'm a Londoner,' said Lois. 'But I don't like football, so that's all right, I suppose.'

She teased him gently until it became an unexpected flirtation. She looked away from their eye contact which had gone on for a few seconds too long and was horrified to find herself blushing. No, it couldn't be a flirtation. He was far too young for her.

'Where are you off to?' he asked.

'To the kitchen to see whether there's another beer to offer you.'

'No, later this month, I meant. I saw you put in for leave.'

'Vienna.'

'Why Vienna?'

'Why not Vienna?' She tempered her tone. 'I love Austria, but I've never been to the capital. And it's not Moscow.'

'Mozart,' he said, surprising her. 'I don't know anything about Vienna except it makes me think about Mozart.'

'Do you like music?'

'I don't know much about that either, not really. I play the piano a bit. But not classical, not much anyway.'

She had seen him at the upright piano in the Garden Block mess a couple of times. Boogie-woogie music, it might have been.

'I don't suppose you'd like to go to a concert with me, would you? A piano concert tomorrow night?' he asked abruptly.

'Well, I—'

'You don't have to, if you don't like piano music. I just thought I'd ask.'

'No, I mean, yes. I would like to go. That would be nice.'

She didn't have the heart to knock him back. Johann would understand. He took other people to concerts, for all kinds of reasons.

The Great Hall of the Moscow Conservatory was magnificent, said to be one of the finest concert halls in the world. The evening was the final of the inaugural International Tchaikovsky Competition. It was full to the rafters of Soviet officials and perched in the best seat in the house was Khrushchev himself.

'However did you manage this?' Lois asked a dinner-suited Rory. She resisted the temptation to brush a speck of dust off his black lapel.

'The Ambassador was sent ten tickets, and he hasn't forgotten that I did some musical accompaniment for one of the plays. It wasn't much, but he seemed to like it.'

'Good for you,' she said, meaning it. She stared around, looking for H.E. and his wife, and wondering slightly awkwardly who else from the embassy was here. The Minister was at a reception at the Israeli Embassy, so he was accounted for, but she fully expected Burville to pop up and note the company she was keeping. *Let him*, she thought. *Where's the harm? Rory's a nice lad, and the Ambassador likes him.*

She ought to have known Johann would be there. The press corps was out in force, primed to report the incomparable superiority of the Soviet music scene. He was sitting next to a woman in purple satin yet speaking to a man on his other side. Perhaps the journalists were all seated en bloc. She was too far away to catch his eye.

Tension was palpable as the first finalist came on stage, then gripped tighter as the second, third and fourth followed. The music was superb. How would anyone outdo the Russians and their mastery of technique? But the event designed to demonstrate Soviet cultural superiority ended in triumph for a young virtuoso from Texas, the twenty-three-year-old Harvey "Van" Cliburn – and a masterstroke from Nikita Khrushchev.

Cliburn was a tall, gangly fellow with a long neck and springy hair. He looked like a polite American youth on his best behaviour, rather out of his depth, but his performance of Tchaikovsky's *Piano Concerto No.1* and Rachmaninoff's *Piano Concerto No.3* brought the audience to its feet for a full eight minutes. Astonished and moved by the ovation,

Cliburn spoke briefly and haltingly in Russian, reading from a piece of paper, then sat down at the piano and began to play some more.

An awkwardness spread through the hall. What was he doing? The musicians in the orchestra behind him were unsure what he intended. The boy began to play an elegiac air, and there were murmurs from the audience, then gasps of pleasure as they realised what he was playing in his own arrangement. Lois recognised the song, too. It was "Moscow Nights", the song Johann had sung as they skated.

The faces of the audience, young and old, were completely changed. Enraptured by the music and the song-like quality of the American's phrasing, they were transported. They seemed to ride the waves of sound, the sadness, passion and hopes of the country they had once known, still present in the timeless yearning melody. As the last note hung in the air, a choked sob burst from somewhere behind her, an animal release, and then the auditorium erupted.

Cliburn went off-stage and the clapping continued. It turned to an insistent beat, asking for him to return. A woman next to Lois wiped tears from her eyes. Other, younger women cried out, and some of them ran down to the stage. When it was time to announce the winner, there was hesitation and consultation. The judges were in a quandary. Finally, they asked permission of the Soviet leader. Could they award first prize to an American?

'Is he the best?' the mighty Khrushchev asked. Cautiously, the judges said he was. 'Then give him the prize!'

The crowd erupted with pride and genuine pleasure. It was a rare public demonstration that East or West, human emotions were the same.

She tried and failed to spot Johann as they filed out of the Great Hall past a statue of Tchaikovsky and banks of pale flowers flown in from the south. Was Pal there somewhere, too, keeping a close eye on the Texan protégé?

Once they were outside, Rory fidgeted with the cigarette he hadn't yet lit. How had he known what she was thinking?

'Who exactly is this chap Johann you've been going about with?'

'You know as well as I do who he is.'

Lois watched the embarrassment rise up his handsome face.

'All I know is what others have told me. He's German and a journalist. And I've seen him at America House.'

'Well, then. You know all there is to know.'

A match. A wobble of the hand on the box before he struck it. Lois watched the flame, his lips on the cigarette. None of the polish of the Oxford and Cambridge types, but he took everything in, and you could tell he was thinking all the time. Nobody's fool, then, for all that he was still young. Too young for her. He was what, twenty-four? In October, she would be thirty.

Rory exhaled. 'All there is for an onlooker to know, but not for someone who spends time with him one-to-one.'

Was there a slight aggression in the way he said that? Was it possible that he was jealous? Lois pushed the thought away. He was just a colleague.

'Come on, shall we go and have a drink somewhere?' she asked more breezily than she felt. That's what colleagues did, after all.

'Where do you like?'

It was almost guaranteed that Johann would head to the Metropol.

'The Ararat?' she suggested. The Armenian restaurant was popular with the diplomatic crowd.

'The Ararat's all right. Shall we get a taxi?'

Mid-April, and it was still snowing. More solid than sleet, not formed enough to be snow. The pavements were shiny and slippery as fish sprinkled with salt before cooking.

Sonia tried to start another row when she arrived back at the flat, wanting to know where she had been and with whom, then sulky and cross when Lois declined to be drawn.

'It's as if you don't trust me,' said Sonia.

Lois pointed to the bugged wall, but Sonia was not to be deflected.

'You never tell me where you're going… just off without a by-your-leave.'

'I wasn't aware I needed your leave, Sonia.'

'Well, I like that! Miss High and Mighty now. Who was it who had to show you the ropes only a few months ago, and looked out for you?'

'Please, Sonia. Not now. I'm tired, and all I want to do is have a soak in the bath and fall into bed. If you want to chat, come in while I'm running the taps,' said Lois pointedly.

But she didn't want a conversation. Sonia only wanted to register her disappointment, maybe to engineer another session of pouring out her woes, which were many and varied. It actually seemed to give her pleasure to make Lois more uncomfortable, to induce feelings of guilt that she was not sharing her own grievances.

But Lois wasn't having it. 'Suit yourself.'

Of course, Sonia changed her mind then and followed her into the bathroom. 'I hear you're going to Vienna.'

Lois silently cursed the girl as she prattled away. Now that the play was over, she seemed to have no other interests but flatmate baiting. Sonia needed attention, Lois realised, even of a negative kind. It was a sad personality to be stuck with, but impossible to help. Every kindness shown to her was sucked into an unfillable void. Lois found it utterly draining.

'You know what,' went on Sonia. 'I like the sound of a trip to Vienna. I think I'll come along. It could be fun, couldn't it?'

Not even an eager request, a favour or a suggestion. Was she daring Lois to object?

'I thought I'd go on my own, actually. We all need our time away from everything, don't we?'

The expression of surprise that met this showed this was clearly a novel concept to Sonia.

'You can't want to be on your own!'

'I like being alone. Really, I do.'

Sonia narrowed her eyes. 'I know what it is. You're not going on your own, are you? Who are you going with?'

'Do you mind, Sonia? I want to get into my bath now.'

'Are you going to share a room with Johann?'

Lois turned away to turn off the water. Steam rose in billows. She hadn't attended carefully enough to the hot tap.

It wasn't any of Sonia's business, but she ploughed on. 'I can see by your po-face that I've hit a nerve. Well, we can share a room, then. We're good friends, aren't we? Seems a shame to pay for two rooms when we could have the money to enjoy ourselves with.'

'Sorry, but I'm not sharing a room with anyone, Sonia. I'm having a holiday, and that means having some space to please myself.'

'I thought you wanted me to get to know Johann better?'

She had a cheek. How nice as pie she was outside the flat. Everyone's friend. Especially to the important people, those who might offer her some advantage. All deliberate, so that none would question her if she blamed Lois for being difficult. Sonia was deceitful and manipulative, but why was she doing it? She had told no one Johann was going with her, yet somehow Sonia knew.

Could she really be the mole? As she soaked in her bath, Lois found it hard to believe so, but stranger things had happened.

She dropped, heavy and warm, still slightly damp, to her knees by her bed, hands clasped as she did when she was a small child. She felt the hard ridges of the rug and cold air on her limbs. In a city where cathedrals were now museums and open-air swimming pools, she prayed. She could not do this without a guiding hand.

It wasn't a bluff. Sonia's permits for Vienna came through. Left unchecked, the wretched girl would dog Lois's every move. The only thing to do was to tell her to invite someone else so she would have another person to go around with.

Johann, understandably, was furious.

'Is there really no chance she could be the prey?' he asked.

'I know it seems like it, but she has no access. I'm certain not.'

'Why is she doing this?' asked Johann. 'Is she a silly young woman who is jealous of you?'

Lois raised her palms. 'Hardly. Why should she be? She's the one who comes from a wealthy family, lives in Chelsea and has smart friends.'

Johann smiled inscrutably.

They had taken the metro out to the gardens of the monastery at Donskoye. It was a beautiful spring day. Beyond the Garden Ring, beyond the grey, forbidding suburbs of dormitory blocks for grey-faced workers, out in what felt like near countryside, it was astonishing, thought Lois, how alive you could feel even strolling past tombs and statues. For once the reliquary did not seem oppressive. An elderly man in dark serge actually smiled at them as he passed.

'I was at the Van Cliburn concert,' she said. Everybody was talking about the extraordinary young man and Khrushchev's unexpectedly magnanimous gesture.

Johann looked up. The sky was a deep blue.

'The world is full of surprises,' he said. 'But the young guy's not exactly a hick who got lucky.'

Again, Lois wondered where he'd picked up that phrase. They spoke English together more and more often now.

'He started taking piano lessons at the age of three,' went on Johann. 'From his mother, who had studied under Arthur Friedheim, who in turn had been a pupil of Franz Liszt.'

'A direct link down from Liszt… how wonderful. I didn't know that.'

He still hadn't said that he was there that evening, too. Should she mention that she had seen him, and ask who he was with? She decided not.

'There's definitely a leak coming out of the mansion,' he said abruptly.

They didn't miss a beat as they walked past an elaborately scrolled family vault.

'Any context?' Lois felt the sun drain.

'Chancery.'

'Where does this come from?'

'The Americans.'

'The cousins – or your Pal?'

'The latter.'

'Don't sit on the details, then. Give me something. You mean Burville?' About whom she had been able to find out nothing meaningful.

'I don't know.'

'So they don't know either, or your guy isn't saying?'

'Who would you say is most vulnerable to being led into bad places?'

Lois had already made her assessment of this question. 'Of the junior staff… Eric. Purely an instinct. But—'

Johann nodded. 'Understood.'

'He has the access. Documents. Cyphers. Telegrams.' She didn't want it to be true. But it had been impressed on her during training: it was so often the junior members of staff, with fewer emotional reserves, with less money and status, who were vulnerable. It was so often those one would never suspect.

'I'd like to meet Pal properly,' she said.

'That may not be wise. Anything he has can come through me.'

'What if I needed to contact him urgently, and I couldn't get in touch with you?'

'Ach, not gonna happen. And it's better you don't.'

'I don't know how you can say that. There might be any number of reasons. What if you had an accident and were in hospital? Or were marched off by KGB goons?'

In the end, very reluctantly, Johann gave her the failsafe. Pal ate at the Café Lyra every Wednesday evening between five and seven, no matter what.

'If you stand by the telephone booth and catch his eye, he will come over for a brush-past.'

If she had no other options, and only then, she would find him there. On no account should she attempt to run into him there for anything less than an emergency.

'How does he know that Zhi— Alexei will be going to the Atomic Energy conference in Vienna?'

'I assume he has a channel to him.'

Which the British did not, though they could have had. Why had Tony Fielding decided not to follow up?

'He might not be on the level,' said Lois, answering her own thought.

'What is there to lose if he doesn't? We go, we have a break from here, and we come back no worse off than we were, hey?'

14

Thursday, May 1, 1958

Up at 5.30am, which we thought rather a lark, like being on holiday. Collected the girls from the buildings and went down to the National, where their doors opened before 7 only to East German delegations. Finally got in and hung around (French dels. too) until they gave us coffee & Tony Fielding got us into one of the 'businessmen's rooms and we had a good view of the parade.

On May Day, tanks rolled in formation through Moscow's canyons of anonymous granite architecture and past a colossal portrait of Lenin. Rocket missiles tall as buildings and engineered to strike fear into the world were towed through cheering crowds. The might of the Red Army was on parade on this most patriotic of public holidays, followed by open trucks carrying victorious farm and factory workers. Celebrations extended well into the night. In the National Hotel, where he had organised their viewpoint, Tony Fielding managed to avoid speaking to Lois alone and she hoped that was because he regretted his drunken approaches to her on the night of the embassy show.

Lois and Sonia were up at three o'clock the next morning (it had hardly been worth going to bed). A taxi came at four to take them to Vnukovo Airport. The cab driver fell asleep at the wheel momentarily and nearly had them in a ditch. Johann had booked on an earlier flight the day before, refusing to travel with Sonia. The saving grace was that Boyd the Canadian was following on.

The six-thirty flight lumbered away more or less on time. The uniquely peculiar smell of the Aeroflot fleet and the sugared petrol taste of the boiled sweets they were given to suck on take-off made Lois feel sick. First stop was Kiev for coffee, Lviv for breakfast and trouble with the Russians over traveller's cheques, then on to Budapest where they were on the ground for only ten minutes refuelling.

They reached Vienna at one-thirty local time. Luggage collected, they crossed town on an airport bus and dropped by the British Embassy to get some money and their hotel reservation.

'I can't see why you didn't book direct,' Sonia squawked too loudly, drawing attention to herself.

Lois had not wanted to make any booking more than necessary from Moscow. Best to keep as much below the radar as possible.

'We get better rates this way,' she told Sonia. It might even have been true.

The Pension Schneider was not smart, but it had crisp, clean white sheets and it was within Lois's slender means in Innere Stadt, a delightful jumble of narrow alleys, quirky old houses and small picturesque squares that opened suddenly to reveal churches, palaces and parks. It was the scale of it that was so familiar and comfortable after the stern military boulevards of Moscow. Frau Schneider was more reserved than dear old Mutti F at the Gasthof Bräu in Zell, but she was recognisably a rural Austrian, with her clear, appraising gaze that did not flinch and common endearments built into her greetings. The street outside was quiet and the windows opened. What more did they need?

Lois breathed in the heady scent of fresh air and freedom. She would never take it for granted again. And she would find a way to lose Sonia, though she couldn't be too obvious about it. So she played nice and led Sonia along the clean, light streets to the revolving door of a grand café where the warm air greeted them like a hug of rich coffee and chocolate cake and tobacco. One delicious creamy sip of *Kaffee mit Schlag* and life was instantly more human.

Back at the hotel in a daze of tiredness and residual frustration, Lois told Sonia she just wanted to lie down. Lois went to her room and allowed Vienna to envelop her in a cloud of white pillow and duvet. Sweet haven indeed, at least for now.

She slept until nine the next morning, took breakfast in her room – relishing the solitude – and set out alone.

After the months of privation in Moscow, the sheer plenty in the shop windows on Kohlmarkt in Vienna's Goldenes Quartier was almost dizzying. High fashion, fine jewellery twinkling with precious gems, elegant leather handbags: each glory seemed to reassure her nothing had changed in the outside world. Not that she would be able to afford any of them. But the proof that beauty and aspiration still existed was enough.

She found the place she was looking for tucked behind Graben, next to another perfumed coffee house, and slipped inside, knowing she would pay the price for not getting up earlier and appraising Sonia of her plans and not caring. This was what she had been longing to be able to do, and on her own. What utter bliss: a decent hair salon and a new permanent wave! She felt so much better when her hair was styled. It had been getting wilder by the day in Moscow, with no prospect of any remedy but the home cuts and perm applications that, in their desperation, the other women inflicted on each other in the evenings at Meshchanskaya and Sad Sam.

Afterwards, pleased with the results, she made her way to the Burggarten on the Ringstrasse and sat on a bench with a sight of the Mozart monument where the park came calling on the Hofburg Palace. The marble statue of the composer struck a languid pose on a plinth. The trees were in blossom and birds sang.

Johann was late.

Lois sat on her bench, still and patient. They would have plenty of time together. It was true that Johann had seemed distracted the past few weeks, but that was the deadening effect of Moscow. Here, now, in the lush Viennese spring, was there anywhere more romantic?

Fifteen minutes passed, and then thirty. Relaxed in her thoughts and the green landscape, she was unconcerned. But when Johann did appear, almost an hour after the agreed time, he looked unusually perturbed.

He sat down beside her. 'I think I'm being followed.'

'Who by, here?'

'Perhaps it was just that prickling feeling I cannot shake off.'

'Did you go to the drop?'

He shook his head. 'I didn't want to lead any watchers there.'

'Are they here now?' Drawing on all the training she had, Lois did not look around.

'No, don't think so. I had to go through a lot of manoeuvres to get here, though.'

It seemed unlikely that he was being tailed here. He had been conditioned by Russia to be paranoid. The Moscow curse.

'They don't know me,' said Lois. 'I could go.'

'You might have to.'

'You might have asked me if I wanted to get my hair done, too!'

Lois's independence and self-sufficiency may have been qualities required by Miss Harcourt and others, but they were her weak spot where Sonia was concerned. Unfortunately, the key to success was to give Sonia what she wanted. Lois let her yap on.

She wished she were here alone with Johann. Their far-fetched plan aside, she had realised something important as she sat in the Burggarten waiting for him. She had reached an age when she had often wondered if she would ever find her love, would ever be a married woman, and she had decided that if it were not to be, she had better make the lack worthwhile with a meaningful career. But Johann had changed that. She was falling for him, and she was beginning to see a way that she might have both personal achievement and a lasting relationship. What had seemed impossible was right there in the spark between them, and in their secret bond. He could be the one.

'You're doing it again!' cried Sonia. 'Tuning out while I'm talking to you! Boyd's flight's been delayed. He won't be here until tomorrow now.'

They couldn't leave her on her own. In pursuit of mundane excitement, that night the three of them went to the Prater. Over meadows crossed by the Danube streams, they were drawn inexorably by tinny, resonant music to the carousels and the famous Reisenrad, the fairground wheel. Johann was as charming as he could be, given Sonia's presence. The only hint of his unease came when she made an inane comment about the thousands of refugees Austria had helped after the crushing of the 1956 Hungarian revolution by the Soviets.

'The Austrians should have done more, not less!' Johann turned on her before moderating his tone. 'The Soviet military used brutal force to crush a revolt for freedom. But Austria was forced to close the border to prevent any help from sympathetic groups here. Austria only regained its state treaty and full sovereignty the year before after a decade of occupation by Allied forces. It had to retain its neutral status.'

'All our fault as usual!' Sonia threw her pretty throat back and gave him the full benefit of a studied tinkling laugh.

'You don't know what you're talking about.'

'Well, of all the—' No one was allowed to pull Sonia up.

'But Austria did allow people fleeing Hungary to enter Austria,' said Lois gently, hoping to diffuse the situation that had flared up out of nowhere. He should know better than to let his frustration and annoyance with Sonia show so much. 'The Austrian humanitarian effort was acknowledged worldwide.'

'Except in the Soviet Union and its satellites, of course,' muttered Johann. 'Their story was that Austria had allowed "reactionary elements" and weapons to cross the Austrian-Hungarian border and so violated its neutrality.'

Luckily, Sonia seemed to decide she would not win any kind of argument with Johann.

'Look, there's a dance floor!' she cried, too enthusiastically.

Relieved, Lois suggested they went over. They did better than that; they waltzed and cavorted and Johann was two-stepped off his feet with no time between songs to catch his breath. The plucking, insistent zither music pulled them round, and the big wheel turned and for a while they were nowhere else but there, caught in the cogs of a spinning park.

Later, back at the hotel, they had trouble getting Sonia to understand they wanted time to themselves. Was she just being thick-skinned and or deliberately obstructive? It was past midnight before they were alone outside Lois's room and Johann finally took her in his arms. Lois was so pent-up that it must have shown in her unrestrained reaction to his embrace. Johann looked at her with new interest.

'I'm glad you feel the same,' he said. 'Away from Moscow, everything is different, isn't it?'

She nodded. She had never known quite where she stood

with him on a personal level. He was always so sure of himself, yet he kept part of himself unknown to her. The dreadful truth was that made him all the more attractive.

That night was the first they spent together. In the morning, she allowed herself to admit gloriously, if only to herself, that there could no longer be any doubt about it; she was in love with him.

15

Monday, May 5, 1958

Wunderschön, fühle mich richtig auf Ferien zu sein.

'What are we doing this morning?' asked Sonia over breakfast in the pension's plain dining room.

Lois, wrapped in her own delightful thoughts – Johann's sure touch was imprinted on her skin – felt miraculously energised (though Sonia's company was wearisome as ever). She buttered a roll without looking up.

'Well, you're meeting Boyd, aren't you?' Thank goodness for Boyd and his imminent arrival. 'And I'm taking the tram and then a bus north to Kahlenberg and the Wiener Wald.' Sonia had several times stated her disdain for public transport.

'I like the sound of that. I'll come with you.'

'I don't think you will have time.'

Sonia stared. 'You are a funny person, Lois. What on earth does Johann think?'

Johann had given her instructions while he established his credentials with the foreign press cohort gathering to cover the Atomic Energy conference.

'He's working today. I need fresh air and the spring trees.'

Sonia insisted on walking as far as the stop with her. Lois let out a great sigh of relief as the tram pulled away.

At Kahlenberg, after a winding scenic route up a green hill, the bus drew up on a wide parking strip. Lois alighted to find herself high above the metropolis. The Danube was a silver snake crawling over the flatlands stretched and swollen by the city that covered the southern horizon. From this carefully composed vantage point, St. Josefskirche auf dem Kahlenberg, the church on the top of the hill, was a steep stroll up the cobbled Höhenstraße. But Lois would not take it, not yet. She put on her wide-brimmed hat and sat on the far stone wall to take in the sublime sweeping views. She read a book and waited patiently for a group of smartly dressed men to gather by a bus marked *Privat*. She saw the bus carry the conference delegates away down the winding road. Her timing had been perfect. Nothing was ever quite how one imagined or feared. No point in worrying or overthinking. She wandered over to the cobbled street and began the final climb.

The church was serene in pale sunshine. A zinc-green spire rose from a single elegant tower. She made sure she was not being followed. The other passengers on her bus, mainly women with baskets, had long disappeared along the way. There were a few tourists holding cameras like she was, two couples and a threesome of young men, but she could not see them.

Lois passed the bench under the lime tree. The safety signal was there, a chalk cross on the wooden seat. She looked carefully, casually, all around, and went into the church.

All was profoundly quiet inside. She took a side aisle up to the front and gazed at the statues of the Virgin and a stirring painting of a battle that she did not understand. Cool incense-laden air. Still no one else around. Under the last hassock of the ninth pew back on the right, she pulled out a folded piece of paper and tucked it deftly, unread, into her handbag.

Lois sat for several minutes staring at the flickering candles on the altar, calmed and sustained as she always was in church. Then she walked softly towards the great door, dropped a few pfennigs in a wooden box by the votive candles and lit a thin taper.

She had to wait forty minutes for a bus back, but she had a cup of coffee in a café, then sat on a bench in the sun, luxuriating in the vista and the unaccustomed spring warmth. *Wunderschön, fühle mich richtig auf Ferien zu sein* she wrote in the little Pepys diary. And she did indeed feel wonderful, as if she really were on holiday.

Back in town, she bought some stamps and several postcards of the Vienna Woods, and one of the Mozart monument. She wrote one of the former to her parents, and the latter to Miss Harcourt, via Elsie, to let her know that she was having a wonderful time in Vienna, that her journalist friend was with her, and they were hoping to see all the sights there were to see. She posted them quickly and kept the others to leave around the Meshchanskaya flat when they returned.

Johann met her in the old town, and they walked arm-in-arm to Bäckerstraße to a good old-fashioned café, the Kaffee Alt Wien.

'Well done, *Schatzi*. You were all alone?'

'I'm sure.'

'None of the usual types from our home city?'

'Nothing like that.' Even if anyone had been following her, what would they have seen and what conclusions could he have drawn? 'You sound surprised.'

'I'm surprised this drop worked, to be honest. A Soviet in his position will be watched almost continuously.'

A pause.

'I guess Pal's on the level with us,' said Lois.

It was an early supper to be savoured: schnitzel with lemon and deliciously sweet young vegetables. The months in Moscow had made her obsessive about varied and tasty food. Afterwards, they wandered the green meadows of the Stadtpark as dusk fell. The river glittered. One path led the eye into enticing trees, another opened a vista of water and the promise of softness and grass.

The message she had brought was brief.

IAEA. Men's cloakroom at 1.39.

She actually laughed at the sheer mundanity of it.

'By the way, can I borrow your Minox, just in case? Mine's not working.'

She reached into her shoulder bag, took out a handkerchief to cover it and passed him the tiny camera. Even outside Russia, some rules were never relaxed.

'*Trust no one but Johann.*' It always came down to Miss Harcourt's warning. But as the paths twisted and led them back on themselves, Lois found herself still fretting about their parallel investigation. Were they being led astray, off course down a blind alley? Then there was the added complication of their more intimate relationship. Joyful and exciting as it was, she worried that it might open them up to being compromised – even if it was a compromise of their own judgement. But equally, maybe they ought to seize some happiness where they could. Who knew where it might lead, or what the next day might bring. Vienna was already the beautiful guardian of their secrets.

They spent that night crumpling the pristine bedsheets of his room, as if that night was all they would ever have.

The next day was another lovely confection of warm sun and breeze. The conference opened at the Atomic Energy Agency.

Sonia and Boyd left a message asking her to join them on a coach trip and were put out when she declined. Boyd made a thoughtlessly offensive jibe about Lois being up to no good on her own in Vienna.

But what a difference it made, losing Sonia. Lois went shopping. Her money went like wildfire. There was so much to buy in the shining shops with their enchanted windows, the cakes and fruit glistening like precious jewels, the sheen of opulence on the latest fashions.

By 1.39pm, she had eaten a fat, juicy ham sandwich in the Stadtpark, looking at her watch too often. Picturing Johann and the Russian. Her head started to ache. She rubbed her temples and gazed out at the green trees and grass, the people strolling in the park. Normal people, walking and talking and laughing.

She went back to her hotel room and slept.

'You saw him?' That was the first question she'd asked, of course, as soon as they met at seven.

Johann nodded.

'And?'

Café conversation swirled around the clatter of plates and cutlery and for the first time since arriving in Vienna, she found it oppressive.

'He's awkward. Getting desperate, I think. He didn't bring anything. He couldn't.'

A waiter interrupted with bowls of goulash and carraway dumplings.

'I'm going to speak to him tomorrow. At the Helenental.'

'How will you manage that? Can he get away so easily?'

'Another trip for the delegates. Saturday afternoon outing. Helenental is a very lovely little valley with woods and a river. There will be plenty of walkers. I should have a chance to speak to him as we go along.'

'I'll come too.'

'No, Lois, you will not.'

'What if it were a good idea to let him see me? Show him that I listened to him, and I am ready to talk now I know who he is?'

'It's too risky, Lois. Leave this to me.'

She was up early to catch the bus to Baden, then felt she was too early, so she carried on to Bad Vöslau, had a lemonade there and caught the bus back to Baden, arriving as the clocks were chiming midday. She bought a guide map, some sandwiches and apple juice and lingered by the bus stop, waiting to spot the cars or coach that brought the delegates.

A coach pulled up twenty minutes later. They were an unprepossessing group, for the most part. The guides were dressed in authentic Austrian hiking clothes. Johann, amusingly, had dressed for a country walk with all the awkwardness of an urban journalist.

They set off in one big group for the path to the river, the River Schwechat, according to the map, that would eventually drain into the Danube. Lois let them go and then tucked herself in behind a rambling club. They pushed on nimbly, stopping now and then to admire the lush surroundings.

Through clearings in the trees, the ruins of two castles hoisted crumbling towers into the sky, one either side of the river, the watch stations of the path since the twelfth century. Lois held back as the path led through a crumbled courtyard and the group imprisoned themselves in ivy-covered corners and some climbed the tower to take in the views.

The Helenental was indeed a pretty valley. The air was fresh and verdant. The forest path was gentle and the babble of water a delightful companion. Now beyond the castle, the Atomic Energy Agency group dawdled ahead. She found a spot behind a spruce tree and sat down when she saw them stop in a glade and tablecloths were spread by the guides.

Lois ate her own lunch with her nose buried in the map, reading the guide notes. Beethoven had walked along this route while he was composing his *Sixth Symphony*, she learnt. The storm in the third movement had been inspired by the unfortunate turn in the weather he had experienced on this very path. Johann probably knew that already.

She began to feel sleepy as the group ahead lingered. She could see that smaller factions had formed, deep in conversation. Johann was out of sight. Eventually, their picnic was cleared and they got to their feet. Lois was ready to move on as soon as she judged it wise. Perhaps she might even overtake them and linger by the Cholerakapelle, which was the obvious destination of the path.

In the end, that was what she decided. She picked her way through the trees above the path and climbed a small hill to the stone chapel that was once a popular place of pilgrimage. A bell hung prettily in a tower topped with an oddly spiky dome that made her think of half a sea urchin. It had been built to offer thanks for the lives of those who had survived a terrible outbreak of cholera in Vienna and Baden in 1830 and 1831 which claimed thousands of victims.

Lois waited patiently, admiring the stained glass windows, then the interior, for the scientists and politicians and pressmen to pant up the incline. She had a moment of doubt when ten minutes went by. She had misjudged their stamina, their interest in completing the walk… She heard them before she saw them.

Some came inside, but Johann was not among them. She folded her map and went out quietly. Pushed her new sunglasses back to the bridge of her nose.

Not all the group was here. There weren't enough of them. No sign of Johann.

Lois took the path down, passing others who were making the final assault. Perhaps he had found a chance to speak to the Russian. Perhaps the Russian was no longer fit enough to do the climb up to the chapel and Johann had quite naturally volunteered to stay back with him. She was making wild guesses.

Finally, she saw Johann. He was standing by a lichened stone memorial, speaking to a man who had taken off his coat. She had to engineer a way to have a closer look. A stout man in early middle age. No hat. A square grey face – a Moscow complexion at the end of a long winter.

He was the man on the train.

Lois scampered back down the path, heart knocking to be let out.

At Baden she went into the nearest café. In the ladies', her face stared back hot and dusty from the mirror. She washed it and combed her hair. At the bar she asked for a strong coffee and a large glass of water, and whether the waiter happened to know the time of the next bus back to Vienna.

She had so much to say to Johann, and so many questions to ask. But that evening he did not telephone her room, nor did he knock on her door. He must have seen her. He was angry with her, she knew it. But this was more important than any of that.

At seven o'clock, tied in knots by waiting, Lois rapped on his door.

No answer.

Nine o'clock. At the desk in the foyer, she enquired casually whether Herr Dreschler had returned, and was told that he had not. Nor was he back at ten when she knocked on his door again.

Monday was the closing day of the conference. A final dinner was planned at the grand Café Central after the final speeches from the United Nations representative and the director of the International Atomic Energy Agency, the text of which had already been released to the press, the wording carefully reiterating the statement of the first General Conference only the previous year: "The main objective of the Agency is to accelerate and enlarge the contribution of atomic energy to peace, health and prosperity throughout the world."

It is so lovely to walk without looking over one's shoulder, thought Lois as she reached the Kärntner Ring. Tram tracks on each side of the wide, elegant boulevard were lined with trees. The street had a secluded atmosphere despite the traffic. The other side of the road was almost hidden. Number Eleven, Kärntner Ring was once the Grand Hotel Wien, the first Grand Hotel in Vienna. It opened in 1870 with a magnificent three hundred rooms and two hundred bathrooms, steam elevators and a telegraph office that in itself was a sensation at that time. More recently, the hotel had been a billet for Soviet troops who checked in from 1945 to 1955. Ownership had passed to the Austrian government, who rented it to the newly minted International Atomic Energy Agency.

'Lois! Oh, Lois!'

Surely not. Oh, please let it not be.

'I saw you waiting for the tram, and you looked so intent that I was curious where you could be going with such determination,' trilled Sonia.

Lois was momentarily speechless.

'Where's Boyd?' asked Lois.

'Gone to some dull museum. Natural History. Unlike him, I've no interest in butterfly bothering. And then I spotted you on your own! Where are you going?'

'Nowhere, just wandering,' said Lois. 'I've always loved trams, you see. You can see so much from them without paying tour prices. I never know where I'm going to end up half the time.'

Sonia narrowed her eyes. *She doesn't believe me*, thought Lois. That was the trouble when you had been in Moscow for any length of time, you got cynical about everything and suspicious of everyone and once you had begun, there was no going back.

'You're in a world of your own again, Lois. I'm worried about you, you know.'

'There's absolutely no need.'

'But I can't help it, you see. It's clear as anything to me that Johann's going to let you down. You're in love with him, so you're oblivious. But all the signs are there.'

It was a disgusting thing to say. Just another of Sonia's mean games.

'As I'm the one who actually knows him, I think I should be the judge of that.'

'If you say so. But don't say I didn't warn you. Now, shall we go and have a coffee in that nice-looking café over there?'

There was nothing for it but to agree if she didn't want more unpleasantness in the weeks to come. In order to avoid spending any more time with Sonia than strictly necessary, Lois had to claim she was meeting Johann for lunch, that he'd told her he had a romantic surprise. In the light of that, Sonia left off her needling predictions about him and prattled and moaned about Moscow over the delicious, pungent coffee. Apart from the glorious baroque surroundings, they might have been back at Meshchanskaya, stuck fast in the mire of Boyd's shortcomings and the mean look someone at the office had given her.

By the time Lois had directed Sonia to a stylish dress shop some miles away, the foyer of the Atomic Energy Agency echoed emptily. Either speeches were still going on or everyone had left for lunch.

'Can I help you, Miss?' A man on the concierge desk challenged her with iron politeness.

'London News Agency. I have an urgent message from the editor for our reporter,' she said.

'You can't go in now. You'll have to wait out here.'

She found a bench seat behind a pillar where she could observe most of the doors and wondered what to do next. A large poster vaunted *Peaceful uses of atomic energy* over pictures of plant growth and fertilisers. The sound of clapping intensified followed by a hubbub of voices.

Delegates began to emerge from the conference room. Lois stiffened when she saw Johann in the middle of a group of voluble men, presumably the press corps. He saw her immediately but continued with his conversation. When he did come over, she saw he was slightly out of breath, a sheen of sweat on his forehead. He hurried her out without a word.

They were halfway up the street before he told her, furiously, 'Alexei has gone.'

Johann rubbed his hands over his face as if he had not slept. Strain showed in sooty smudges under his eyes. Lois would not ask him where he was the previous night. It occurred to her that if Russian soldiers were billeted in the building after the war, only leaving a few years ago, that might mean that someone who, say, was with military intelligence, might know very well the internal lay-out of the building. Perhaps Zhigunov had left without recourse to the foyer. She started to say this, but he interrupted.

'The Russians left early. Some of the press are reporting that they walked out. That the Soviet scientists presented papers with nothing new for the West, that they only came for our knowledge. Come on, Lois, you can see what this means, can't you?'

'I'm not a mind-reader, Johann.'

'Please tell me you are not missing the main story?'

She said nothing.

'Go back, look at all the steps that have brought us here.' But, she realised, he was not so much pushing her to answer as he was thinking aloud. 'Is this a test, or is it a trap? The fear has always been that the biggest fish would swim away unrecognised while the net was cast in the wrong place... What exactly does Boyd do in Moscow?'

'I'm not sure, exactly.'

'I knew I had seen him, damn it!'

'Boyd?'

'The Russian. One of the security detail who watch the Canadians. He was the one on my tail. Perhaps there are others. They have most likely been following you, too. Perhaps they suspected Alexei might try to defect here.'

Johann hailed a cab. Within minutes they were back at Schneider's. He led her up to his room and stood by the window without speaking, watching the street below. Lois sat in the only armchair. He was completely still for a moment, then picked up his jacket. He put it on again and patted the pockets. Far away, remote from her.

'Where are you going?'

'Don't ask. Just stay here. Watch this room.'

'Johann!' she protested. 'Tell me what's going on!'

But he left. Lois found the resolve to wait patiently despite her anger. She picked up a book he had left, a paperback thriller in German. Put it down, unable to concentrate. She was supposed to trust him, yet he would not trust her. She was beyond fury, yet what could she do? She took her diary out of her handbag and caught up to date. Afternoon faded to evening.

A knock on the door startled her.

It was a young woman, decidedly not a chambermaid or other hotel employee. Very beautiful, with Slavic eyes and high cheekbones. Lois knew even before her eyes travelled down to the embroidered peasant blouse, open provocatively to show that she wasn't wearing a brassiere, that the girl was Russian.

She was clearly knocked off balance when she saw Lois. She had expected Johann to be alone.

'*Guten Abend*,' said Lois, playing the innocent.

The Russian looked beyond her, into the room. Lois saw her checking the mirror at the dressing table. Her eyes slid from side to side as she backed away.

Lois came forward beyond the doorframe in time to see a large man in an ill-fitting suit try (as much as it was possible) to flatten himself against the wall of the corridor, then walk around the corner. The girl backed away, awkwardly followed him, stumbling slightly in her high heeled shoes. In a matter of seconds, they were gone.

Lois went inside and shut the door. 'It's not just Alexei who knows you're here, Johann,' she murmured.

It could have been a mistake. But Lois did not think so.

Draw your opposition out. It won't be who you think.

What better way to stop Johann than to engineer a classic compromising situation, allowing him to be accused of reckless wrong-doing? Plant something incriminating in his possessions. Get him locked up and investigated. Lois persisted in her thought process. Whoever the mole was, whoever it was who wanted to stop anyone contacting Alexei, they didn't want their flimsy diplomatic lines disrupted. They would put the Russians on to you to make their relationships stronger. "See, we're not all against you? My enemy's enemy is my friend." They were all fighting their own secret corners. *Paralysis,* she concluded, *that is the goal here.*

And there was nothing to do but wait. Night fell but Johann did not return to his room. Eventually she wrote him a note and let herself out. Would it have been better or worse to have gone back to her room sooner? Her senses warned her as

158

soon as she got out of the lift and walked along the corridor. A familiar smell hung in the close air.

Key in hand, she slowed as she approached her door. Tensed for what was coming. Unlocked the door and waited, standing well back. Then cautiously pushed it open slightly. Listened, ready to run. Sniffed. It was unmistakeable, that Moscow stink, all the stronger and more recognisable for the respite from it: the Belomorkanal cigarettes, the body odour and badly washed clothes.

She pushed the door further open. Could see her suitcase open on the floor and the bedclothes strewn. Lois listened intently, trembling, for a moment then set off down the corridor to the stairs, down to the reception desk to ask for help.

The stout porter came back up with her.

No intruder remained, only the warning: the snarled mess of the bed, her possessions, the ripped lining of suitcase, and the knife stuck in the pillow.

The porter, visibly shocked, could not understand why she did not want the police called immediately. Lois made a rapid, shaken inventory of her things, assuring him there was nothing missing, that the suitcase lining was unfortunately torn already (a lie). Any important items were in her handbag, which she had with her all day.

Still to the incomprehension of Frau Schneider and her apologetic concierge, Lois was moved into another room where she lay awake all night and was up at seven for a hurried half-breakfast. She made another abortive call to Johann's room. At eight, she took her booked taxi to the Air France office for the bus to the airport. She found Sonia there for the same flight, stroppy as usual, though this time because she had been told her seat was not next to Lois's. With this small mercy, Lois had no choice but to get on the plane back to Moscow without being able to contact Johann and lie to

Sonia about the wonderful time they had had the previous day.

Worry seared into her stomach and tensed her shoulders. She was seated next to an Austrian doctor bound for Leningrad with a delegation – what really went on at all these conferences that pulled back the Iron Curtain far enough to slip through? They chatted politely, Lois straining to appear at ease. The trip to Vienna had been a disaster. Who knew what damage had been caused? They landed in Moscow at nine that night. The taxi ride with Sonia back to Meshchanskaya felt like a return to prison. Dense blackness outside the cab window only intensified her fear. Was she in deeper than she thought – what game was it she was really involved in? Never quite as confident as she made out, she relied on determination to push her through, she realised. But she could not back down now. She had no choice but to go on. But would taking this chance to prove herself prove only to be her own undoing?

Twenty-four hours later, Lois returned to Vnukovo Airport to meet the flight Johann should have been on. She waited until all the passengers had come through after the Vienna plane landed. Then waited longer, in case Johann had a reason for holding back until he would mix in with the flight from Rome that followed shortly after. After the legations and businessmen from Paris had dwindled, and the last stragglers had resolved their inevitable difficulties at customs and been met and transferred to their hotels for observation, Lois felt stupid and, worse, her desperation was exposed in the echoing chamber of the arrivals hall.

What had happened to him? How could she help him now? Or had he betrayed her? No, surely not. He was protecting her. She saw him by the window in his hotel room, the tension in his broad shoulders, the strain around those blue, blue eyes.

She saw him energised in the streets and cafés of Vienna, and then again, earlier, in that room, that bed. Only a matter of days ago he had loved her. She had found her lasting love. One day, when all this was over, they would walk hand-in-hand in the mountains, and they would never speak of this foreign adventure that was their unbreakable bond.

She closed her eyes against present reality. Alone at the airport, she was in a daze of indecision. Meat-faced Soviet officials were getting suspicious, beginning to prey on her vulnerability, harassing her with disgusting suggestions, smirking when she tried to explain in bad Russian about a friend who must have missed his flight.

Nothing for it but to find a taxi home.

Two nights later, Johann had still not returned to Moscow.

16

Tuesday, May 13, 1958

Vienna hangover. Lasting for days, it seems.

On the fourth day that Johann failed to return from Vienna – Lois had called repeatedly, frantically gone round to his flat after work, telephoned his office only to be told that he was still on leave – she was called into the Head of Chancery's private room to find Tony Fielding already there, perched on the edge of Burville's imposing desk, one hand in pocket, affecting nonchalance but primed for action. In his red rollneck sweater and vintage naval coat, he was a friendly buccaneer who might at any moment draw his cutlass and relish the fight.

In contrast, Hugh Burville was standing by the bookcase, sleek and seething. His mouth and jaw were clenched as if he could hardly allow himself to speak for fear that he would lose control. The veneer of politesse was at odds with the hardness in his eyes; she was only surprised that he didn't lead her to the secure chamber and let rip.

'How was your trip to Vienna?' he asked glacially.

'It was very nice, thank you.'

'Much sightseeing?'

'A fair amount.'

'And where's your German friend now?'

It must have been Sonia, that was her first thought. But what had come out that necessitated Fielding's presence in the room? The only way out was to play dumb as truthfully as possible.

'He missed his flight.'

Burville exchanged a glance with Fielding, who immediately looked down and crossed his arms.

'Trouble getting back?'

'I think he must have.'

'Tell me how you two got so friendly.'

Lois explained with innocent helpfulness that she liked to keep up her German, and she enjoyed his company.

Burville wanted to know what she had done each day in Vienna, when precisely she had seen Johann and what they had done. With the controlled fury of a schoolmaster interrogating an errant pupil, he took his chair at the desk and made notes on a single page of blue draft notepaper resting on a marble tile. Lois rounded her shoulders, submitting to the punishment, making herself smaller and more intimidated. Playing down to his expectations.

At length he said, 'There's a rumour that Dreschler has been honeytrapped.' He watched her reactions like a hawk, eyes fixed and glittering. Still Fielding said nothing.

'Where – here?' She did not have to manufacture her surprise. How could he know that?

'In Vienna.'

'That seems… rather unlikely.'

'How so, in your humble opinion?'

'Johann is… very experienced. He knows how to handle himself.'

'In what way, exactly?'

'He's a newsman, pretty cynical. I shouldn't think he'd fall for anything like that. Besides, he was with me.'

Burville assessed her, paying attention to her bust and waist. Again she could not help but be reminded that women were divided into the beautiful and decorative young, and the older and useful. Safer for current purposes to be consigned to the first group, if less satisfying to the intellect.

'What have you been telling him, Miss Vale?'

She felt sick. 'What do you mean "telling him"? We talk about all kinds of things. Travel, books, music, poetry.'

'You never discuss your work here?'

'I would *never* discuss embassy matters with an outsider,' she stated resolutely.

'Does he have any… unusual contacts with Russians?'

'No more or less than any of the foreign reporters here.'

'Russian women?'

'I should hope not.'

Burville picked up a paper knife and held it reflectively for a moment in mid-air. 'We can't rely on hopes, Miss Vale.'

He stared hard at the knife. 'Why did you not report the break-in of your hotel room?'

A shadow grazed Fielding's face as he listened carefully to her answer. Her every inflection was being judged.

'I… nothing was taken. I didn't want to make a fuss, to miss my flight the next morning.'

'Report it to me, I mean.'

'The same reason. I didn't want a fuss. If I should have done, I'm sorry.'

'What else have you thought too unimportant to report since you've been here, that's my question…'

Lois stood a little straighter. Shook her head but said nothing.

The knife went back on the table. Burville looked away into the middle distance. It was a trait she had noticed among the more experienced dips. He was deciding whether to tell her something, or whether she was too much of a risk.

'If Dreschler makes it back, I want you to come to me at once.'

She nodded.

'I'll be watching you,' he said.

Not as carefully as I will be watching you, she thought. Tony Fielding had said not a word. That was far more concerning then Burville's icy interrogation.

Suitably chastened and outwardly grateful for Burville's intervention and understanding, Lois retreated to her anteroom. She carried on as normal in the office, though her heart skipped beats and the pit in her stomach gnawed like a wild animal.

It was hard to believe that Johann had fallen for some set-up. The girl in the Slavic blouse was so obvious, so half-baked, that even at the time she had questioned how real it had been. But Johann had not been himself in Vienna, she could see that now. Apart from physically, she had not got to know him any better, and the more she went over what had happened, the more true that seemed. Her reckless willingness to sleep with him had clouded her judgement and she felt ashamed. As for her room being turned over, had the report come from a watcher at the hotel, or an informant inside it reporting to the MI6's man in Vienna? What she did know for certain was that Johann's disappearance could potentially take her down as well. If so, who was behind it?

The Minister made a discreet comment to show he was aware of the situation with her German journalist friend but would not interfere. Some of the girls were a little standoffish for a while, almost certainly thanks to Sonia. They asked where Johann was, of course, and why Lois no longer went about with him – what had happened in Vienna to the great romance? She managed to fob them off with half-truth. She and Johann had decided to cool it down; he must be on a story elsewhere.

At a tea break she managed to time perfectly, Ellis Wachorne asked her to make up a doubles four with his wife Flora and John Mowberry for a game of tennis after work. He proved himself every bit the lithe sportsman of Lois's first impression, leaping and running and dextrous with his racket. It was a nice chance to get to know Flora Wachorne better: she was petite and seriously pretty with green eyes that sparkled under her fringe of straight blonde hair cut in a short elfin style. She clearly shared her husband's sense of fun, the two of them larking around between points, teasing each other and very much in love.

Unexpectedly, Lois felt envious. She found herself wondering what it would be like to be one of the diplomatic wives, seeing the world while their husbands took the strain of working. They smiled proudly as they stood by their man but were rarely recognised for their own achievements, she reminded herself. The Minister's wife, the polished embassy hostess who ran his home and had brought up their children, had once been his capable secretary. But the rules were that the foreign service did not employ married women, and that was that. No matter how high-powered women were, they had to give up their jobs upon marriage. Was Mrs Waller happy? She seemed so. Though how could anyone really know? But the Wallers had had a run of interesting and successful postings, no doubt thanks to her quiet contribution. They were a partnership. Though she had never thought it before, Lois suddenly wanted nothing more than to feel safe with a man who truly loved her.

The Wachornes trounced her and Mowberry over two short sets. After a few days of decent weather, the enclosed embassy garden was almost balmy that evening and the game good-natured. It was good to be outside in congenial company, so the men swapped partners for a further knock-around.

Lois and Wachorne chatted as they hit balls back and forth. Wachorne was curious about what had held Johann up in Vienna, too, it seemed. Or was he just being friendly? She might have thought less of him had he pretended to know nothing of a matter that was clearly being discussed at high level. Lois meticulously told him no more and no less than she had told Burville and Fielding.

'Good shot!' he shouted, as she hit a hard, net-skimming forehand down the line.

'Needed a few more of those in the match!' She laughed.

'Oh, you're a decent player all right, Lois.'

There was no mistaking his underlying meaning. She turned to look at him, but he was already chasing down the next ball, blond head away from her, racket arm outstretched. He said nothing more that was not merry and amusing. The evening ended in the library bar, drinking beers – still in their tennis kit – and chatting about sporting events and comedy films. Lois told herself she was being oversensitive.

Rory was also interested in Johann's whereabouts, which had the effect of making her avoid him. Clearly, this was the opposite of his intentions, but he seemed unable to stop himself once he had mustered the courage to approach her. On the subject of Johann Dreschler, he was dogged.

'Johann and I weren't that serious,' she insisted for the umpteenth time. The awful but self-evident truth of that twisted her insides.

'That's not what it looked like.'

'Well, it's what it was.'

Now Rory seemed to suspect Johann's motives in getting close to her. 'Did he ever ask you for details about your work?'

'Never. He knew better than that.'

When she told him to stop asking about Johann, he took offence and did not speak to her for days.

He was right, though. Everywhere one looked were new possibilities for betrayal. How could they ever hope to catch water in a sieve? Behind the diplomatic statements and threats, public hopes for peace, the parades of strength and progress, behind the stories supplied by clamouring newspapermen and broadcasters, theirs was a dirty game playing out in back alleys and lavatories.

Without Johann, she felt profoundly apprehensive. Moscow became once more a lonely place of unremitting threat. The apartment blocks that leaked and creaked and were hacked about by the diplomatic community had been built by German prisoners of war kept enslaved for years after the war (if they made it back at all). The feared Lubyanka, headquarters of the KGB, cast its dark shadow over the city from beyond the Red Square: a monumental edifice to fear with only two windows on the top floor and a central clock like the eye of a camera. People died in there, were murdered in cold blood. Inside were no innocents, not even those who had done nothing wrong. The Russians in the street knew it. They all knew it.

Two thugs followed her when she set out for St Philipp's church to check the dead drop. She diverted from her usual route and circled back, slowing her pace when she reached one of the crowded main boulevards. The *veniki* stared as she passed: the broom ladies, old and middle-aged women in long black skirts and headscarves who quietly toiled, sweeping in the pay of the KGB. While the backstreets remained untidy dumping grounds, the *veniki* were the state's eyes and ears on the streets, detailed to report any un-Soviet activities or overheard conversations. Lois went into a café and then queued for a while outside a shoddy store, and tried again but could not shake off her tail. She aborted the mission.

The only way to survive was by compartmentalism, as Robinson had impressed on her. Not only for security in work matters, but in the personal sense. One had to learn to lock away unpleasant facts when they were not required, so as not to be unnerved by them.

The days churned over with too much to do: several jobs going at once, home to lunch and change for cocktail parties and dinners in the evening. She had ceased to be amused by the parade of party clothes worn for work by the junior staff in the afternoons. Sonia was her usual trying self.

Trudy, always so sensible and unobtrusive, told her discreetly that Sonia had been coming round to the flat she shared with Frances and working herself up into a febrile state, accusing Lois of taking trinkets, being oversensitive and unstable, of being careless about what she said in the flat. And that she was concerned about Johann's character and motives.

'She is jealous of you, you know,' said Trudy. 'She also says Rory called round when you were out, confirmed the worst about you, and made a play for her.'

'Rory doesn't even like her!' burst out Lois, unexpectedly, even to herself.

At a party a few days later, one of the frenetic gatherings in someone's bottle-strewn flat, Rory told her about the evening he called round on the off-chance of finding her in, and Sonia launched herself at him.

'That's funny, that's what she's been saying about you.'

'No. The other way round.'

'I see. Makes better sense to me now,' said Lois. A warm spike of hope had surged up, catching her by surprise. Nothing here was ever quite what you thought it was. They went over to the sofa and sat down.

'She's trying to make life difficult for you,' he said, 'and I have to tell you that she's on a winning streak. H of C had a word with me yesterday. He was keen for me to confirm her stories.'

'You didn't, I take it?'

'Of course not.'

The one glimmer of light was that Valerie's posting was up soon, and when she left there would be a spare place in the flat upstairs. Lois thought long and hard whether it would be wise to move in with the gimlet-sharp Nan, who had noticed her struggles to get on with Sonia. No doubt Nan would prove a different kind of challenge, but on balance, it was worth the risk. Nan was a lot more reasonable and self-sufficient.

Lois took the chance and proposed the move.

Sonia screamed and shouted at her, not caring who heard it. 'What have you said about me? How do you think this makes me feel?'

'Why are you like this?' asked Lois.

'Because I'm scared!' wailed Sonia.

'We're all scared,' said Lois. 'But we just have to get on with it.'

'I feel like I'm falling apart. I'm frightened I'm having a breakdown.'

'You need to see Dr Harrison,' said Lois as gently as she could.

The most honest conversation they had ever had, but it had come too late. The existential threat of Moscow caused so much social combustion. Lois had made an enemy, but the relief of removing herself from the flat and Sonia's immediate company was enormous. The question remained why Sonia, so unstable and needy of attention, had been sent out in the first place.

In mid-May, the England football team arrived for a match against the USSR, complete with cohort of pressmen from the nationals, all of whom were eager to drink and gossip. For a few days, no party was complete without the hacks, with occasional sightings of the players. The man from *Empire News* was nice, but he said none of them knew anyone from the German press corps.

The match was played on the Sunday afternoon. Somehow she ended up sitting with Rory, and thanks to him understood that it wasn't a bad game, but the Russians shouldn't have had their equaliser. The weather was fine, too. They went back to the embassy and had a cup of tea, then a drink in the bar, and watched the film show, which was *The Ladykillers*. All the England team came along afterwards at eleven, though there were complaints that there weren't enough girls. Lois found herself talking to two northern lads called Brian Clough and Bobby Charlton, after Rory had engaged them in a lengthy and forensic discussion of match tactics and league games the previous season. Rory was confident and clearly enjoying the opportunity, while the players seemed to appreciate the conversation, young Clough in particular, who confided he had been nervous about attending a party given by stuffy diplomats.

It was another side to Rory she had not seen. All passion for football spent, Rory gallantly brought her home, and Sonia came in at dawn.

The following Sunday, Lois was invited to spend the day at Perlovka, a *dacha* long used by the embassy. The old country lodge stood in its own grounds just outside a village of wooden houses within the twenty-five mile radius outside Moscow for which no special permission to travel was needed. It was a breath of fresh air, with walks in pine woods and trees in the garden to sit under while reading. Nan and Valerie were going, and the inseparable Trudy and Frances, Frank, Eric and Rory. The admin officer Kit Woodward and his wife were joining them, adding rank.

It would be a chance to relax, though they could never be absolutely certain that listening bugs were not present. The weather was set fair. It would be a lovely, relaxing day – and it was always good to escape Sonia.

They arrived in the office bus to find the door already open. Music blared from the gramophone in the empty sitting room and the sound of voices drifted from the orchard beyond.

'What the devil?' Woodward scurried ahead. The men followed.

They found Tony Fielding chopping wood and Ellis and Flora Wachorne setting up a pockmarked old archery target. In the sunlight, Flora's blonde hair glowed and a peach-coloured dress showed off her wonderful creamy skin. She and Ellis were laughing together as ever as the stand toppled over on the uneven ground.

'You didn't put yourselves in the book!' Admin Officer Woodward was clearly put out that the system had not been used. He scratched his balding head and pulled a reproachful face.

'I thought it was empty this weekend,' said Fielding brightly. He made no apology.

'So sorry, Kit,' said Wachorne. 'Obviously a mix-up.'

'Does it matter?' Fielding brought the axe smartly down on his own question.

'Suppose not. But we're quite a party already, and it should have been in the book.'

'Oh, we've another on board as well.' Fielding looked around.

Sonia stepped daintily out of the dilapidated summer house.

Lois went for a walk with Nan and Valerie. Fielding chopped more wood and lit the stove. Margaret Woodward, kind and matronly in a huge apron, set to in the kitchen making scones that turned into rock cakes, and heating stew. Another embassy wife who made herself quietly useful, apparently without complaint or recognition, thought Lois, in grateful anticipation of good English home cooking. Was Mrs Woodward's life in Moscow easier to bear or harder in other ways than her own? She had no pressure of official work, let alone a tricky clandestine mission to navigate, yet there were two children at boarding school back in the UK to miss and worry about. How did she feel about that? Yet there she was, in the kitchen, making sure the party was well fed and largely oblivious to her efforts. The churn of dull but necessary chores naturally fell to her. No wonder all the married men were comparatively cheerful.

After an excellent lunch, they lounged in the garden on ancient British deckchairs, chatted and played cards. Fielding and the Wachornes attempted archery with heavy wooden bows and blunt arrows, Sonia scampering around making a show of herself bending over in tight pink capri pants to collect the failed shots. They were all drinking vodka and making more noise than all the rest of them put together. Lois resolutely concentrated on reading *War and Peace*, but it was yet another losing battle.

What was Sonia doing here with them anyway? A few more pages in, Lois felt a sudden stinging on her bare arm.

'Ow! What on earth?' A long graze started to seep blood. She sat up.

An arrow lay on the grass.

Sonia stood ten feet away, lowering a bow. She was laughing hysterically.

'Take that, Lois, you deserved it!'

Lois stared in panic as the woman reached around her back and produced another arrow.

'Just so you know, I had to tell Tony and Ellis about you,' said Sonia. 'How you always behaved so disturbingly in the flat. How you go off alone, even though you used to tell me you were meeting someone first. Then the way you did everything to lose me in Vienna. What were you up to there, eh, Lois? I didn't want to have to tell. I wanted to be your friend but there's something not right about you – and certainly something not right about Johann Dreschler. You made me do it, and they were certainly very interested. Made me go through everything I could remember, which was plenty. Just as well I was there to keep an eye on you, wasn't it!'

The garden seemed to darken. Lois felt herself sway. No one else seemed to have noticed what was happening. Sonia placed the arrow in the bow and grinned. Lois remained rooted to the spot, as if in a dream when she knew she had to run but could not.

Sonia's little doll mouth contorted as she pulled the arrow back, pointing it straight at Lois. Yet as quickly as Sonia made the gesture, Fielding ran up from behind her and pinned her arms to her side.

As relief flooded Lois's veins, Sonia was screaming with drunken laughter. She turned her head to Fielding and kissed his mouth ravenously.

'Oh, you big, strong, gorgeous man! The best one I know!'

He pulled back. 'What have you done?' was his only response.

'You know I want you, don't you, Tony? And she…' Sonia was shouting at Lois, 'she has been poisoning everyone against me!'

Others started to move toward, drawn to the scene.

'Calm down, Sonia. That's enough.' Fielding's reprimand

had the effect of instantly deflating her. Her legs seemed to buckle, and she went limp. Fielding was now holding her up, a rag doll in his muscular arms. 'Are you all right? How bad is it?' he asked Lois urgently.

'Just a scratch. It's nothing, I'm just...'

What was she "just"? Bleeding? Alarmed? Infuriated?

Flora Wachorne rushed up, examined Lois's arm and ran back to the house. Lois watched Fielding settle Sonia in a chair apart from the others and kneel down beside her. Within the minute, Flora was back with warm water, a clean tea towel and some iodine. She had inspected the wound and tended to her almost as quickly.

'It's only superficial. You'll live.'

'I know. I wasn't worried. But thank you.'

Flora patted Lois's uninjured arm. Her wide smile showed lovely even teeth.

'Stupid thing to happen, though.'

'Yes, wasn't it.'

She had been training as a nurse when she met Ellis at Cambridge, she told Lois. She qualified but they married before she could take up a hospital job.

'I couldn't resist him, you see.'

'Nor I you, sweetheart!' Her husband came up from behind, wrapped his arms around her and dropped a kiss on top of her head.

Lois wanted to ask Flora how she felt about the vocation she had trained for and then abandoned. Did she ever feel she had missed out by not following it through – or had work been, as for so many women, only something to fill the days until they found a husband? But Lois didn't ask. Sonia's words about not being too familiar with the higher-ups quelled her inquisitiveness. And anyway, who was she to judge what made other women happy? Ellis Wachorne really did seem to be a

175

loving and considerate spouse; quite the catch, indeed. Odd, thought Lois, that she was so interested in the wives suddenly. It must be the sheer normality of being in the countryside and the domestic nature of the house in the woods.

They stayed chatting pleasantly with her for a while but not a word was said about Sonia until Lois felt she could hold back no longer.

'Whatever Sonia says, I haven't said anything untoward about her. It's been very hard, but I haven't.'

'I know,' said Wachorne.

One by one, they all came up to ask what exactly had happened. Rory was outraged and solicitous. Sonia had made an utter fool of herself. Nan, in particular, also wanted to know what Sonia thought she was doing by throwing herself at her boss. Lois calmly told them all she was fine.

'Just as well she's no Robin Hood, eh?' Fielding stood four-square in front of her, arms on his hips, and shot her a piratical grin.

Lois smiled. 'Just as well she didn't actually aim at my arm.'

'Indeed... yes, I see! Could have been much worse. She's asleep now. Sorry, should have noticed she was drinking too much.'

Silence. Lois held it longer than was polite, but he did not oblige by explaining what Sonia was doing here with him in the first place. But nor did he ask anything that might make her uncomfortable.

'What are you reading?'

She held up her book.

'God help you,' he said.

Someone had put a Rachmaninov recording on the gramophone. The music made the sunlit afternoon lush and full of soft air. Fielding sat down on the grass, and they talked about novels and biographies.

'When I first arrived, everyone was reading *The Brothers Karamazov*. The whole diplomatic corps was ploughing through it – there was quite a competition to see which nation could get the most out of Dostoevsky. Give me John Buchan or a Neil Shute thriller any day!' He spoke amusingly and asked her questions as they naturally occurred about her life back home. Neither of them mentioned Sonia. Tony Fielding was utterly charming and engaging and revealed nothing of substance about himself.

At teatime, Frances revealed an interest in reading their teacups. Lois was told she was to have a trip but would meet much opposition for a while. The prediction in Nan's leaves – to much hilarity – had her running away with a dark man and finding happiness on an island.

Fielding and the Wachornes left early to take a tear-stained Sonia home. The rest of the party stayed until after eleven, chatting more freely, playing cards, and talking of trips to Kiev and Yalta. Lois enjoyed Rory's company, too. He was by far the best looking man, yet the least relentlessly sure of himself and his views. Practical, too. When a fuse blew on the plug for the record player, it was Rory who stepped forward to find a makeshift tool and replaced it with a minimum of fuss.

'Thank you for a wonderful day, Mrs Woodward,' said Lois as she helped pack up. 'I haven't eaten so well since I don't know when.'

'You're very welcome, my dear. It was my pleasure. Especially seeing you younger ones relax, not easy for any of you.'

'No, it isn't. But I'm sure it's difficult for everyone, wives included.'

'That's true. But I have Kit by my side and so I'm lucky. We're a team. Between us we keep going and look on the bright side. We're going on leave in a couple of months, and we'll stretch it over the Christmas holidays when the boys are home from school, and that will be marvellous.'

'You must miss them.'

'Of course, but they're of an age when they'd rather be playing rugger matches and going on cycling tours with their friends and being independent anyway. It all works.'

Margaret Woodward reached out awkwardly and put a hand lightly on Lois's shoulder. Her eyes suddenly watered, even as she gave a little laugh.

'Probably why I enjoy looking after the young singles here so much. I'm glad you had a nice time.'

As each hostile day brought no news of Johann, Lois checked the dead drop at the church as often as she felt it was safe. She became the most religious young woman at the embassy. Gradually she stopped thinking she saw him among the figures in the distance blown like leaves into the corners of Red Square or walking the paths of Gorky Park.

At night, worry turned to sleepless anger and then to numbness. But sharing with Nan was infinitely better than living on her nerves downstairs with Sonia. She could only hope and pray that if Johann telephoned the old flat, Sonia would have the decency to give him the new number. On the embassy doctor's orders, she was now on bed-rest leave while her health was evaluated.

Then, at last, when she had all but given up hope – she hadn't got to know Johann better in Vienna, quite the reverse – a postcard from Vienna arrived at the office in a brown envelope. She was to meet him on the steps of the Bolshoi at 6pm in a week's time; he had forgotten he had tickets for the ballet. But Johann never forgot tickets. Nor did he ever ask to meet that early at the theatre. He would always pick a bar or restaurant for a rendezvous at six.

On the appointed evening, she waited close to a pillar at the designated time, tense as a tripwire wondering who was watching. But Johann did not come. Lois was terrified that she had fallen for a ruse and been enticed to show herself in the open. But she did not inform Head of Chancery. Neither about the postcard nor the abortive meeting.

The next day, a Wednesday, she batted away suggestions from Rory and Eric to go for a drink in the library and slipped off to the Café Lyra straight after work.

17

Saturday, May 24, 1958

Messing about on the river.

The Moscow Northern River Station at Khimki was a Venetian palace reimagined by Stalin's myth-builders. A central tower raised a star to the heavens on a long tapering spear that looked like a radio transmitter. Perhaps it *was* a radio transmitter. A wide quay, grand as a royal terrace, formed the river frontage of this monumental edifice, though its park-like setting was marred by the vista of cranes and industrial ugliness upriver on the otherwise mundane Moskva-Volga Canal.

Lois alighted from her taxi cursing the excessive fare extorted from a Western woman on her own. Yet her spirits lifted at the sight of the water and the building's romantic air. From this port, the Baltic, the White Sea and the Black, the Caspian seas and the Sea of Azov were all accessible. Muscovites proudly called it the five seas' port and held that the landmark terminal building looked like another ship about to set sail.

It was Saturday afternoon, and a line of people had found their smiles as they stood waiting to board an old pleasure boat painted white and blue. Lois studied the unfinished men with bulging necks, badly shaven, their unpolished shoes, badly fitting clothes, un-pressed suits and pockets pulled out of shape. He wasn't there. Of course he hadn't come. She'd known it all the way here as the taxi fare burned through her meagre allowance. No, wait. There he was, standing on the quay.

She walked in his direction. He strolled nonchalantly over to the crowd by the boat, giving no indication he had seen her. She was relieved, though. He hadn't been thrilled to see her at the Café Lyra but here he was, as good as his word.

She bought a ticket and boarded, wondering how far this tired steamer was going to take them. Two men hopped onto the gangway and ran on board at the last minute. All too probably they had been in the car that had followed her taxi from Red Square, despite all the effort she had put in to avoid being followed from Meshchanskaya. Plenty of likely candidates on his trail, too, no matter how careful he had been.

From the deck, she watched him go up to the bar in the interior seating area. Lois stayed where she was, at the edge of a group of women in headscarves leaning against the rail, waiting for the boat to cast off. Folk songs were piping from a speaker. As the old tub started to move downstream, Lois sauntered idly inside to the bar. The man she still knew only as Pal was standing at the far end of the counter. He did nothing to show he had seen her. There was quite a queue; Russians loved to drink on high days and holidays. Finally it was her turn to place her order. The cup of coffee, no saucer, was banged down so it slopped. She picked it up wordlessly, moved along the bar.

He turned then. 'No brandy?'

'I prefer not.'

'You English?'

'Yes.'

'On your own?'

'Yes.'

'You wanna go outside with these?'

'Why not.'

He steered her to the rear deck of the tub where there were fewer people. They stood at the rail looking out at the water.

'Thank you for coming,' she said softly. 'I wanted to know… have you heard from our mutual friend?'

'Whoa, lady. Lemme take a drink, get my sea legs first.' He observed her over the rim of his raised cup. It was also the first time she had seen him properly. The brush-past at the Café Lyra had lasted only the time it took for him go through his pockets for some change for the phone booth and quickly tell her where and when he would meet her.

She studied him in return as she took a sip of weak coffee. Johann was right: the veteran FBI man looked like a small-town car dealer on a big trip abroad. His face was curiously unlined, bearing the remains of a healthy suntan, though the whites of his eyes were yellowing and bloodshot, and the skin beneath was pouched.

'I hope you know what a dangerous game this is,' he said.

'I'm just a secretary.'

'A secretary who sees around corners.'

'I can think for myself, if that's what you mean.'

The boat chugged past industrial plants and corrugated iron defacements until all that was left to offend were dull flat fields and covering trees. A sharp wind whipped their words away. No one could overhear.

'You went with Johann to Vienna.'

A nod. Just how much did this Pal know? What had Johann admitted to him about his mission, perhaps even their joint mission?

'Guy who works for the US Embassy has you flagged as dubious. I wish I hadda known earlier.'

'Sergei gets his information from a silly idiot who's not coping well with the pressures of Moscow.'

His gaze was unwavering. She held it, searching for a sign of sincerity or threat. A chill wind caught the edges of her sleeves and burrowed in.

'Do you know where Johann is?'

'Last I knew, Vienna.'

She turned away, looked out at the riverbank slipping away like everything else.

'Maybe there was a reason he couldn't tell you.'

'Must have been, mustn't there,' she said.

'Your Foreign Service still has some bad guys in place.'

'I think we all know that.' Lois kept her tone and posture neutral, not only for Pal but their watchers, too.

'Yeah, but. Listen, we know what we know. We can prove a lot happened. Same way we proved the secrets of the atomic bomb were being whispered in Stalin's goddamn ear by some high-minded scientists with communist sympathies before most of the intelligence services in the West even knew what the Manhattan Project was.'

Suddenly he was rattling like a machine gun. His eyes narrowed. Waxy jowls rippled. *This is what excites him, keeps him going*, she thought.

'But guess what? Every time it gets brought up, the legends in your Foreign Office kick the can down the road. They deflect; they say they're working on it. Working on it, my ass. Sorry, not in front of a lady, but it gets me kinda worked up. They're not working on it, someone – at least one someone, maybe more – is working on protecting the bad apple. This goes right to the top, and I don't care who knows that we know.'

He looked as if he could do with another drink, though the puffy grey bags under his eyes were surely the result of too many already.

'What happened, exactly, to you two and Alexei in Vienna?'

The boat juddered slightly as the wind strengthened. A gust

swept and pitted the river. A queasy feeling rose in Lois's stomach which might have been the movement of the boat, or might not.

She gave him a brief but truthful summary of the Vienna trip.

'Maybe you should look at the stiff who runs the MI6 station in Vienna,' he said when she had finished.

She met his eyes again and they stood, wordlessly. Their fellow trippers were shivering in the chill breeze, beginning to make moves inside.

'You have proof of that?' she asked.

'No proof. Only instinct and logic and the kinda small details in stories that get passed around. Your guy in Vienna might want to make life as hard for you as he can. Deduce what you will from that.'

'When did you last hear from Johann, then?' she asked, as coolly as she could.

'Last week.'

'From Vienna?'

'I surmised. He didn't correct me.'

She was loath to seem weak, but she needed more. All at sea on a boat trip from Khimki. They were among the last on deck now. Steep banks of grass concealed any vista.

'He filed a story from Budapest. You didn't see that?'

'No.'

The American shook out a couple of Lucky Strikes from a packet he pulled out of his pocket. She bent her head to his lighter.

Was Johann keeping her in the dark to protect her because lines of communication were insecure, or was there another motive? It wasn't entirely clear whether this was a sideshow, or relevant to their main task.

'The guy who tried to make contact with your mansion on the embankment…' Pal examined the end of his cigarette after exhaling deeply. 'Your jokers coming up with a plan to ask him in any time soon?'

Lois shook her head. 'I could be wrong, but I don't think so.'

'On whose orders?'

'Above my clearance.' She hesitated. 'You're still in contact with this man?'

'Just about.'

She took another chance. 'What news of Nayland?'

A long drag on his cigarette and longer exhalation. 'So you know about that.' A sigh and a flip of ash over the side. 'No good news.'

'He went in the river?'

A nod. 'Officially, he came out here, he went back home, job done. Obviously, rumour has it otherwise, but so far that has been contained. To those of us who know better, he's proof that someone don't want Alexei talking.'

'And that someone… is not necessarily a Russian?'

They stood for a few minutes in silence. The dull brown banks of the canal spooled past slowly like caterpillar tread under an army of tanks returning from exercises in the mud under a uniform grey sky.

'Look, maybe Johann's just stayin' outta trouble.'

Lois wrapped her coat tighter around her, said nothing.

'A lot of intel makes no sense. Are the people pushing it crazy, or stupid, or not what they should be? Only way you know for sure is you get yourself on the ground and see for yourself.'

'Is he working for you?' she asked.

A long hard look. 'We're on the same side. The side that's done with bullshit.'

'That why you're being so honest?' Flatter him that he was persuasive.

'Sure.' A pause. 'Look, everyone's building their own empire, the good guys as well as the bad.' He sighed, as if giving up his part in it. 'Just to let you know, you won't see me again. I'm heading back to New York soon.'

Lois swallowed hard. So many questions she wanted to ask. Even normal questions like where in America he came from, and how he had ended up here in this moment, on a boat heading towards the Volga with at least two members of the KGB watching them morosely from the other side of the deck and the two youngish thugs sharing a newspaper on the rail. But if he cut back with the same, she would have told him she was from Devon, her father was a dairy farmer, and she'd had enough of life in the English countryside by the age of fifteen. So what was the point?

Was he leaving to protect himself? He knew things she desperately wanted – needed – to know. About Zhigunov, too. But there were rules. Too many questions and she would compromise herself. Best not to reveal what she didn't know.

'New York. Not Washington?'

'I don't work out of DC.' He flicked a glance over at the duo with the newspaper. 'What you have to know,' he said, hardly moving his lips, strangling the words like a bad ventriloquist, 'it's a corrupt system. There are good men in the CIA, but there are more good men who have left the CIA over this. And the same goes for your intelligence services. They stop at nothing to protect their own bad apples, and there's the compromise right there. The moment the good operator steps over the line and follows orders knowing he's doing wrong, he's theirs. Nothing is ever simple.'

'Even if it's a bad deed for a good reason,' she murmured.

He raised his palms. 'There you have it.'

'And they stop at nothing.'

What did they do to Nayland before he was dumped in

the Moskva? Lois tried and failed to stop herself thinking of that. Cold-blooded murder had achieved exactly what it was supposed to. Fear was a great inhibitor.

'Some stinkin' lousy snakes that crawled into this business and sometimes you gotta get down on your belly to see 'em. Look, don't worry about Johann. Johann's a great guy. Funny how reporters can find out information so much quicker than incompetent intelligence services. Perhaps it's because they aren't forever trying to cover their damn backsides.'

There wasn't much more to be said.

'What ya wanna do when we get back to town – have a few drinks, find a nice hotel somewhere, just the two of us?'

'I most certainly do not! What do you take me for?' She raised her voice, and several people looked their way.

'OK, lady, have it your way. You're all the same anyway.'

She glared, turned on her heel, flushing red, and strode inside. She found a window seat and sat, resolutely alone. Over the other side of the cabin, Pal stretched out on bench seat and closed his eyes, conspicuously relaxed like a lizard in the sun. Lois let the movement of the boat soothe her. Nothing she could do but sit tight, let the world and all its contradictions go by.

Three hours later, still ignoring each other, they alighted back at Khimki.

18

Saturday, June 7, 1958

Went to church but found little comfort. The wanderer returns.

Women noticed things that men didn't. All women knew that. *It ought to be taught to men in basic training*, thought Lois. They were also compassionate, which might be an advantage at times, but it could well be a failing, too. She'd ended the boat trip with a sneaking regard for Pal's brass neck, and the certain knowledge that he had lied to her.

She would not go again to the Café Lyra.

When she managed to get there, the dead drop at the church remained barren.

Another long week passed before Johann finally returned to Moscow like a parcel that had been lost and damaged in the post. He'd lost weight. His face was weatherbeaten, as if he'd been living rough. Shadows flowered like bruises under his eyes.

Finally there had been a coded note in the dead drop, asking to meet her at GUM, the department store, and this time there was a fall-back position. He did not turn up at GUM. The fall-back it was, then. An hour later she was in

Gorky Park where they had skated, and he had sung to her. The ice was now a muddy stream, thick with insects. No fairy lights, no music. Only a few months on, but it might have been another country, another era.

Johann had changed, too, it seemed, from the man who had seemed to promise so much. Her trusted associate, her true love, her untrue lover, the slippery fade-away. It was a lukewarm greeting, with a brush of the cheek he might have given a sister. Rain began to spot on the path, on their coats and faces. Johann seemed oblivious to everything.

'I thought there were to be no secrets between us,' said Lois.

A loudspeaker blared instructions on how best to advance the glory of the magnificent Soviet Union, drowning her words.

'What happened in Vienna?' she tried again.

'I was followed. Set up. You know that. We never got close to a handover from Alexei. Only thing I got was compromised. Had to lie low. Only back now to pack up and leave Moscow for good.'

She was furious but managed to contain herself. What about their special bond, what about their love affair? Did those count for nothing – had she been mistaken, or worse still, used? But a flare-up would achieve nothing.

'Any luck in Budapest?'

Johann hesitated, the blue eyes clouded. 'I'm guessing you talked to Pal.' He sighed. 'Budapest was an in-and-out. I had to justify being away from Moscow with my editor. Listen carefully. Alexei is going to a conference again, this time to Sukhumi. September. Don't ask me how I know.'

'That's exactly what I *do* need to know, Johann.'

'I went to Kiev then took a train south to the coast in search of some Germans in Sukhumi. It's a resort on the Black Sea coast with a reputation as a playground of the Party elite, pride of the Soviet republic of Georgia. The border with northern Turkey is a hundred miles or so to the south.'

Johann was not weatherbeaten, she realised. He was tanned from the sun.

'There's a nuclear laboratory in Sukhumi.' He was speaking fast, with the same flatly informative style as Burville under pressure. 'On an estate built for the brother of the last Tsar, Nikolas. A beautiful place set in lush gardens close to the sea. It even has its own neo-classical concert hall.'

Lois let him speak.

'Who lives there now? I'll tell you. German nuclear scientists. Once there were two hundred and fifty of them. Living and working there – their families, too. They were needed, you see, to keep the balance of power after the end of the war. Germany was defeated. What to do about the scientists who had been working on rockets and bombs for the Nazi regime? Their work was valuable. The Allies and the Soviets were in a race to capture them and their technological advances. Many of them were spirited away to America, but Mother Russia also gathered as many of these orphans to her bosom. *Ach, ja.*

'Soviet intelligence chose according to greatest need. Manfred von Ardenne was the son of a Prussian army officer and head of an electron physics laboratory in Berlin. Gustav Hertz was an experimental physicist who had won the Nobel Prize in 1925 and was director of a research laboratory at the Siemens Company. It might have been dressed up as an invitation but there was no option to decline. They were taken to Moscow and brought to Lavrenty Beria, who was not only the head of Stalin's secret police but also in charge of the nation's nuclear programme. This delightful fellow gave them a choice: Siberia or Sukhumi, in the Abkhazia region of the Georgian republic, where both Beria and Stalin both enjoyed holidays in their dachas. Not a hard choice.

'The scientists – none of them wanted to be in the Soviet Union. They knew the cruelties of the Russian front. But effectively, they were prisoners of war allowed to pursue their scientific research, no different from the slave labour of the German foot soldiers put to work building apartment blocks in Moscow. In Sukhumi, they were building centrifuges to separate uranium isotopes. They were now a vital component of the Cold War. They had been set the task of building a nuclear bomb, and they succeeded. It may not have been entirely due to them that the USSR is now a nuclear power – a certain Klaus Fuchs and his KGB controllers embedded in Britain saw to that – but the centrifuges they made were crucial to produce the fissile material required for a bomb.'

Johann was breathless by the time he finished. Tension strained the skin tight around his eyes and mouth.

Even now, appallingly, she wanted him to kiss her, to pull her into an embrace that would enable her to offer a show of resistance then allow herself to forgive him. But all that was over now, if it ever had been anything real.

'Are they still there?' she asked into the space between them.

He half shrugged, resolutely separate from her. 'A house was built for Hertz on estate land. It was said to be a replica of his family home in Germany, but I'm told it's empty now. He was treated well, as these events go. He had servants, though, as ever, they were KGB informants. The Germans had served their purpose and began to be released a few years ago. I was told most had gone by '55, though there is one man, an Austrian,' a weak smile, 'who married a local woman and has stayed on.'

'But the Russians are still using the research facility?'

'Of course. There are now German-trained Soviet nuclear physicists working there. It's not quite so secret now. They say it is used for research into civilian uses for nuclear power. I have heard, though I don't know how accurate this is, that they are doing pioneering work on mini-reactors. Smaller and smaller… more and more potential uses, in more remote places.'

Johann raked a hand through his hair. It had grown since she'd last seen him. He had been compromised, he reiterated.

'Are you saying what I think you are?'

He was. 'It would always have had to be you – not me, not Pal – *you* who met him on the big occasion. A woman who is just a secretary and doesn't get followed.'

Lois thought back to the times she hadn't dared go near to the dead drop at St Philipp's. The rendezvous on the boat with Pal, and the two watchers who emerged from the car behind her taxi to Khimki and joined them on deck.

'How does this square with what we were sent to do?'

'It's all connected.'

'Says who?'

'Pal says Alexei has proof about the Moscow traitor.'

'Then why doesn't Pal produce it and save us all the bother?' she snapped.

'So will you do it?'

It was far too dangerous. A crazy plan.

'OK,' she said.

'*Ach*, don't look so frightened. I am not abandoning you, no matter how it seems. I promise you I will be in the background. I'll watch out for you. The Sukhumi conference is the second week of September. Take two weeks holiday from the sixth. Stay at the Intourist hotel. I will get a message to you there.'

He told her the location of the dead drop where he would collect any material given to her by Zhigunov. Under no circumstances was she to attempt to travel with any of it. Foreigners' luggage was too vulnerable to being searched.

'By the way, I'm sorry I kept this so long.'

It was her Minox camera that he had borrowed in Vienna. They said a heartbreakingly formal goodbye.

That night she wrote another letter to Miss Harcourt, usual method. Her German boyfriend had ended things, she told her. She was taking it badly, as she had had high hopes of the affair. *Wasn't that the truth*, thought Lois bitterly. Her tears had been silent retches in the sanctity of her bedroom.

If it looks like a romance, then so much the better. It wasn't even difficult to pretend. She would not get it wrong again. Neither could she bring herself to stop loving him, not quite yet.

The Minister went to Leningrad on a week's "working holiday", followed by leave in the Caucasus with his wife. As soon as she had settled the travel arrangements despite the repeated efforts of Intourist to sabotage them, Lois went along to the butler's pantry to see Bill Stoneley.

She took a folder containing a handwritten draft on flimsy blue paper of the Minister's report on Soviet scientific research stations, asked Stoneley to clarify certain phrases, and made sure he knew she was available to work for him when she had completed the task of typing it. Using the same report as cover, she wandered along to the Chancery Registry and pulled out files on atomic research in the Ukraine, international nuclear conferences, and Soviet innovations in warhead rocketry. She spent an equal amount of time going through each of them but concentrated hardest as she scoured one in particular for any cross-references to Avrely Zhigunov.

She went carefully. For the first two days, she looked up no file that Waller had not already requested. On the third day, her searches in the Registry's barred cell had become so routine that Mac the Registry chief clerk popped out, leaving her alone except for the guard by the door. Her fingers flew over the section devoted to the GRU. "Z" section. Heart thumping. Found a reference. She forced her shoulders down; she must never come across as excitable. Took the chance. Lifted out the file and sandwiched it between four others. Buff brown files, steel-edged to hang from the drawer.

'Taking that lot?' The voice from behind made her jump.

'Not sure yet, Mac. I might just sit here and skim through a couple first. No need to book them out if they don't hit the brief.'

'Be my guest.'

Zhigunov was indeed some kind of military spokesman, quoted in all four entries, all of them cuttings from Soviet publications, with translations. All were short – the longest came to ten paragraphs – and were dry official statements on outstanding progress by the USSR's nuclear inventors and experts and calculated in their brevity to instil pride and confidence. He was hard and to the point, the epitome of a military man. No mention or trace of the letter from a potential defector. That meant there must be another less obvious file needing higher security clearance to access.

It was a race against time while the Minister was away. Burville was most put out that she was not pitching in with Chancery work. He cast a few disparaging remarks about her, which found their mark when repeated to her by a malicious Sonia. To show her willingness to make amends, she made sure to ask Tony Fielding and John Mowberry over tea in general company whether they could make use of her and was relieved when Mowberry accepted her offer. When Burville got to hear of it, he came into Mowberry's section spitting fire.

'I need you for my excess load, Miss Vale,' he said, voice ominously measured.

'Thank you, sir. That will be lovely,' said Lois, with a silly enthusiastic smile.

'Lovely?' Burville had already turned away, but he span back. 'This is serious work, for God's sake!'

'Sorry, sir.'

'Get yourself into Registry,' he snapped. 'I want all files on Malenkov, Molotov, and Kaganovich pulled out, and Bill Stoneley's analysis of continuing opposition to Khrushchev.'

Punishment indeed, but exactly where she wanted to be.

'Grafting for H of C,' was all she had to say, and Mac could not have been more helpful.

She worked thoroughly, checking as many files as possible. Where *was* Zhigunov's approach letter?

In the bug-proof room, Burville dictated fast. Not only did she keep up, she had to correct him at one point. Did so stupidly, without thinking.

'Malenkov was Stalin's chosen successor, not Molotov,' she said. 'Sir.'

They had been sitting at the conference table, but he sprang up as if he had been stung. His face fixed and glazed, he stared at her. Dignity fought with distaste. She was quite right, he averred.

'Very good, Miss Vale. Waller said you were remarkably good.'

But in saving him from making a mistake, she had made one herself. A tic pulsed in his clenched cheek. He tested her ten minutes later by deliberately (she was sure of it) mixing up the two again. Her own pride did not allow her to let it go. It was Molotov, not Malenkov who had opposed Khrushchev over agricultural development of the USSR's virgin land. She had read one of Bill Stoneley's reports and her memory was as reliable as ever.

Burville checked his papers, issued frozen praise. 'I see you are right again, Miss Vale.'

It would not make her life any easier, and she had only

herself to blame. She had revealed too much about herself. He retaliated by giving her twice as much work as was reasonable.

Refusing to be defeated, she stayed hours late at the office that evening to finish typing for him though her back was aching from the tension and her eyes were stinging. The subject matter was terrifying. The KGB was the largest secret-police and foreign-intelligence organisation in the world. Researchers with access to Communist Party archives put the number of KGB personnel at more than four hundred and eighty thousand, including two hundred thousand soldiers in the Border Guards. Larger than all Britain's armed forces put together by some margin.

The arms race was building up nuclear warheads for rockets that could travel thousands of miles. But was it a bluff? There was a faint possibility that Khrushchev's aggressive claims had little basis in reality. It was calculated bluster, in order to keep the West in a state of fear that Soviet expansionism would dominate the globe.

Lois prayed hard that night, for all the people of the world.

19

Tuesday, June 10, 1958

A car trip to New Cherry Town with Bill. Yet again, he proved a perceptive companion. Interesting conversation with some Russians as we wandered around, all out in the open. Bill knows the game.

Novye Cheryomushki translated as "New Cherry Town". Under a radical initiative, model housing developments were going up rapidly in a suburb to the south of the city.

'Could you take some notes as we go around?' asked Bill Stoneley over Camp Coffee and biscuits. 'The Russians are certain to approve more if I look like one of the "delegates" I'm hoping to bring out to see it. Good will all round! Go on, have another, I'm going to.' Crumbs trickled down his front. 'Apparently they're using engineering methods to build rather than bricklayers, and the whole project is going up at record speed because it's a competition between construction teams each working on their own housing block! Fascinating – and we might even learn something.'

He drove them out to the south of the city in a monstrous old American limousine that pitched and rolled like a boat. A car followed them, but Stoneley made no attempt to lose it. Stalin-era apartment buildings gave way to a flat, muddy stretch of land. He made a circuit of the construction site and drew up at a central point next to a painted hoarding, making it clear that he had no reason to hide. The wide chassis of the car continued to shake for a minute or so after Bill pulled the key from the ignition.

'Novye Cheryomushki – they might even plant some trees. The key to everything is to remain open-minded.' His keen eyes twinkled as he surveyed the shells of four-storey apartment blocks. 'Space for a small park – see? Be called a garden square in London, wouldn't it? Space for children's playgrounds, places to stroll and sit on benches, maybe an inspiring statue of Lenin.'

It was an architectural competition, not a construction race, Bill informed her. Seven blocks of flats, each one built using a different system of prefabricated materials, usually variations of concrete pieces that slotted into place like toy building blocks. At the end of the year, each block was going to be judged on solidity, cost and speed of construction, and one would be announced as the winner. The best would be a template for more housing blocks, to be replicated across the Soviet Union. What happened here would determine the method of building hundreds of thousands, possibly millions, of new homes for workers.

He danced across puddles, nimble on his feet as big men so rarely were, openly taking photographs with a large Leica. He had swapped the deerstalker hat for a straw Panama more appropriate for late spring, although not in Russia. Beneath the shadow cast by the brim, his pink cheeks jinked as he moved.

No one came over to challenge them. If they had watchers, they were keeping well back. It seemed Bill was right: their visit was welcome.

'They *need* this. Desperately,' said Bill. 'They're sitting on a catastrophic housing shortage. Before the Revolution, eighty per cent of Russians lived in the countryside. But enter Stalin. He unleashes the swiftest, most brutal industrial revolution in history. Rural folk are starved out of the countryside. They flock to cities to find work in the new factories. But where do they lay their heads? They're forced to live in basements and tents and even in trenches. The problem was only beginning to be addressed in 1940 when war came knocking again. Thanks to the Third Reich and their efforts to kill them all and destroy their hard-won homes, millions were left with nowhere again.'

He certainly sounded sympathetic. But who wouldn't be? Righteous indignation fuelled his feet, and Lois strode after him.

'Stalin's soaring giants on the Moscow skyline were an outrageous vanity project! Delusions of grandeur for Party bigwigs and well-controlled bureaucrats. One thing Khrushchev has got right is his decree against architectural excess. Industrialised construction, that's the way to go.'

The contrast between the Stalinist boulevards they had driven down to get here was undeniable. The area felt lighter in every way. Lois could picture how it would look when it was finished, as Bill described the plans – he had certainly done his work before coming. The metro station, the planned outdoor spaces, the health centre, the school, the shops and cinema. It would be lovely if it was well-maintained. Hard not to think it might be better than some parts of London that were still bomb sites.

'Sweet?' He offered her a tube. 'Vitamin C, good habit to get into.'

She accepted.

He took one himself and went on. 'This is a huge advance for the Soviets… not only in terms of modern amenities for the ordinary man and woman, but for their social needs – the privacy they simply haven't known before. Hard to overstate what an advance this is…'

His admiration was catching. As she filled her notebook with shorthand, Lois found herself wondering why Western cities couldn't do this. Bill was in no doubt: the Soviet way of making progress – an egalitarian, centrally planned, mass-production economy – was producing results.

Each separate area would have a factory or a research institute. Eventually Novye Cheryomushki would be a hub of the USSR's scientific-military-industrial complex.

'It's impressive,' said Lois. 'Now if they could only stop trying to control their people by fear, and do more like this, we might even believe their system could work.'

'But it does work.'

That was a lie. She knew it was a lie. It was the very opposite of what she had typed in his open source reports. Bill must have read her thoughts on her face.

'We see a Soviet defector, a Soviet asset, as a good man. The only difference is ideology – correct?'

She supposed it was.

'We have been told we are on the side of the angels and communism is the darkness. But what if it were our system that was corrupt and theirs seemed to offer the better way forward?'

Stalin's mountains of the dead. The gulags and the work gangs, shuffling exhausted through the snow, their histories ignored and rewritten. Bill's premise wasn't true, it couldn't be. Yes, there was unfairness and imperfection in the British way of life, but the war had changed a great deal. Those who had fought and lost people they loved wanted more for themselves and were bent on working to achieve it. They were free to try, at least. Nowhere was perfect, but there wasn't the universal despair of the powerless in a controlled state that there was here. She didn't understand how the so-called intelligentsia back home could possibly believe in communism; she could only conclude they had never tried living behind the Iron Curtain or troubled to use their common sense. They all knew about the lies and repression and hardship and want of basic freedoms, yet seemed to despise their own decent people as much as the Soviet elites did, with as little understanding of human nature, their own included.

But she recognised the discussion for what it was: a breath of fresh air. Bill Stoneley was first and foremost an academic. His job was to open up the debate, to put forward differing viewpoints. Dogma on either side rarely served truth.

'Do you think the potential Soviet asset who sent his letter of introduction with the students is genuine?' she asked casually.

'Who knows? If they're still looking into him it's because the Service always wants a spectacular win. They want the Americans begging for their flow of information. But spectacular wins don't often happen. They usually mean getting involved in foolhardy exploits by old-style adventurers that have little chance of success and run the risk of endangering the steady work.'

Lois made a point of staring round at the construction in progress. 'But *are* they still looking into him?'

'Oh, I should think so – don't you?'

'I wouldn't know.'

A truck had arrived and was being unloaded. A sack of sand burst as it was thrown onto the ground and shouting ensued. Bill took a few light steps in front of her, then turned so she could not avoid his eyes.

'You were seen with Johann Dreschler the other day, by the way,' he said evenly.

Lois felt the ground give under her.

'By a contact of mine. Not one of Burville's, luckily for you.'

'It was an unexpected… and very quick… goodbye.'

'It had to be. He's done some digging down south, apparently. The Soviets are never at their most forgiving when they have to refill a hole.'

'Bill, you have to trust me – I can't speak about it – and now it seems I have to trust you not to say anything. Will you – will you keep this strictly between us?'

He gave her a long assessing look. Perhaps he was thinking of the man who went into her train compartment by mistake. They turned a corner and were looking up at the concrete structure of an apartment block. He did not respond. Then she realised Bill had stopped walking.

Facing them was a KGB man, broad and tall in the standard issue garb. A face like a savage dog. Hard, bright black irises, a red burst in one eye. Another man stepped out of an unfinished doorway and blocked their way.

A sound behind told Lois that another was at her back, coming closer. She heard him breathing. She felt a sharp solid jab into her spine and assumed it was a weapon. She did not turn, concentrated on reacting like an innocent woman. Allowed a gasp of shock to escape, a supplicating look to her colleague. For his part, Stoneley was impassive.

A further prod in the back made her cry out, but carefully: not too loudly, not hysterically.

'What's happening?'

'You come with us,' barked the man in front. Harsh, guttural voice. Speaking to her.

Stoneley moved forward. 'No! Speak to me. We are here to see this magnificent new building programme. We want to show the West what good progress the Soviet Union is achieving.'

He was brushed aside. Spoke again in fluent Russian.

It did no good. Lois was pulled roughly around. She saw

now that her assailant was younger, most likely stronger than the thugs who faced her, despite his weak, doughy chin.

'She is my secretary and my responsibility. I insist on accompanying her!' said Stoneley, first in English then in Russian. 'Please, this is a misunderstanding. We have come to see only what your newspapers have already shown.' He held out his large tourist camera. 'Here, you can have the film, see that we have done nothing wrong.'

'You,' said the first man, ignoring him, pointing at Lois.

Lois was pulled roughly from behind and made to walk. She was marched off into a concrete cell of a room on the ground floor of the block and motioned to stand with her back to the wall. For a moment she was sure Stoneley would be forcibly held back, but he followed. He too was placed against the wall, this time facing it with his hands up, splayed on the gritty surface.

A nerve-shredding pause.

'You take boat from Khimki Station,' began the KGB officer. He brought his face so close to hers that she could smell the mouldy bread on his breath and see the pits in his grey skin.

Lois aimed for incomprehension. She shook her head without aggression.

'You meet man on boat.'

'I'm sorry. I don't understand.'

'Man on boat. Yank man.'

Lois understood one thing very well. The Russians might know very well who she had been seen with. Their shadows had been blatant, after all. But under no circumstances could she allow Stoneley to connect her to Pal. Nor could she lie, which would only lead to more complications. She fervently hoped that her precautions had been adequate, and she had not been followed the evening she went to the Café Lyra.

'I did speak to a man on the boat, an American, but I did not know him.'

She was aware of Stoneley listening intently. *Volunteer no information you do not have to give.*

'Who this man?'

'I do not know. I had never met him before.'

'What his name?'

'He did not tell me his name.' That much was true, she had never known it.

'What you talk about?'

'Living in the Soviet Union.'

A snort of derisive laughter. 'What you talk about?'

'Nothing. He made a move on me.' She glanced at Stoneley's back, hoping he would be able to translate if necessary. 'He wanted me to go to a hotel with him.'

Smirks.

'I was not interested.'

They had agreed the staging of their meeting and how it would end. Their shadows would either have reported the argumentative end to her encounter with Pal or would corroborate it when questioned. And now for a little more acting. Lois burst into tears.

'I've done nothing wrong, Mr Stoneley! When I took the boat trip all I wanted was a little time on my own out of the city; it's been so hard here!' The pantomime was for the KGB. Bill wouldn't buy it for a second.

Forget the embassy protocol of having at least one other person with you whenever you went out. (Lois had broken that rule repeatedly, right from the start.) By appealing to the man on her own side, showing her fear of him too, she neutralised the Russian's demands. Stoneley, apparently more exasperated with her than frightened of the KGB, let loose a volley of frustration at her naivety that – to judge from his impersonation of Burville at his most pompous halfway through – was intended as nothing more than a show as good as hers.

'Just trying to scare us,' asserted Bill laconically as they walked back to the car. 'They try it on all the time.' He opened the passenger door for her. 'You did well there. Not many who would have been so composed under fire, as it were.'

'Glad it looked that way. I'm actually shaking.'

He settled himself behind the wheel, no small task. As he switched on the ignition he turned to her.

'Look, Lois. It takes one to know one, right?'

It takes a worm to catch a worm?

She said nothing.

'I hope you know what you've stepped into. Because my nose tells me something ain't right, and you're not the problem. Be very careful. I'd hate to see—' He stopped himself and spoke again objectively. 'There's no safe place.'

An uncomfortably long pause was filled by the engine rumbling.

No safe place. Especially for those with much to hide, he might have added.

Summer came in waves of heavy, golden warmth and torrential rain. Young women released from their bulky winter coats walked arm-in-arm. The men in the streets wore light baggy suits with tie-less shirts or loose mismatched jackets. Women threw off their headscarves and boots, and legs emerged in sandals and short white socks. Others, less trusting, in these oppressive, stifling few weeks of summer, were still wearing galoshes.

Flower stalls appeared on street corners, gay with peonies, forget-me-nots, and buttercups brought in from the country. Drink vending machines appeared in Gorky Park. Where was Johann now? Lois put away her winter clothes. Most were now reminders of misplaced optimism and ill-conceived romance. From the suitcase under her bed she unpacked summer dresses.

On the streets and paths through the parks, last year's fashions from London and The Hague and the frocks she'd made herself from Vogue patterns elicited sad and suspicious glances from the Muscovite women.

The days lengthened until it was still almost light at midnight. For a few weeks they were under a spell of veiled twilight and birdsong at 3am. This was the time the river moved, unmoving, and a song was heard, yet not heard, in those beautiful silent nights, as the song lyrics told. "Moscow Nights", still playing everywhere, stripped bare the Russian soul and tore Lois into pieces. Where was Johann now?

The Queen's birthday party on June 12 brought Khrushchev himself – a short, round little man with warts on his face – to the celebrations in the embassy garden.

'Peasant stock from the Ukraine. Once a metal worker. A herdsboy as a child. Went to school for a total of four years. Decidedly no sophisticate.'

This languid summation, overheard by Lois as they descended the steps to the garden, came from John Linton, speaking to Vere Sinclair. They were still nothing more than names and faces to Lois, but they hadn't checked who was behind them. Slackness or their usual arrogance?

She watched as they paused just a second, exchanged some wordless message, and launched themselves on the party. Celebrations continued long after the Russian delegations had departed. The international diplomatic community threw themselves into the biggest event of the British calendar. Music and dancing went on until 4am, a Moscow night in summer when darkness never quite fell.

20

Saturday, June 1, 1958

Panic stations this morning with a lengthy Khrushchev letter to go out; four of us worked on it & it was ready in time; home late, only to dash out again on the Kremlin visit. The museum & churches were quite interesting, but oh, so tiring – and the Gruesome Twosome in the Mausoleum weren't receiving after 4pm. A relief for me, though there were some very disappointed Russians who had apparently come a long way for the chance to see Stalin sharing a resting place at last with their hero Lenin.

Cup of tea with Nan – and then I was quickly out again with her to see The Monte Carlo Story *with Dietrich & de Sica at America House. What a contrast! Enjoyed it very much; came straight home & managed to get my letter home written in bed.*

Lois was a failure. She'd found nothing – how had they ever thought she could succeed? A high level of awareness of the listening devices in the embassy walls ensured there was minimal chance she would overhear a crucial conversation. She'd been rumbled by Bill Stoneley – twice – and the only person she could realistically watch was the Minister. Her work for Waller had yielded nothing untoward and no mention of Zhigunov. Yet was it, after all, Waller they suspected?

She sat in bed looking at her writing paper and pen on the tray. The cheerful letter to her parents was sealed and waiting in the drawer by her side. There was no getting away from it, she would have to write to Miss Harcourt as well. Better now, while she had peace and quiet, and then she would have Sunday free to try to relax.

Dear Elsie, she wrote. *Sorry not to have written earlier, but I've been having such a busy time of it here.*

There was so much she wanted to say yet could not. Not just for reasons of security, but because she did not want to compromise herself by admitting weakness. The whole system was rotten, the world over. *They* – the big *they* in London – had finally worked out that the people on the routine end of the work, the unsung lower orders and women were those who could spot immediately when something was wrong or out of kilter – it was astonishing, really, given all their grand education, how long it had taken some of them to catch on – but there was no network in place for people like Lois. In Miss Harcourt's own words: '*If you are caught there will be no safety net… Should it go wrong, you will be branded a traitor to this country…*'

She got a grip of herself and wrote:

To tell the truth, I've been a bit down after my romance with the German journalist fizzled out. I'd thought it was going well, but he left town for a while, and I didn't hear from him. Then, last week he reappeared. We had a sad goodbye with an air of finality about it. He's leaving for good. I didn't know what to think, really. Just one of those things? It was more than that, or so I thought.

In other news, I enjoy the work for my boss, and he does seem a very nice man, very straightforward, so far as I can tell. Though, as recent experience has shown, can one ever tell? Only way forward is to keep my head down, I suppose, and try to spot the rotters sooner.

Apart from Head of Chancery who gives every indication that he dislikes me intensely (I don't like him either), the only problem colleague seems to be a girl I shared a flat with at first, Sonia. She worries me rather – a very uneven temperament. I fear she is struggling with the pressure here; she doesn't have the inner resources to cope and resents that somehow I do. I have tried my best with her but have had no effect. If anything, she's on a downward spiral and unfortunately has decided that I have played a part in this.

Lois paused, as if for breath. The words had tumbled so rapidly onto the page. She needed to stop a moment and gather her thoughts. Why did Sonia, for all her advantages, lack the capacity for self-sufficiency that Lois possessed? How did Lois have it? Because she had had to, she told herself sternly. She had nothing to fall back on except a loving family. The experience of hard, uncertain times had made her stronger. Sharpened her evaluations of others and any difficult situations. Experience had taught her she could and should trust herself.

She sat back and closed her eyes for several minutes. Then she read back what she had written. She fiddled with the pen for another few moments then got up and fetched an ashtray. She placed this on the chest of drawers. From her handbag she retrieved her lighter but not her cigarettes. She folded the letter and burned it.

Only when the paper was ash did Lois light a cigarette to mask the smell and settle back to dash off a much curtailed, less emotional version.

She felt drained the next day on a group outing to Tolstoy's house at Yasnaya Polyana, a hundred and twenty miles from Moscow. On the grey office bus there, her failures and other dreary thoughts weighted her down and she fervently regretted having agreed to go. The countryside was flat and uninteresting, a sea of mud broken up every ten miles or so by a cluster of wooden shacks and picket fences that passed for villages. No wayside inns, no forests or pleasant woods, no petrol stations, no signs advertising local attractions and the distance to them, no factories or large-scale farming, just intermittent hedges and untidy plots of struggling crops. Life here had not improved for centuries, and the blanket of winter snow would only be a kindness to the dismal landscape.

Under a watery sun, lowering clouds and a gnawing wind, the house where the great author wrote *War and Peace* and *Anna Karenina* was a charming white confection with a roof the colour of cloudy emeralds. Lois wished she had time to read either of them.

For most of the following week, she was exhausted by the work, the late nights, the drinking, the stress headaches and the feeling of being on edge that never truly lifted. Recognising the symptoms was half the battle, she decided. It was just the endemic Moscow Twitch. She could ride it out. She would have to.

Demonstrations outside Western embassies were becoming more common. The West German Embassy was attacked on June 23 in retaliation for a protest outside the Russian Embassy in Bonn after the show trial and execution of Imre Nagy, leader of the Hungarian Revolution of 1956 against Budapest's Soviet-backed government. In a show of iron power, Nikita Khrushchev had given the order "as a lesson to all other leaders in socialist countries", it was said. An episode of "unparalleled infamy", according to the Western press. Emotions were running high, and the Russian mobs were emboldened. Burville let it be known that it was only a matter of time before they were targeted.

Nothing for it but to redouble her efforts. At tea urns and in corridors, she spoke to everyone, especially those she judged loose-lipped or vulnerable. She did her best to linger in Registry and carefully observed the reactions of those who came in and found her in the caged alcove that held the most secret files. Who was oblivious to her presence and who failed to disguise annoyance under the usual quick working smile? The only person whose reaction gave her pause for thought was an unlikely contender. It was Rory Kendalmoor.

The July the Fourth ball at Spaso House, the palatial eighteenth-century residence of US ambassadors to Moscow, was another big night for the diplomatic community: a glittering feast; an excess of caviar in crystal bowls and cocktails; a sumptuous buffet and dancing to Russian music as well as the latest American hits. The men were handsome and sure of themselves; a pretty young woman was much sought-after and might have all kinds of opportunities.

The interior of the mansion, built in the New Empire style during a time of the grossest excess, boasted a main hall eighty feet high and topped by a domed ceiling from which was suspended a crystal chandelier said to be the largest in any Moscow house. The parties there were legendary. People still spoke with wonder and reverence of "a real shindig" before the war, when it was decided the entertainment should feature performing seals. On the night, with guests gathered expectantly in a darkened hall beneath the chandelier, the three seals made their entrance: one balancing a miniature Christmas tree on its nose, the next balancing a tray of glasses, and the last a bottle of champagne. The performing seals executed flawlessly a variety of tricks, to rapturous applause. But then the seals ceased to cooperate. Chaos ensued, as guests chased flapping seals as they moved surprisingly fast through the grand rooms, knocking over tables and chairs, and slipping out of grasp.

Whoever planned the July the Fourth ball in 1958 might well – mischievously – have planned to emulate this memorable event. Lois and her party from Meshchanskaya arrived to be greeted by a performing monkey wearing a baseball cap and white and blue striped shirt holding a tray of nuts. Another three monkeys and their Russian trainer, all in baseball gear, were swigging root beer and eating popcorn at a table in front of a Yankee Stadium scoreboard.

Lois was whirled away by familiar faces from America House. She talked and danced for hours with as many Americans as possible, all the time trying to spot Pal. There was no sign of him. She supposed he had already returned to New York, but knew no one she could ask without drawing suspicion on herself.

She was beginning to flag when the orchestra itself seemed to run out of steam. It gradually stopped playing and then a terrible noise came from the drums. Conversation stuttered and then laughter broke out.

Lois was dancing with a middle-aged American, more from duty than pleasure. He had no sense of rhythm and feet that seemed a law unto themselves.

'Well, I'll be… the monkeys are having their turn!' he said.

So they were. Marine guards ran up to try to contain the exuberant primates, though without much luck. Some of the guests joined in, but the monkeys were too quick. They were having fun pelting the dancers with olives and peanuts.

'The darned trainer's drunk,' chortled Lois's partner, blithely unconcerned. He nodded over to where the man slumped in the corner, cap over face, suddenly passed out in the Russian way. 'I bet there was vodka in his root beer. Hey, what you know, perhaps the damn monkeys are stewed, too!'

'Whose crazy idea was this anyway?' asked a distinguished-looking senior US diplomat as he rushed past.

'I think you'll find it was your wife's, sir!' He laughed and turned to Lois. 'When a suggestion comes from one of the senior wives, it can't be ignored. The Moscow Zoo flat-out refused to cooperate, but the Moscow Circus was more amenable to furnishing her whim – for a price. Obviously more than enough to keep their man happy... oh, my good Lord, what's happening now?'

With their master indisposed, the monkeys were making a break for it into the reception hall and up the grand staircase.

'Go, Yankees!' shouted a wag.

One of the child-sized baseball stars swung up the outside of the banister and the tiny waiters took up peanut firing position on the landing as a swarm of men in dinner jackets and Marines led the offense.

Lois was still laughing when Rory materialised at her side. 'I've never seen anything like it except in the films!' he said, wiping away tears.

That set her off again, which in itself became funny, and they convulsed with silly mirth like a great release until they were almost holding each other up.

'Come on.' He grabbed her hand, and they raced upstairs to see the next instalment.

The last monkey was recaptured in the Ambassador's wife's dressing room where it was reported to have made a fine mess, and the ball resumed on a mellow note. Lois had an unexpectedly lovely end of the evening with Rory. They danced a bit and ate some caviar, then sat out in the candlelit garden. The conversation was relaxing, undemanding, of no importance at all. Films and songs they liked. Things that made them laugh. She wasn't working so hard to impress as she always did with Johann. Neither was Rory awkward. At

213

no time did he put her on the spot with any clumsy lines of questioning. For the first time she wondered, unlikely as it might have seemed initially, whether he could become a friend. She certainly needed one.

21

Thursday, July 17, 1958

Demonstrations at the American Embassy yesterday and today,
nastier today. Heard that at request of King & P.M. of Jordan,
British troops had returned there – so we must expect demonstrations
too.

H of C began to flap.

Friday, July 18, 1958

Bit of excitement today. Front gates closed in morning; petition
from No.5 Furniture Factory handed to H.E. lunchtime.

Protesters gathered at 2 & by 4.30 they really got going,
banners, fist-shaking, pouring through into courtyard. The Min.
unperturbed. Had to plead papers away from him, took them
into secure zone. Left from the back into Garden Block with Rory
after a silly, tension-relieving game of hide and seek – he hid in a
fireplace!

Cypher machines clattered non-stop, and urgency stalked the
corridors. The trouble had begun in Baghdad, Ambassador
Mountbeech summed up for the staff crammed into Chancery.

'King Faisal II of Iraq was executed during July 14
Revolution, along with a number of members of the Hashemite

Royal Family. His younger son died in London on the 11th, though that was kept out of the papers as long as possible. The overthrow of the monarchy was a coup d'état by units of the Iraqi Army who were supposed to be en route to Jordan in answer to a call from King Hussein for military assistance during the escalating crisis with Lebanon.'

The Minister had urged Lois along to hear what H.E. had to say, and now he was standing in the doorway between the Chancery guards.

'News of American troops landing at Beirut means further potential tension with the Soviet Union. There have been demonstrations at the American Embassy, and they turned noisier and more violent today. King Hussein of Jordan and his ministers requested the support of British troops, and these have duly been sent. We are battening down the hatches in expectation of the same treatment.'

The protests outside were noisy and full of fury and fists punching the air but the only physical breach of security was the storming of the gate, which the Russian militiamen on duty had apparently done nothing to stop.

The more worrying breach had been invisible. Gone was Hugh Burville's slick confidence. The first stones against the Chancery windows and placards waving in the courtyard, and Burville had panicked, issuing curt orders then countermanding them. The internal telephones stopped working. Then so did other electrical devices. A juicy row with Tony Fielding followed, in which Burville shouted down his suggestions before having to admit they were better than his. To steady himself and reassert his supremacy, he lashed out at unfortunate members of the junior staff.

By six, the demonstrators had grown tired of shouting at a lifeless building (little did they know) and melted away. The embassy's own security guards kept watch for any opportunist move by the last diehard demonstrators while a lively party attested to British mettle in the library mess. The noise rose through the cavernous rooms as Lois passed through the Kharitonenko Mansion like a ghost, taking the Minister's most sensitive papers to the locked cage in Registry for the night.

Each door she passed on the empty corridor was securely locked. No one was in either of the cloakrooms and lavatories. The cypher room was now bolted and silent. The door to the sitting room attached to the Ambassador's upstairs office was closed but yielded when she tried the knob. She had stepped too far into the room to retreat when Rory popped his head above the arm of a chair and turned to see her. For a second, he looked as surprised to see her as she was to stumble across him.

Challenge first, and quickly. Never volunteer an excuse, especially if it's untrue.

She stepped forward brazenly. 'What on earth—'

He was kneeling in front of the fireplace. It had been blocked up and now hosted an electric fire. He bent down again and put his ear to the black-painted board above the ugly metal contraption. She watched his face as intently as he was listening.

'See if you can hear anything,' he said.

She went closer, leant in. It was hard to be sure, and she said so.

'At first I thought it was something in the chimney behind the mantelpiece – a bird, maybe, or even a rat,' said Rory. He turned to look behind them. 'Close the door. I'm going to have a look.'

Was it any different from digging into the walls for bugs? She didn't ask whether he should have permission from the Ambassador. Did Rory know as well as she did that H.E. – in a bravura show of nonchalance – had summoned the

Ambassadorial Rolls Royce and gone to a dinner at the French Embassy?

It wasn't scratching. It was crackling. It might be from residual electrical power surges, Rory explained, enunciating while barely making a sound. She was almost lip-reading. Surges that could be used to take out sensitive equipment. That could be what had happened. The demonstrations were just a distraction.

'Just a possibility, of course. Or rather my suspicious mind. But it's not the first time the equipment has died at a vital moment.'

She liked his suspicious mind. 'And no proof can ever be found,' she mouthed.

He shook his head. 'I need to collect some tools. Hold the fort. Lock the door behind me.'

He was back within minutes, working fast with a screwdriver. Next the black panel; not as easy to loosen screws that had been painted over.

Rory put his hand inside, asked her to hand him the torch.

'Interesting,' he said, half into the blackness of the wide chimney. His voice had a muffled echo, barely audible. He was now on his back, shining the torch upwards. Then he turned over. Swore. He pulled himself back and sat up.

'Well, I'm no sweep, but I've never seen wires like this inside a chimney flue.'

'Wires?'

'At the back. They go up as well as down.'

'Are you going to cut them?' Stupid question. She kicked herself at the moment she spoke.

'Absolutely not. We need to work out what's at the end and how it works. They're not ours, that's for sure. But I need to wait until I can get the rest of the team here.'

The locally engaged Soviet staff had long gone home. It was as good a time as any. He could not risk a phone call, so he went down to the duty maintenance and security detail, leaving her alone again with the discovery. She switched on the torch and saw for herself the thick black fabric-encased cables, one of which was damaged, perhaps by insects. It lay frayed on a rough brick ledge level with the floor, badly set on wooden joists, next to a small metal device that she guessed was some kind of transmitter or amplifier, or both. Below was a cold yawning drop.

Again, Rory was back within minutes, this time with two technicians. Lois watched, heart in mouth, as they manoeuvred themselves into the space behind the fireplace. The slightest of the technicians was all but swallowed inside. They emerged filthy.

One of them conferred silently with Rory.

Rory strode along the embankment at an athletic pace that seemed to match the intense focus of his preoccupation. She had seen what she had seen and could not un-see it, he seemed to have decided.

'There's another receiver on the floor below pointing at the Chancery,' he said.

'Is this normal Russian bug technology or something new?' she asked. What if it were not Russian? Was it possible they had been installed by a traitor in the embassy? Would it make any difference if they were? The permutations chased themselves around and around in her mind.

'Not the usual. But with some of the usual components and all the defective hallmarks. This one might involve microwave signals. We know the Russians are beaming microwave attacks at the US Embassy and at us. We've known about it for quite a few years now. The Thing at Spaso House. It was a Great Seal, given to the Americans by the Russians – a dance troop that performed there, or something apparently innocuous – but it had an implant in it, a bug. The microwaves were latching on to the frequency and activating it. Using radio frequencies like radar to pick up a target, they can read everything we are doing. Any device with a moving metal part can be picked up and analysed from a distance.'

'Like a typewriter?'

'Exactly. We all know that each letter on a keyboard has a set place. And as such it resonates very slightly differently according to that place on the machine.'

'They can distinguish that? Such a tiny differential?'

'I believe so.'

They were walking faster and faster. She was almost running to keep up with him. Dusk had set lights glowing the length of the Moskva Bridge.

'If that's the case, they must also know the signature patterns of each individual typist.'

Rory stopped abruptly. 'I hadn't thought of that. You mean, each typist has her own way of typing that is unique to her... that makes a difference?'

'Typing has a rhythm, with certain quirks. Yes. Everyone is slightly different, just as no two people have exactly the same handwriting.'

'And if the listeners have so little to go on in the first place... we're dealing with tiny clues...'

'Mechanical oscillators.' He was back in the grand scheme, it seemed. 'That's how they're doing it. It sounds scarcely credible, I know. But I'm convinced I'm right. Unintended radio frequency. A sensitive microwave receiver somewhere nearby can pick up the vibrations on any electronic device – your own radio, perhaps – and send them to be decoded. It's pretty advanced stuff but that is what the Russians do, I'm convinced of it.'

'Can you track when they are doing this?'

'Technically it must be possible. But it's a needle in a haystack. You would need to keep up a constant scanning of radio waves.'

'Wouldn't it be easier to come up with a silent typewriter?' asked Lois.

He turned and stared, as if he couldn't believe no one else had thought of that. But that wasn't it. He looked at his watch and cursed mildly.

'I had no idea that was the time – I'm late! So sorry. Do you mind?' he asked, wheeling round to go back the way they had come.

'What's—'

'John Mowberry's poker game. I have to show up. Thing is, I took rather a lot off the others last time, and it would be very bad form not to give them a chance to win it back.'

'I didn't know you were—'

But they were practically running back, and conversation was all but impossible. He found her a taxi back to Meshchanskaya and they said a hurried goodnight.

Lois sat back in the cab, wondering why she felt disappointed. So Rory was a good poker player, too, was he? One thing was for certain, he had hidden depths. If the embassy was under attack, he was determined to find the evidence. She had never seen him so animated. He was no longer shy; he was a quiet warrior. The technicians had shown him a deference they did not usually bestow on junior members of staff. He'd instructed rather than requested them not to speak about the discovery for now. The thought occurred that he might quietly be from a similar special department to her own, and neither of them would ever say a word. Then she realised. Somehow she had been given the wrong name in London. There was every chance that the mysterious junior MI6 security officer named "Goodrich" was Rory.

Lois wrote to London via Elsie again that night using an

urgent code mark and invisible ink between the lines to pass on what Rory Kendalmoor had discovered in her presence. Was it possible the leak was actually a siphoning-off from outside using advanced technology?

The Minister had to know, of course. She had decided she must tell him, preparing a plausible veil of misrepresentation to explain her knowledge of the situation. But he got in first. When she arrived the next morning, he was at his window, a wolfish stare locked in the direction of the Kremlin, and music already blaring. Oddly, he asked her nothing about the reason for her presence at the crucial moment of discovery. The dilemma, he mimed to a bracing burst of his favourite military march by the band of the Coldstream Guards, was whether to cut the wires or play them. They would have to send word to London for the official decision.

If they played them, the Ambassador and others who conversed in his sitting room could plant some useful pieces of disinformation. There was always an upturn after a setback. A positive to be gained with the right frame of mind. He seemed curiously energised at the prospect.

'After all, we're only here to be spied on, aren't we,' he said.

Impossible not to wonder: *was* it him? Could Waller possibly be the culprit? The spiral of questions began again, gripping ever tighter. *A clear head*, she told herself. *Smile, shoulders down. The willing secretary.*

22

Friday, August 8, 1958

The days are rolling by quicker and quicker. Frightening. Seeing Rory quite a bit these days. Radio games and other amusements. Feeling lighter and more sociable.

August days began warm and humid, and simmered up to what felt like boiling point. Lois fretted as the days passed. Somehow or other, she had to get to the Black Sea. Apart from any other consideration, she'd have to book her leave before anyone else claimed that week. Then she needed to ask someone to go on holiday with her, or she wouldn't be allowed to go. Nan, perhaps? Whoever she went with, she would risk having to confide some version of her purpose. Typical of a man not to understand straightaway why a young Western woman could not go to Sukhumi alone.

Lois went through the motions at a birthday tea party in the Garden Block mess, all the time preoccupied with the implications of a potentially workable solution. When she did not run into him at the tea party, she found Rory in the guards' room. He always seemed more comfortable with the "men" rather than the "officers". He was a riddle in a mystery in an enigma (as Churchill had famously said of the Soviets) all right. But he said he was glad to see her, and, after some small awkwardness in front of the guards, asked if she wanted to take another stroll along the river.

He was playing it cool but Rory, it transpired, was also in need of support.

'The Ambassador knows all about insecure comms and brushed me away when I tried to warn him. Come to think of it, he didn't even seem curious about the microwaves bombarding the American Embassy when that came out. The Yanks were getting it in their new premises in Tchaikovskaya, but he made no attempt to discover whether our place was being attacked,' he said. 'Is he more interested in playing the radio game?' pondered Rory. 'That's the only explanation I can see.'

'Radio game?'

'That's what the old hands who worked transmitters during the war called it. Knowing the channel had been compromised and playing to the gallery. Feeding in all kinds of false information and elaborate fake trails.'

'Turning a disaster into—'

'An advantage, yes. Let's say the Ambassador knows that his office is bugged and his phone is tapped – but he doesn't care. He decides he can live with that because he understands the rules of engagement in Moscow. He can use it to gain the initiative. Whenever he speaks to anyone, he understands that he is speaking directly to the Russians, more specifically to the KGB. And he tells them what he wants them to know.'

'All theatre,' mouthed Lois, disingenuously. 'He loves putting on shows, so…'

'But it's dangerous. Leaves us wide open to other security breaches. Once they have the wavelengths… I cannot believe it's sanctioned.' He stared into the distance. 'A lot of the office's internal problems have stemmed from the rivalry between departments, especially between MI5 and 6. Some of them are old battles left over from the war, some of them from bloody prep schools as far as I can see. Neither one fully trusts the other and mistakes are made because of it. At the top level, it's all personal.'

She wasn't going to argue with that.

'The Americans have the same problem. I know that from when I was in New York. Even when the FBI was closing in on Burgess, clues were missed not only because he was being protected by someone on our side, but also because the American agencies were fighting each other. Protecting their friends and their own backs rather than doing their jobs properly. Makes me sick. But look, forget the class war for a minute,' he seemed to be talking to himself, 'and make what we can of it. Because, don't you see, if we have this problem, you can bet anything that the Russians do too. This is what I've been thinking… what if the KGB and the GRU are actually deadly rivals?'

She let that sink in, unsure where they would be able to go with this, even if he was right.

'We could exploit that?'

Rory nodded. 'We could.'

'With the Ambassador's play-acting. Or Chancery's.'

'Exactly.'

'Draw them out.'

'But you can't pull out the wires, see. We have to pretend we don't know. Accept it, knowing it's put the embassy under almost total surveillance.' Even though they were outside, Rory was speaking softly. She had to lean in close to hear.

'Everyone knows that it's not secure,' murmured Lois, thinking of Waller.

'Perhaps we now know why.'

Surely the leaks couldn't be coming from Mountbeech himself, deliberately? That would be far too blatant, too shocking. Or it would have been unthinkable only a few years ago. But after Maclean, anything was possible. If it were still unthinkable, she would not be here. Yet when the anomalies were considered… H.E. was old school through and through, more's the pity for all of them.

They walked on, lost in their separate inner worlds.

The fact that Rory didn't flirt with her, that he treated her only as a trusted colleague and friend, made what she had to do both easier and much harder. Easier because the way he was behaving made him far more attractive to her than anything else he could have done; harder because she was going to have to take a gamble.

'I was wondering what you were doing tonight,' Lois said boldly.

They cut that night's dull party and simply walked in the dusk. Once again they did not discuss anything of any importance. There was only the close heat, and the music and the game of edging closer to each other. A band was playing in the dusty little park near Meshchanskaya. She caught his hand in hers as they walked, and he did not release it. A shy kiss on the grass led to another. Then embarrassed, as if he might have overstepped the mark, concerned too late about who would have seen them, he pulled away. His kiss was sweet, and his diffidence moved her. Both left her wanting more.

They went to see a film together the next night, and he took her out to dinner at the Praga the night after. A few days later, they played tennis after work. Rory was a surprisingly good player; perhaps it was another facet of his adeptness with practical matters, dispatching winners onto the lines with the same skilful practicality he used on radios and wiring. When they flopped on the grass afterwards, she still slightly out of breath, she showed him the advertisement in *Pravda*.

It showed a smiling girl in the sunshine resort of Sukhumi. For most Russians, it was a lifelong dream to spend three days on a train to visit this subtropical beach resort on the Black Sea, complete with palm trees, botanical gardens and citrus plantations, and backed by the high alpine peaks of the Greater Caucasus Mountains. The Soviet Riviera, the closest any good Soviet citizen could get to paradise. It was rumoured that only very special workers who had pleased the regime with exemplary devotion to the communist cause would be beneficiaries of a voucher enabling them to travel and stay at Sukhumi. Stalin himself had kept a dacha there, his favourite of all the escapes at his disposal.

Rory dropped his eyes to fidget with the strings of his racket.

'Are you missing Johann?' he asked.

'A little. But that's not why.' She reached out and touched him, first on the shoulder, then the face. 'I liked Johann,' she told him. 'I enjoyed his company very much. He's interested in many of the same things I am. I liked going out with him to the ballet and to concerts and for dinner. We drifted into a friendship that wasn't quite what it seemed to everyone else.' *Or to me*, she thought sadly.

Rory looked up.

'Let me prove it to you,' she said. 'Come to Sukhumi with me.'

At first, the Minister would not grant her leave. He raised no end of objections – his schedule, the workload – but eventually relented when Bill Stoneley stepped in and explained that Lois could combine her holiday with some vital observations and data collection on his behalf. (Whatever his motives were, she would have to live with them.) The mounting tension before any departure – the permissions that came through as late as

227

possible, the tickets withheld until the day of travel, the ever-present possibility of leave being cancelled in the event of an emergency – was doubled by the risks she was taking.

23

Friday, September 5, 1958

Off to Sukhumi! Cannot wait for a holiday by the sea. Nan smacked me down for being "sickeningly cheerful", but I couldn't help myself.

Lois dialled down her show of enthusiasm. Whatever awaited, the prospect of warmth and the semblance of a holiday was irresistible. As was the thought of nine days alone with Rory, strangely enough. The more time she had spent with him, the less the age gap and other differences seemed to matter. She was getting frighteningly skilled at compartmentalism. If anyone was sceptical about this rapid escalation in their romance, nothing was said, or even implied. Even Nan, the one who avoided any romantic entanglements in case they might jeopardise her career, seemed to think it perfectly acceptable for Lois to grab some excitement when she could.

Their tickets finally came through at lunchtime. Lois managed to scribble a quick letter home, and another to Elsie as an insurance policy, outlining her travel plans. Their passports were stamped, and she raced home to get packed and ready in time.

It was pouring with rain when Rory came at 9.30pm.

Streaks of yellow light trickled across a black and watery Red Square. Half a mile from Vnukovo Airport, the taxi caught a flat tyre. There was no time to wait for the driver to change it, bad-temperedly, too slowly, in the soaking downpour. They made him flag down another cab that was heading for the terminal, and caught the flight with minutes to spare, having wasted more time wrangling over excess baggage payments that seemed entirely calculated to harass foreign travellers, judging from the luggage Soviet passengers were hauling. Then, at last, they were off into the night. They toasted each other in vodka, then slept the sleep of exhausted escapees until the plane put down for a stop at Krasnodar.

Disappointingly, the sky was overcast in the morning as they flew along the Black Sea coast. The plane smacked down on the runway with a shocking rattle, and they disembarked dazed down the stairs. Even the September sun seemed tired and truculent in the usual Russian way as they walked across the tarmac.

From the outside, the Intourist hotel was impressive but inside there was a squalid lack of attention to details, especially in the bathrooms. But they were shown to adjoining large rooms with a shared balcony that looked over crystal clear sea, inviting in the heat and soft breeze. In Lois's room was a scuffed white baby grand piano. Rory surprised and delighted her by sitting down and playing a piece in the classical style he told her was called "La Petite Waltz".

Sukhumi was a place of strange combinations and unexpected delights, decided Lois as she tried to take it all in. Pine trees and palm trees. Cedars and tamarisk on the shore. The piers at Sukhumi looked like Soviet submarines with art deco entrances. Lenin was commemorated in a mosaic mural and holidaymakers strolled the seaside promenade. Old men played backgammon in front of coffee shops. Smoked whole fish hung in stinking clusters on iron hooks outside food emporia.

Men in flannel pyjamas – a popular form of beachwear, it seemed – strutted past peasant women selling lottery tickets. Other women in black Muslim garb sold sunflower seeds in twists of paper. Sweet Georgian champagne and ice creams – a choice between vanilla and chocolate – were available from colourful stands.

The first afternoon, in a daze of tiredness, they ate blinis and *syrniki* dumplings and noted with relief the availability of beef stroganoff for dinner, always the safe option on the Cyrillic menu. They lay poleaxed on the beach at Medicinsky Plag, never realising the sun was so hot or that they were growing so red. They swam and the sea was glorious. The views of mountains across the bay evoked the French Riviera. The beach was stony but chairs or flat wooden beds could be rented for pennies.

Lois laughed. 'Have you noticed?' She was feeling so light-hearted, so intent on boxing away her concerns until they were needed, that she was nearly giddy with living for the moment. 'Most of the swimming costumes have been made by the same state factory!'

Four women had already come past sporting the identical swimsuit in buttercup yellow and purple. A version in orange and apple green was also popular. Most of the Soviet bodies on display were pale and ample, testament to the comforts afforded to those who qualified for a booking.

The next day they paid the price. They were both queasy, red and sore. Definitely too much sun. They had a late breakfast and idled in the hotel before sallying forth for a short walk along the shore on a road that seemed to lead right out of Sukhumi. They made sure to learn the Cyrillic on the sign: *СУХУМИ*. It was another easy day. Well, they had more than earned it.

For dinner they found a café with dancing on the roof but didn't stay for long. They had a choice of two beds to share and no beady eyes noting which one they chose, but despite some welcome embraces on the balcony, trying to avoid painful areas of sunburn, they had each retired to their own room.

A Czech delegation arrived at the hotel and filled the restaurant at breakfast time the next day. There were no tables left so they were shown to an overflow room at the back. Rory was quiet, but she had no idea whether he was moody or just being himself. It was a niggling reminder that she did not know him well at all. He went off by himself to buy some film for his camera, and Lois was glad of the time alone to think.

She tidied and made a final check around her room before closing the door. The tells were set: a hair or a crumb of paper on each drawer and her suitcase. At the concierge desk, she enquired casually whether there were any messages (there were not) and sauntered out to the café where they had agreed to meet. The photographic shop was within sight, to one side of the exuberantly excessive fountain in front of the theatre. Plenty of tourists were taking photos of themselves in front of griffins spewing water into the three-tiered cascade. Succulent small palms flourished beside it, and the elegant white theatre building was no more Russian than modern Greek.

Another coffee in the sunshine, could anything be better? She closed her eyes, soaking up the warmth, sweet bitterness on her lips.

'What the hell's he doing here?' Rory burst in on her thoughts, standing over her, his temper far from improved.

'Who?'

'Your German, of course.'

'Johann?'

Rory glared at her.

'Johann's not here,' said Lois. 'You're imagining it.'

'I just saw him.'

'Where?'

'Over there by the card shop.'

Lois raised her hand as a sunshade and stared over. It was the hottest day yet, or so it felt.

'It can't have been him.'

Rory began to say something, then held back. Neither of them wanted an argument, not when everything was so lovely. Lois got up and slipped her hand into his.

Despite their sensible plan – have a dip in the sea, cover up, then go back to the hotel out of the sun for afternoon – they didn't leave the beach until three, too tired and sun-drugged to make decisions. All they could do was sleep on top of the bed in her room, as if they were sleeping away all the months of tension in Moscow.

They went back to the rooftop restaurant in the evening, the one with the dancing. It was an unfortunate idea. A rowdy group of Russians began talking to them, ordered champagne for them. Were they delegates, too, or just a group of colleagues on holiday? They did not say, and she did not want to ask.

A couple of them spoke good German and soon they were giving her the inside track on the resort. The loveliest sections of the shore, with fewer stones and gently shelving beach, were reserved for those high up in the Communist Party, or with connections to those who were. Beaches were designated for the young: the Pioneers and Young Octobrists, groups of children who could be recognised by the red or white caps. There was a class hierarchy every bit as well defined as in the West, it seemed.

They hadn't been taken to the foreigners' beach? There certainly was one. It was ruled over by a woman in a large white hat and uniformed militiaman. Was that to stop foreigners speaking to Soviet citizens? asked Lois cheekily. The champagne had hit rather. No, the only reason for this arrangement was so that the beaches did not become overcrowded. Though there was an official and an unofficial reason for everything.

They all raised their glasses and clinked them in naughty merriment. The procedure at Sukhumi harbour was that all boats were taken out of the water every night and dragged up the shore overnight. The official line was that this precaution prevented damage from unusual winds or currents. In practice, it ensured that none of the boats could easily be used by potential defectors set on reaching Turkey and thence to the West.

Lois was grateful for the information, not that it would make much difference to anything, just notes for Bill and his endless Soviet compilations. She must be sure to pick up a railway timetable before they left.

A huge car arrived and waited for the merry Russians.

'Come with us,' they urged.

Lois was tempted – the champagne again. As they walked back, Rory was furious with her. He rightly pointed out not to forget they were in Russia, but he needn't have used that tone, and they had their first argument. The only good that came out of it was that Rory could see she was just an ordinary young woman released from the pressures of an extraordinary overseas posting and letting go rather too far.

In other circumstances, it would have been an idyllic September holiday. Summer lingered, balmy and sensuous. While others were toiling at their desks, they were lying in the sun, laughing in the face of another looming Moscow winter. It was a jolt about Johann, though. Could it really have been him? Maybe just a man who looked a bit like him. Rory was obsessed, but hardly knew him well. Nevertheless, Lois was on high alert.

Whether Rory picked up on her preoccupation or had his own twinges of guilt at so much self-indulgence on the beach when they could be gathering general information, he suggested the next morning they go to "see the monkeys". It was a sweet nod to the night something had clicked with them at Spaso House on the Fourth of July. The shared memory of the animal chaos made them laugh again.

The Institute of Experimental Pathology and Therapy had been conducting ground-breaking tests on monkeys since the 1920s, including research into cures for polio, typhus, and cholera. It was a Soviet research institute that had the rare status of being open to the public. According to one of Bill Stoneley's reports, it was also the training place for the monkeys blasted off into space by the USSR's pioneering rocket programme. He would be delighted she had seen it, and if she could snatch some photographs for him, so much the better.

Following the Intourist instructions, they crossed the railway line and walked past the Botanical Gardens. The entrance was marked by a row of aged men and women offering paper bags of chopped cucumber and peach intended as delicacies to feed the primates.

Rory paid a fee, and they followed a tour guide who spoke some impenetrable Russian dialect through pretty trees and foliage to a collection of buildings. The prettiness of this garden on a hillside above the sea was blunted by the rich, rotting smell of animal faeces and, from somewhere inside a building, the cries that might have come from terrified children. Lois felt her stomach turn and wished they had not come. But they kept walking down the path, now hand in hand, neither wanting to look at the other, withdrawn into their own personal distress. Iron bars in the green arbour: cages of prisoner monkeys, some howling in anguish, a few making an effort to move, others gnawing at orange peel like bitter, wizened old men endowed with knowledge no one cared to know. Others, distressed and banging their heads against the bars and fighting, were eating stones. Seven thousand of them, their guide managed to convey by scratching the number in the solid, fetid air.

Now and then a breath of sea breeze lifted leaves but made no dent in the stench. Their throats were dry and their eyes moist. But as Lois and Rory progressed further from the building where the scientists performed their experiments, acrobatic macaques swung and leapt with loose grace from the ceiling bars of the cages. Kingly gorillas stared with amber eyes, and enormous baboons sat watching the rank and file of the patrons come by, the tourists whose admission tickets kept them in captivity and fruit.

It was upsetting, like an animal version of the sanatorium on the hill above the town.

Lois made an excuse to go back to the hotel, excusing herself with some vague feminine complication she knew Rory would not want to discuss. And yes, as part of her had known there would be, sooner or later, there was a message for her with the concierge.

In her room she concentrated on the envelope, the familiar handwriting, before she ripped into it. *I am too tiny in this world, and not tiny enough*, she read. *Drink in the bar 8pm? The usual. Cheers!* No signature.

So it had been him, and he would know that Rory was with her. Why had Johann allowed himself to be spotted? 'A nice triangle,' she could hear Rory saying.

She moved fast. Fetched the book of Rilke poems from the bottom of her suitcase. She had followed protocol and brought it, however unlikely it had seemed she might need it. She flipped to page eleven, the number of the words in the quotation. Four lines down, the number of letters in the repeated word. She made a further calculation, and then transcribed the message using words and letters in the poems: *Alex. 8pm, east end of the esplanade. Safety sig 2, 20. Box drop.*

There was no hint as to where Johann was staying or how she could contact him, but he had promised to watch over her. That gave her more confidence. He would be as good as his word, even in the shadows. She had to believe that.

Her first problem, to which she still had no firm solution despite many sleepless hours at night, was how to get away from Rory for the evening. Various possibilities had presented themselves to her: a flaming row, during which she could flounce away; she could call London and ask them to arrange an urgent message from the office in Moscow asking him to stand by to assist in a situation that had arisen in his absence. Or she could come partially clean and admit that Johann was in Sukhumi. This had the benefit of using Rory's own eagle-eyed observation, proving him right, and for this reason might be the best option.

Or she could take him into her confidence. 'If I tell you something, you must promise never to reveal it to a living soul.' Could she actually do that? What would be the consequences?

Over lunch with a view of the sparkling bay, Lois told Rory that he had been right. Johann had called at the hotel. He had left a message with a telephone number. Lois produced a page of hotel notepaper with a number on it and his name. (She had scribbled it herself.) That was why she had been so long, sorry. She had spoken to him, very briefly, told him that she was with Rory now. Johann had not taken it well. So tonight – it had to be tonight, he was booked on a boat trip this afternoon – she was going to see Johann, to tell him to leave her alone.

'What the hell's he doing here? Why now? Did he follow you?' Rory was understandably furious. It was clear this was more than coincidence. 'What's the game here, Lois?'

She did her best to calm him.

'I'm coming with you.'

'You can't!' she cried. The words rang out like a slap. 'I'm sorry. Honestly, it would make everything ten times worse. He's jealous of you.'

'But there wasn't anything between you.'

'Not now. At one time there was a possibility there might be. He's proud and I have to let him down gently. You need to show him that you have nothing to fear from his presence, because I'm with you.' She hated the tangles, but she had chosen her path and had to follow it to the end.

He remonstrated some more, but she shook her head.

'Please, don't let's argue. I have to do this. There's no way around it.'

'There are times when I feel you like me, really like me,' said Rory. 'And others when I wonder if you even have a heart.'

That stung. She had always known there would be times when her higher loyalties could inflict wounds on personal ones. Perhaps one day she might be able to explain, but that would not be up to her, of course.

A walk in the woods at the back of the bay proved more difficult than they imagined. Roads petered out and then one which eventually didn't was officially barred. They found a way by sinuous paths to the top of a hill thick with undergrowth where they stopped to eat and read. They spotted lizards and a snake. Then straight down to the beach, where they were alone in the sea, and a certain scene in *From Here to Eternity* seemed miraculously to occur to both of them at the same time.

She pulled him down on top of her at the edge of the waves. Rory was a fine young man; she did not have to act her excitement and daring. Surely he could have no doubt how she felt about him after that.

They had an early supper, though neither could eat much. Lois left Rory at the table with a full carafe of Georgian red wine and promised to return as soon as she could. It wouldn't take that long. She would be back soon. At seven-thirty, past the men playing dominoes and backgammon outside the waterfront cafés, she set off for the esplanade alone, backtracking, in and out of shops, checking all around her, through one café to visit their conveniences and out by the service door at the rear, vigilant as all her training had prepared her.

24

Friday, September 12, 1958

A walk along the esplanade as darkness fell. Sat and talked on the beach.

The colonnade of classical pillars on the Sukhumi waterfront framed a tall palm tree. Beyond this delightful folly, the sea flirted and showed off its sequins in the last of the evening sun. Well-baked couples and groups drifted along the promenade. Ice cream vendors were still open and doing good business. A sense of holiday freedom stretched like a smile across the town, good Soviets, Abkhazians and Georgians drinking wine together before the singing started.

Waves whispering at her side, Lois made her way west into the sunset. Mauve and apricot clouds streaked the sky. Feathery tamarisk trees stood in silhouette. As one, the lampposts on the sea wall came on, twin globes stretching ahead like a string of old pearls. Lois counted the lampposts. Under the twentieth, a paper sandwich bag was weighted by a stone on the concrete seat built into the wall. The safety signal check in place. He was there, up ahead, and had not been followed.

She was alone. This far along the esplanade was deserted.

Night was falling rapidly. She thought Johann might show himself, just briefly, but there was no sign of him.

The promenade ran out. She waited, hardly daring to breathe. As she scanned the darkness, a piece of it detached, stood up. The figure waited. She hesitated then advanced. It was Zhigunov. He put a finger to his lips, and she moved forward noiselessly until they were face to face. He looked harried. His face thinner than she remembered, its features carved shadows in the dying light.

'Come, this way.'

The end of the stone promenade had crumbled, demolished by stormy waters in winter, she supposed. Zhigunov offered a hand and together they climbed down onto the black rocks beneath. It was possible to walk across the stones to a tiny beach hidden by trees. A maximum of three people could have lain out after bathing there, in a cave of bushy hornbeams.

She hardly dared breathe. He made silently for the tree cover then sat on a fallen trunk, gesturing for her to join him. He had become still, a cold granite presence. A man who had lost the habit of smiling.

'I am going to tell you what very few are ever allowed to know,' said Zhigunov without preamble. His voice was low, the tone conversational yet disconcerting. The voice of the man on the train, coming back to her with every particular inflection and imperfection. 'Will not be what you are expecting.'

The terrible thought rose that she had been lured into a trap.

'First, I tell you this: it was I who killed the American Nayland. I love my country. I do this for my country.'

It was a trap. It was a set-up, and she had made a very bad decision.

'Nayland was dangerous man. He want talk to me, ask questions, decide if I can be trusted. He is the one who should not be trusted. CIA understand nothing. If I did not kill him, I would have been exposed to my people.'

Silence, the only refuge. She wanted to ask how and exactly why and when he had killed him but did not. She was frightened, of course, but she did not want to halt the flow of information. Nor was his manner threatening. Just as on the train, it was almost confiding. He was not offering himself to theirs, she decided; he wanted her for his cause.

'All is built on lies. In this, we are all equal, all over world.' He gave the start of a laugh, a single derisive note. 'Keep telling there is crisis and danger in the world, and peoples will do anything you want. They want believe that leaders are on their side. But is not true. Forget balance of power. It is balance of *terror* that is used by *both* sides, on their own people.'

Compartmentalise the shock of his confession to the killing of the American. Concentrate on committing his words to memory.

'Cold War is wonderful distraction. What if same people who control the Soviet Union are the people who control you? Differences between us manufactured. Is brilliant mirror, a confidence trick of unsurpassable scope! No one will believe it. But I can tell you who is in control if you can be open to the truth.'

The sea shuddered, iron grey as the Moscow sky. Waves receded, clutching vainly at pebbles.

He seemed to be waiting for a reaction. There was power in his stillness and silence. Careful! Trust had to be earned. Or was this part of his game, the one he had started before she had even reached Moscow? Blackmail, manipulation, political opportunism, he was saying, all were available weapons to the unscrupulous. And some men couldn't help their addiction to power over others, for an exhilarating hour or for a lifetime.

She nodded, not finding much to disagree with. Shaking, she was shaking, she realised. Concentrate. Commit to memory.

In regular circumstances she would have been prepared with a detailed and lengthy briefing, might have been equipped with a functioning recording device. This was way off the books.

'"Look over there!" they say,' went on Zhigunov. 'They are like magicians; they attract your attention one way while quickly doing something they don't want you to see. What if what looks like an error is not an error? What if hidden in plain sight in the guise of a mistake?'

The name of the traitor. She just wanted the name. If only it could be fished out of the flow, its British body dropped dripping in front of her like Nayland. But Zhigunov was still setting the scene. She had been told the Russians did this when they had a chance to speak with Westerners: they became philosophers and lyricists, performers avid for an audience that would be all too quickly gone.

'So we must look at tactics they use against us and turn it back on them. How we can do that? Think. But advantage is always on their side. You see, Miss Vale, there is a cynical and manipulative international club. People who don't care about destruction they cause.'

'You're right,' she whispered. Give him something. 'It's not just the Soviet leaders.'

'Money, power and control. Everywhere. Truth is whatever people are led to believe will benefit them. Governments, military – the "facts" only what they want you to believe. Each side is told they are doing good, that they are fighting evil. We make mistakes not because we cannot see the truth but because we do not want to believe it.'

The darkened headland had merged into the black shifting water. A red glow clung stubbornly to a cloud, just enough to brush pink on the foam of incoming waves.

'We face a common enemy. We must act before it goes so far we can never turn back.' He reached into his jacket and brought out a paper bag from which he took a Kodak envelope. He opened it quickly to show it contained a handful of black-and-white photos and draw her attention to the strips of negatives. 'Put in your bag. Now. Tell your people to look especially carefully at photographs of groups by the lake. Other pictures not important, only show details of location, could be your tourist pictures. This one of group is key importance. In negatives, details of research. I can give more. Current military capability. Nuclear capability.'

'In return for?'

'You, understanding truth.'

On the pebbled ledge of beach fringed by trees they paid their respects to the truth, that near-extinct prey of the warriors. Neither of them lit a cigarette, though it would have been the natural accompaniment to such a conversation. They could not risk the smallest ember glow nor trace of acrid tobacco smoke on the night air.

'Our countries are our families, sometimes also our friends. We choose to love them despite faults. We work hard to overlook weaknesses. Possible even persuade ourselves that these make us love more, that we might perhaps have power to heal them. We need sense of belonging, but this so easy to turn against us. Is no longer beautiful country. Is ugly.'

Music had struck up in a restaurant. Fragmented notes floated over the water. Their watchful tension seemed to undulate with the gentle breaking of waves on stones.

'This war, this Cold War, it begins in 1917. Bolshevik Revolution. Peasants and glorious proletariat rising up in revolt against Tsar Nicholas II and his government. New Communist Russia, led by Vladimir Lenin.' His delivery had a faraway quality, almost as if it were a well-known song to which everyone knew the words. 'But there was opposition. Civil War broke out same year. Red Army for Lenin and Bolsheviks fought

White Army that was for monarchy, anti-central control, for the capitalists and new form of democracy for our country. The Tsar and his family, the Romanovs, were executed and civil war lasted until 1923. Ends with victory for the Red Army and the establishment of the Soviet Union. Russian Revolution has brought communism to the world, influential new political belief system. Soviet Union rose to status of world power, only one that can match capabilities of USA.'

A pause.

'But what if Revolution was engineered outside Russia? Foreigners wanted Russia to be part of a central bank – a bank they control. The Tsar refused. Was murdered. Money pours into Russia to create unrest, to destabilise and bring in the ultimate control – communism. What if these people were the same ones who control the West?' He looked hard at her. 'Is that unthinkable to you?'

It sounded absurd.

'Oh, I would once have agreed with you,' he said. 'A crazy notion! But now…'

'But we've always known what happened.'

'You are lied to. We are all lied to. This is what I am telling you. East, West: we are all on same side against same powerful enemy in the shadows.'

The enormity of what he was saying took her breath away. Either he had gone mad, or – no, there was no alternative.

'When you work out who is in the group photograph by the lake, then you will see it. See who works for both sides, see who supplies funds. That is why they are so powerful.'

The darkness resonated in her ears.

'Can send men crazy,' he resumed. 'I have seen it. Informed and intelligent people can be persuaded easily if they *want* to believe. Equally, when this belief is established and they are shown proof it is wrong, mind fights hard to disprove this evidence. Reason is nothing against desire to retain the belief.'

Silence again. The lapping of water on the shore.

'Is this the proof?' she asked.

He nodded. 'All I can do is to show this: we are not threat to the West. Not in nuclear weapons.'

The music across the blackness was becoming more insistent, folk tunes on guitar and mandolin, twanging and jangling and thrumming in frenzied rhythm.

'They think this is trap, your people. Of course they do,' said Zhigunov. 'Controlling what people think is the key. Controlling them so well that they don't even realise they are being controlled. Cold War is also psychological. Balance of terror.'

His sincerity seemed real. In that moment, it was all real. She thought of the gilded churches converted into museums purporting to show history rewritten according to the demands of political expediency.

'I was told you had proof about the British traitor in Moscow.'

'This man has left Moscow now. His name is John Vassall. Was assistant to the Naval Attaché in your embassy.'

Not a current member of the embassy staff, then. It was both a disappointment and a relief.

'Kompromat and blackmail,' went on Zhigunov. 'With men, homosexual. Now he is ours, but Vassall is still working for your government in London. Do not doubt that Russia has spies in US and UK nuclear development programmes. I offer this as balance and my goodwill.'

At this, the moment of truth, Zhigunov seemed overcome by sudden despair. He put his head in his hands.

'This is black heart of this world. It takes courage to believe. Then to find truth is hard, but to discover what to do with it… that is hardest. Truth should change people, but truth is changed by corrupt societies. People are made to believe lies. Lies enforced by more lies until they cannot live unless they repeat the lies and hate those who tell the truth.'

He did not want to talk about individual men. He was speaking about dead souls, about Gogol. How normal people did not know this kind of evil to be possible. They did not want to know, and that was their tragedy.

'Why?' asked Lois. 'Why are you doing this?'

'Because I have nothing left to lose. Because I believe that in this world there is good and there is evil, and it cannot be that one nation state is evil and another is good. In each, there are people with human hearts. In some hearts there is more good than bad, and in some there is more bad than good. We must believe – we have to show – that there is more good than evil. Otherwise… is nothing.'

Perhaps he was drunk and had been all along. He was beginning to ramble. Then he stopped, abruptly. Held up a hand in warning. Lois stiffened. He moved his head – she saw it in outline as he seemed to listen intently. She strained to hear what he had.

With a sudden strong movement, Zhigunov pushed her down on the pebbles. She went down heavily, bumping her hip, the air knocked out of her lungs. For a few seconds, she could not breathe. His hand was on her mouth. But he was down flat, too, not attacking but protecting her.

Rustling in the undergrowth grew louder. A crack of gunshot came from behind. She might even have heard the whistle of the bullet. Then another shot, and a muffled cry.

Zhigunov was up on his haunches. He listened again then pointed to the sea. Lois held tight to her bag as they slithered and crawled to the edge of the trees on the beach. The stones ripped at her hands, grazed her knees. Her heart pounded as she decided she had no option but to stick with him and trust. *Trust no one.* Right now she had no choice.

Keeping to the shadow line, they seemed to round a small promontory. They emerged on a tumble of black rocks where the sea slapped loudly. He helped her when she could not find a footing, one hand on her back to keep her as low as possible. Then stopped her in a hollow where she could rest unseen while he went further down to the water, then signalled for her to come down.

He had the rope of a small boat. *So that was how he had arrived*, she thought inconsequentially. In the scramble to get in it, she knocked a shin painfully and bit her lip hard to stop herself crying out. Another shot rang out in the dark. Other sounds were getting closer, twigs snapping, the crunch of boots on pebbles. Zhigunov hunched over the outboard motor. He pulled on the starter cord. Nothing happened. Pulled again. Still nothing. Again. There was a splash close by and a hand came from below to grab her.

She dug her nails into the arm. The grip released. Zhigunov lunged in the same second that Lois moved rapidly to the other side of the craft. A knife glinted in a shaft of moonlight. It was Zhigunov who pulled it from left to right across the solid shadow on the sea. The man in the water disappeared into blackness. But she had no time to feel relief. There was another man in black in the water, hair sleek like a seal's. He held the other side of the boat. Now he was rocking it. Zhigunov hurled himself across the wooden slats towards the assailant and took the man's head in some nefarious lock. Silently he held it, moved it brutally first one way then the other. Held it for a few seconds more. The manoeuvre, accomplished in silence except for a few feeble splashes, ended with a push. The body slipped away. Zhigunov the soldier was a shockingly efficient killer.

He went back to the engine. It took three more pulls to spark. Even then, it made barely any noise. It must have been specially adapted for covert operations. They moved off. All Lois knew was that they were heading out to sea. A shout from the shore and a whistle, then another shot and all was quiet but for the rapidly diminishing music and the splutter of the outboard motor.

Moonlight straked the water, always seeming to point to their position. No more was said for a while. She was still alive; Zhigunov had saved them both – for now. Now that the rush of fear was over, if only in the immediate present, Lois felt sick and exhausted.

'Who were they?' she asked at last. 'KGB?'

'No.'

'Who?'

He did not reply. Almost as if he were waiting to see whether she would make connections and work it out.

'Do you know who?' she asked.

'Do you?'

She said nothing.

They churned through the water. After what seemed like a long time, they turned back towards the coast. According to the position of the moon, they were travelling west. According to her watch, they had been on the water for an hour, but it felt like the whole night. She clutched her bag with its precious contents as if that would stop her shivering.

Zhigunov cut the engine. Squinted at the shore. Listened. Minutes passed. He fixed two oars in the side locks. He rowed into a creek and moored using a chain fixed to a rock. On dry land, he held her back while he scouted the path ahead, came back to get her. They climbed rough-hewn steps to the coast road.

As they began to walk wearily, he slung an arm over her shoulders.

'Like we are lovers,' he said.

So they wandered back in the direction of Sukhumi, apparently in no hurry to conclude a night stroll. His stout form solid against her side. Tensed ready to jump in the dark ditch at the side if they needed to. A few cars passed. An army truck. She felt the tension in his arm as it rumbled by. Truth be told, she was glad of the physical support he provided.

A grey limousine passed. Stopped. Reversed back towards them. With a jolt, she realised it was just like the one she and Rory had been offered a ride in only a few days earlier. What if they recognised her? Her heart pounded uncomfortably. They had so nearly made it. The nearside back passenger door opened.

Zhigunov exchanged a few words with someone sitting in the back. A woman, elderly, judging from the voice. Lois could just understand one basic Russian phrase. It was going to rain, the woman said. She made room on the seat next to her and asked her chauffeur to drive on.

She was the mother of wealthy smugglers, proud Azkhabians, Zhigunov explained when they were dropped off twenty minutes later. They always recognised and helped others who kicked against the Soviet state apparatus. When he hadn't returned the boat by the agreed time, they had known something had gone wrong and been waiting to offer assistance.

The lamps had gone out along the sea wall when Zhigunov stole away along the Sukhumi promenade. Lois studied his weary face one last time.

'What will you do now?' she asked.

He raised a slow shrug. 'Go on. As long, as far, as I can.'

They parted in opposite directions.

Lois felt as if she was walking underwater. At one point she froze, thought she heard sighs and whispers, but it was only the sea. She passed the remains of the Roman fortress on the waterfront, watching every shadow, aware of every movement, every leaf lifted by a furtive breath of breeze. Her bag felt like lead, so weighty were the vital negatives. The lighthouse pulsed slowly, sending a ribbon of yellow light across the bay. Flowers moist and heavy with dew oozed their scents. The moon was another lamp in the string of glowing globes.

A figure detached from a pillar of the colonnade and a chill sliced the thick warmth of the night. Her legs buckled. Someone was coming towards her.

'Where the hell have you been?' asked Rory.

Lois had never been so pleased yet so scared to see anyone. She ran into his arms, but he stepped back violently, pushed her away then stopped himself. He looked as if he wanted to shake her to her senses but held back.

She reached out to him again. He was trembling as much as she was.

'If I tell you something, you can never reveal it to a living soul.'

25

Saturday, September 13, 1958

Today was a good day. Felt the heat. To the gift shop. Couldn't resist a brigand's letter opener! Then to the cathedral. Beautiful serene Madonna and candles alight. Confession, I was moved. Another lovely moment later that I won't forget: the mournful notes of the mouth organ on a deserted beach, with scrub behind & the sea whipping up. Our last night, I'm afraid.

The Minox camera was jammed. She fiddled with it, rubbed Vaseline into the button, cursed, but could not make it work. She had to go out, leaving Rory still asleep in her bed, and buy another film for her own tourist camera. Came back and did her best with that in the bathroom: took photographs of the photographs in the Kodak envelope – '*The best that can be done sometimes*' – four goes, to make sure, of one showing a group by a lake that seemed to show Stalin himself in open shirt and slacks; did her best to get images of each negative strip on the white edge of the bath; used up the film and put the cartridge in the lining pocket of her suitcase along with the other one containing her holiday snaps. Anyone could have such a good time they ran out of film and had to buy a new roll locally.

She put the photos and strips of negatives back in their envelope, hesitated, then with trembling fingers, pulled the last strip out again. It was different from the others, like a summary of all the images, or perhaps the most important ones. The first was of the man who looked like Stalin and his entourage; the next showed an expanded group with another man at the centre next to him; the other two negatives showed documents. Quickly, not allowing herself time to dwell on her motive, Lois folded this strip and secreted it behind the mirror of her powder compact.

When Rory stirred and tried to pull her back to bed, she told him softly that she had to go out, that he should not ask her any more questions. Of course, he protested. He wanted to come with her, offer what protection he could. She had not slept a wink, but she was still thinking rationally. She persuaded him firmly that she should go alone while he stayed where he was to ensure no one came to search the room in their absence. She would be back in an hour, and they would have breakfast together.

Lois left the hotel and turned left into a street lined with palms. Despite her inner turmoil, she forced herself to wander along slowly, lightly swinging her empty tourist camera by its strap.

Had she really had no choice but to confess her covert mission and what had happened that night to Rory? All things considered, she had not. To try to cover up and lie to him in the circumstances would only make things worse. He had known something was up from the moment he had spotted Johann, had waited for her for hours in the shadows of the esplanade, had gathered her to him when he had realised the state she was in, shocked, tearful and shaking, legs badly cut and bruised.

'I love you, I love you,' he had whispered. 'I would do anything to keep you safe. You know you can trust me. Tell me, please, and let me help. We're in this together.'

What would be the consequences of breaking all the rules to confide in Rory? Was it his anguished declaration of love that had broken her defences? Why? What did love have to do with it? Everything, she decided. Not only in the personal but in the highest sense. Even Zhigunov had spoken about the human heart. And what of Johann now?

She took a circuitous route, checking every corner, every shop window, doubling back on herself, still faking delight at the glorious plants and trees as she again made sure she was not being followed. If I were a man, thought Lois, I would put my shoulders back, confidently approach a likely source – a young man who seemed prosperous despite selling only bad nails and screws, for example – and talk him into finding a gun for a stranger in need, no questions asked. Or bribe a man in a dark side street bar to tell me who to seek out, a fixer who knows what's needed without having to be asked. And if I came into a little local difficulty, I could punch and chop a way out with my bare hands. Best not to think of it; no mileage in impossibilities. It was different for a woman, and that was that. She had to be inventive, play not to her strengths but her weaknesses.

She purchased some presents for home in the tourist shop. Taking pleasure in the sunshine, she reached the Cathedral of the Annunciation, admired its Greek neo-Byzantine style and guardian palm trees, well worth a photograph, and wandered idly inside.

She took her time walking around the interior as if lost in thought, then took a seat in the cool stillness of a side chapel to spend ten minutes in contemplation. From her bag she took out the red and blue flowered scarf she had just purchased and tied it over her head. She got up and wandered over to the organ, admired a Madonna and Child, then the confession box. Old wood, not polished. How many visitors would it have when participation in Christian rituals was so discouraged?

Lois pulled open the door to the confession box, sat down inside and drew the faded purple curtain. Quickly she bent forward and felt around, under the seat, in the panels, over the planks of the floor. Her prayer was answered. She slipped off her blue cardigan and trousers and put on a white dress, folding the discarded clothes into the shop carrier bag.

When she stepped out of the box a few minutes later, the envelope was tucked neatly beneath a board under the seat. The Abkhazian knife, sold as a letter opener in the tourist shop, had worked well as a tool to prise open a narrow gap to provide a hiding place. Johann would be watching out for her. The dead drop would be live only for a matter of hours before he collected.

Outside the cathedral, she kept the Russian scarf on, still careful, still taking a twisting way through the streets. A rush of relief carried her along, stronger as each minute passed. Mission accomplished. She smiled to herself at the thought of Rory waiting in her bed. All around was a lush, bright world, sharply vibrant this morning, at the edge of the sea they called black. She could see for miles, achieve anything. She was wholly present and strangely, dangerously happy for the first time in many months.

Then she saw him.

Lois watched with shocking incredulity as he came out of the chemist's shop along the road, carrying a bag, looking straight ahead, emerging without so much as a cursory check. Too busy scouting for a dark-haired woman in a blue top and trousers, maybe. His rules had slackened in the tropical heat, away from Moscow. Was it arrogance or certainty of his safety that gave him that swagger? The knowledge that he had nothing to fear from the Soviet security services? Of all people, here...

She ducked into a doorway and watched him go.

She had the excuse of a restless night to cover her quietness over a late breakfast of eggs and *kachapuri* cheese bread with Rory. Her hunger had passed, the frantic energy drained. Faced with food, all she wanted was the tiny cup of Turkish coffee. They went out to the beach again. She would sleep there, she told herself, this time under a sunshade. It was safer than the hotel. She had the powder compact with her, in her bag.

Were there watchers hidden in the shadows of the trees? They had to assume so. Act naturally. She took Rory's hand and laughed gaily. Whispered to him and then began to run along the shoreline. He caught up with her and did not let her go. She kissed him. He kissed her back. Were they still acting for the camera? If her cover was blown, then she was worthless and what did any of it matter now?

They swam, they slept, they stayed until the beach was almost deserted and the sea was getting wilder. From somewhere behind in the scrub came the sound of a thin tune being played on a mouth organ.

'Hard to go back,' said Rory.

'Very.'

'My posting is up soon. Don't know where I'll be sent next, but if I sent you an air ticket, would you come to join me? Just a single, one-way. I'd want to be sure you'd stay.'

It was hard to tell how much he really meant. They were both so caught up in living for the moment. As she had witnessed so shockingly early that morning, the end or a new beginning could come out of nowhere.

Their luggage was searched at the airport. Lois's heart raced as she saw the mess the Georgian officials made of Rory's suitcase. Her own stood on the table awaiting the same going-over. Finally they turned their attention to hers, pulling the lid up roughly and pawing through the lingerie she had placed on top, hoping that would distract them. She was right. They pulled up a lacy brassiere and grunted lasciviously between themselves, then looked no further.

The flight north became successively colder at each stop.

Lois wrote to Elsie as soon as she arrived back at Meshchanskaya, in order to make the next day's diplomatic bag. A chatty screed about her wonderful holiday in Sukhumi with as many coded details as she could, dressed the rest in allusive fluff between friends, and had it ready for the bag for London in the morning. Regarding Zhigunov, she had done all she could.

She sent the film from her own camera with the letter to Elsie, couldn't risk having it developed in Moscow, of course. That was the best she could do. The jammed Minox camera was such bad luck. Try as she might, even now, she could not make it work. The possibility that the material she had photographed was part of an elaborate, far-reaching hoax was a noose hanging loose at her neck. There were lies, enormous lies, and unimaginably huge lies. There were truths and risks, and blatant propaganda coups. It all hinged on a GRU colonel who had been sent half-mad in the hall of mirrors. And Johann – where the heck was he now?

The name Vassall haunted her. Ellis Wachorne had told her about the clerical officer in the Naval Attaché's office who had had problems. Zhigunov maintained Vassall was still working in London. Had she found the answer to the leak at the embassy at last, only to find it was out of date? Or did she know now who had done his best to compromise and divert the information Zhigunov was offering?

When she closed her eyes that night, trying too hard for oblivion, she was back in a tangle of sheets with Rory, with the open window over fragrant night flowers and the sea beyond. The memory was already freighted with a terrible nostalgia, as if it had been years ago. Love was a dangerous occupation, too, it seemed. Then she saw the chemist's shop close to the cathedral, and the self-confident stride of the man who came out. What was Tony Fielding doing there? How much did he know?

In any other place she might have run; quietly – suddenly. Taken a bus or a train to the first destination possible and disappeared from there. But no foreigner could travel from Moscow without a wait for permits, nor vanish into the wilds of Russia without a trusted support network. Flying was impossible without alerting her colleagues. She was trapped. The only safe path was to sit it out in embassy confines, protected as much as any of them could be by guards and walls, and by keeping her mouth shut.

The dangers of chance happiness were confirmed in the days and weeks that followed. Rory was suddenly very busy. She hardly saw him around the office, and he did not come to the library bar or parties. Neither did he drop by at her flat for a drink or cup of tea. Among the junior staff, the rumour circulated that the office romance had not survived exposure to sunlight. These things happened. A second time for poor Lois, sad to say. Lois was both unhappy and terrified, but she would not chase him down for an explanation. It was obvious, surely, that he had played her at her own game. The question was what Rory would decide to do with her confession.

The beginning of October brought her thirtieth birthday and she told no one, couldn't have taken the enforced jollity – was that it, was she now officially an old maid, an efficient, sexless spinster of the F.O.? In the evening, she made herself join the girls for bingo at America House. Milling around the bar as usual, the press pack was only too happy to make space for her.

Derek Moss of the *Express* bought her a gin and orange.

'Haven't seen your chap Johann around,' he said. 'Gone back to Frankfurt, has he? Might have stood a farewell round!'

'He went ages ago.'

'Got found out, did he?'

She hesitated before laughing dutifully at the old joke. 'Would there have been anything to find?'

'Well, you would know, wouldn't you?'

She raised her glass. 'Thanks for the drink.'

'I heard he got set up and it went nasty.' Moss was fishing now.

'False information, as far as I'm aware.'

He pulled a face to concede while allowing doubt to remain.

They were interrupted by the *Times* and *Reuters*, neither of whom had seen hide nor hair of the *Frankfurter Allgemeiner* for a month, give or take. Lois slipped away gratefully and joined the table for bingo. Trudy won a hostess hotplate, with which she was delighted.

Normal procedure would be to have a quiet word with the Minister to prepare the ground for what would inevitably break, but Waller had undertaken a four-day trip to Helsinki. A semi-confession to Burville would hardly be wise. Bill Stoneley, then. She had decided on the plane back to Moscow that it would have to be him but had second thoughts as she overheard him in the hall, so cheerful and acutely observant beneath the superficial bonhomie. There was too much at stake. Bill had too many tangential connections, knew too many people and was too willing to trade information. Ellis Wachorne, perhaps – but no. Too close to Fielding. Though Wachorne had been his usual friendly self. He and Flora had invited her over to dinner, and it was a lovely evening, just the three of them. Ellis allowed himself to be teased mercilessly about his sporting prowess, his love of cricket and strange obsession with his grandfather's sporting blazers. Funnily enough, she'd been right about him liking Housman. But she had resisted the temptation to confide in him.

No. She had a moral and patriotic duty to pass on what she had but it could not happen in Moscow. Hers was a deep cover mission. She had no choice but to wait until she got back to London. Even then, she knew she would hold back, or rather tone down, the fullest extent of the Russian's world view. That was too all-encompassing, too frightening to contemplate, even if only a sliver of it were true.

So she waited, head down, waiting for the axe to fall. Rory kept his distance, though she noticed how he watched her whenever they were in the same room. It was all too complicated to unravel. Best to leave it. They were but ships that had passed in the night.

The Minister returned to Moscow, but still she held out. Nothing happened. For now, Rory was clearly keeping her confidence. She worked diligently for Waller and typed Bill Stoneley's lengthy reports without comment. She rose above Burville's sniping and avoided Tony Fielding, though she spent more time with Ellis and Flora Wachorne, finding she enjoyed Flora's good humour and inventive cooking very much indeed.

It was still Sonia who unsettled her most. Sonia, who should have had no further hold over her, who shot her knowing looks in the corridors and on the office bus and across the same old grind of forced social gatherings. Lois stiffened whenever she saw her. Eric had been posted back to London at the end of September, so it would not be long before Sonia followed. That was the way it worked in the foreign service: time passed and washed difficult relationships away on its tide; you just had to sit tight and wait. It occurred to her that this was also the way traitorous connections were missed. But instinct told her that the woman would not depart without some petty pay-back. Every day that passed without incident was a blessed relief.

Of course, it was always going to be Nan who picked up on the distress Lois fought so hard to hide. Cool, calculating Nan. It could hardly be otherwise, even with the comfort of individual space they afforded each other and the lack of probing personal questions that seemed to have been agreed without formal declaration.

One quiet evening in the flat, Nan handed Lois a cup of coffee she hadn't asked for, moved the book Lois was conspicuously failing to read, and sat down on the sofa next to her. For all the homeliness of her gesture, the older woman held her spine straight and tense, touching neither arm nor back-rest.

'I know what's going on,' she said, brusque as ever.

Lois looked down at the cup in her clenched hand, not daring to react. What, exactly, could Nan know – and how?

Nan kept a rigid posture even as she sighed. 'It's the way of the world. Maybe it won't always be, let's hope not. But for now, it just is.'

A terrible pause.

'It's the role of us women to do all the work and not get the credit. Yet we're braver than the men in ways they simply can't comprehend, being so sure in their disdainful, stupid assumptions.'

Lois nodded, still uncertain where this was leading. She liked Nan. On one unspoken level, she trusted her implicitly. She respected the perception produced by her almost uncanny powers of observation. On the other hand, that perception was the greatest danger. Yet Nan hadn't cranked up the record player. The room was so quiet they could hear the clock ticking. She would not say anything that should not be overheard. That silence was a bond of trust between them.

'They have not the first clue about so much, especially when it comes to half the human race,' went on Nan. 'That's

261

our strength, being a mystery to them, and remember that it frightens them. Never underestimate yourself – or overestimate them, though I don't suppose you do.'

At last, Lois smiled.

'I'll watch your back, don't you worry.'

Lois felt her eyes water and closed them tightly.

'Now, there's a soothing Brahms concerto on the radio I wouldn't mind listening to. How would that suit you?'

'Very well, I think,' said Lois.

'That's the spirit.'

Sure enough, the inevitable happened on the day Sonia announced her farewell party. Lois was summoned to Head of Chancery's private office and Sonia was hanging around in the corridor with another of her knowing smirks. The doll's features were lit with malice as she stood and watched her knock on Burville's door.

'Time to face the music, Lois. You'll need a good story now,' she hissed.

Lois took a deep breath, stood taller, head up, shoulders back, and ignored her.

Inside the room, Burville affected an air of venomous boredom.

'Once more I have been given some very disturbing information about you, Miss Vale,' he began.

And once more also, Fielding and Wachorne were present, loose and limber and ready to move as players on a substitute bench, silently watching every movement.

Burville released an inquisitorial stare. Lois fought to still her thoughts and remain calm. Vienna again? Sukhumi? The meeting with Pal on the Volga? She would not react. *Don't even allow yourself to feel angry at Sonia. Let them deal the cards. Don't pre-suppose anything.*

'According to Sonia Capell, you have acted suspiciously since your arrival,' began Burville. 'When you shared a flat with her, she alleges you consistently broke rules about going out alone and behaved in an odd manner when you were together in the apartment – also during your trip to Vienna.'

Silence.

'So, what have you to say?' Burville looked her up and down in a way that was calculated to insult.

'I don't know what I have to answer to. It's no secret that I found Sonia impossible to live with and moved out to share with someone else the first chance I got.'

'That may well be the case, but the fact is, she has made some very serious allegations against you.'

Another discomforting silence. It was abruptly shattered by a raucous blast of loud military music activated by a switch on the desk.

'Who was the Russian you met on the Moscow Express during your inbound journey?' demanded Burville. 'You spoke for a while in your compartment. You did not report the encounter as you were required to on arrival.'

'It was a simple misunderstanding.'

'That's not quite true, is it, Miss Vale?'

Still Fielding and Wachorne did not move. Neither took their eyes from her face.

'I have checked with Boyd Givens at the Canadian Embassy, whom I believe you know,' went on Burville. 'It was he who told Sonia that you were seen meeting a Russian on the train by one of his compatriots en route back to Moscow. Interestingly, the same man was seen speaking to your friend Johann Dreschler in Vienna.'

She shook her head slowly. Had Bill Stoneley been consulted, had he said anything?

'I can't answer for Johann Dreschler, and he is no longer

here. All I can tell you is that a Russian man barged into my compartment on the train. He was apparently as surprised to see me in there as I was to see him. He apologised and we attempted to make ourselves understood for a few minutes, then he left.'

'Except…' Burville pulled at his cuffs with studied carefulness. 'If this man was who we think he is, he is a military officer who speaks good English.'

'I can only tell you what happened from my point of view.'

'You should have reported it. Why didn't you?'

'If I should have done, I'm sorry. But nothing happened. It didn't seem important enough to report.'

'I should have been the judge of that,' he snapped. 'You're hiding something, Miss Vale. Sonia may well be a vindictive piece of work, but she's no fool and she's right about that.'

'I just didn't want anyone to think badly of me, that I made a fuss over nothing.'

'Did you see Johann Dreschler while you were by the Black Sea?'

That rocked her. How much did Fielding know?

'I did not,' she was able to answer truthfully. 'Why would you think that? I was with Rory, as you know.'

'What does the name Zhigunov mean to you?'

'I don't know the name.'

He and Fielding exchanged glances. 'We have been watching you, Lois.'

'Why would you do that?'

Fielding crossed his arms and spoke for the first time. His voice was all reason.

'If you confess now, it will be better for all of us.'

How often had she prepared herself mentally for this moment? She made a rapid calculation of what partial truths she could afford to confess. Zhigunov had never been part of the plan. Could she cloak her true mission by admitting her role in the handover at Sukhumi? If she came clean about being dragged into it by Johann, would their connection face further scrutiny and eventual revelation of its purpose? There was no way out but to sacrifice a portion of her involvement.

The silence was shattered as the door banged open.

Sonia burst in shouting, face streaming with tears.

'I am not a thief! You set me up and it's all your fault they think I'm mad! You've poisoned everyone against me, Lois!'

A kerfuffle in the doorway revealed Bill Stoneley right behind her, evidently trying to hold her back.

'She's not what she seems,' Sonia howled. 'Surely you must be able to see that! She writes a diary and half of it just isn't true. She put in it that you,' she looked at Burville, 'had a passion for lady acrobats and *he*,' she turned to Wachorne, 'offered to hang around backstage at the Moscow State Circus with you! And all sorts of other nonsense about people here, like you,' now she was addressing Fielding, 'who apparently wanted to have an affair with her – oh!' She clasped her hand to her mouth. 'I wouldn't have – but she used to leave it lying around everywhere.'

Shaken to the core, Lois stood her ground and shook her head slowly in baffled denial.

'Sonia, you're not well,' said Stoneley kindly.

Sonia was screaming ever louder, directed now at Lois. 'They're saying I'm having a breakdown and I'm being sent home early, thanks to you. You're a bitch! A stinking, lying bitch!' She lunged at Lois and caught her cheek with a sharp fingernail.

Fielding and Wachorne moved as one, but Stoneley had already enveloped Sonia in an avuncular hug that would have been impossible to shake off. He caught Lois's eye long enough to reassure her that he had her back, too.

The doctor was called. It was true, then. Sonia really was

having a breakdown, just as she had claimed to Lois months before. The Moscow Twitch had claimed another victim. Lois would later assert that she had thought Sonia's antics were bids for attention but had later urged her to consult the embassy doctor. Rory was able to recount how unstable Sonia was in the flat with Lois and how kind Lois was to her despite provocation. The new girl who had taken her place in the apartment was clearly relieved Sonia was leaving and quietly asked Lois whether any of her possessions had gone missing while she had lived there.

The inquisition was abandoned; Lois had managed by a whisker to avoid admitting anything to Burville and perversely she had Sonia herself to thank for that. But sooner or later the hammer would fall. Each subsequent day was an agony of wondering whether it was imminent. Fielding knew what he was doing; each day that passed was another twist to the knife that would break her nerve. Yet the recall did not come. There were no more questions from Fielding and Wachorne. Bill Stoneley sought her out, but it was to make sure she was all right (the only one who bothered) and to tell her what Sonia herself never had: that although Sonia's background was wealthy and well-connected, her father had lost most of his money after the war investing in ill-conceived schemes and the country estate had been sold; her mother had lost her mind and was in an institution for the unstable.

'Sonia should never have been sent here,' said Stoneley. 'But she has an uncle in the service, and he pulled strings.'

Rory left Moscow in mid October without saying goodbye. The only surprise was that his posting had lasted so long.

For Lois, there was no option but to go on, the only way she could get out intact. The days and weeks moved like stone. It took all her courage to keep going, waiting for news. Finally, not one but two telegrams arrived, the first long anticipated, the other utterly unforeseen. It comprised a single question:

Will you marry me?

26

Sunday, November 2, 1958

Arrived home; everybody at the station, incl. Ralph & Harold. London never looked so shabby and soot-stained, and I was never so glad to see it.

Home looks very clean and bright, and newly decorated.

Mum & I went to church in the evening.

Tuesday, November 4, 1958

Swan & Edgar's, Regent St. Bought two suits. Reckon I earned them!

Reported to F.O. Miss Harcourt really couldn't have been nicer. A few loose ends to tie up. On leave til November 30, bliss.

Lunch with Peter in Piccadilly, same as the day before I left for Russia. Afterwards, walked the long way back through St James's Park to Charing Cross. So much to think about my head started hurting, but walking helped. Nice to have no one over my shoulder watching my every move.

The meeting with Miss Harcourt went much as expected.

A detailed debriefing covered the salient events and her impressions of the personalities at the Moscow Embassy. The older woman took notes and asked questions. She made no comment after Lois's account of Tony Fielding. Nor was she noticeably moved by the discovery of the wires in the chimney leading to a listening device in Chancery.

'Your letters were a little short on detail,' she said, 'and you made some rash decisions. You were not expected to go that far, not in your position.'

Even with Miss Harcourt, it seemed, women were supposed to know their place.

'How long exactly did the partnership with Johann last?'

'Until the end of our trip to Vienna in late May, effectively.'

'How did you feel about that?'

'Let down, certainly.'

'Not disappointed to leave Russia before your year was up, I take it?'

'Not in the slightest.'

A half-smile intimated a mutual understanding of the risks Lois had taken. Miss Harcourt squared her shoulders. The glimmer of empathy was extinguished almost as soon as it appeared.

'You impressed the Minister. His report states that your work and conduct was exemplary.'

'Good to know, thank you.'

'We'll see what Peter has to say, but I thought it best in the circumstances to have this prepared.' She handed Lois a letter, typewritten on small-sized blue-grey paper. It was a declaration to be signed that she would continue to be bound by the Official Secrets Act, even after she left the service.

Lois read it carefully under a penetrating gaze from across the desk, signed it and took her copy.

'By the way.' Miss Harcourt opened a drawer. 'This arrived for you through another friend of mine. About a month ago. I thought best to hand it over in person.'

Lois glanced at the handwriting on the envelope and put it, unread, into her handbag.

On Whitehall, in the magnificent shadow of the Foreign Office, Lois checked her watch and the scudding clouds above and, deciding to walk, strode out purposefully. Outside the Criterion restaurant on Piccadilly, she stopped for a moment or two to smile at its entrance awning, so like a giant plate embedded in the building, then turned to its immediate left and entered the Underground station. Ten yards into the soot-scented passage was a door marked *Works, Private*. She pushed the buzzer, waited a few seconds, and gained admittance.

Two flights of stairs brought her to a landing and another door at which she knocked three times. She was permitted to enter a narrow corridor that led into a splendid high-windowed room looking out over Piccadilly Circus. It was furnished in the style she imagined would be found in the gentlemen's clubs of St James's: oil portraits on the walls, a long polished table over which hung a candelabra.

The Peter Committee was already assembled: Pearson, Esterby, Trenchard, Ellingwood and Robinson. Or rather, the men known by those names. Who knew what their real names were? Robinson she had last seen at the country house in Shropshire where she was taught to fight communism, but the others were characterless, featureless blanks to her, the faceless men of the Establishment.

Robinson came forward and shook her hand. 'You have done well, Miss Vale.'

Meagre though this praise was, it seemed to stir a distinct undercurrent across the room, however. Foreheads and mouths twitched. Smiling in the face of opposition, he motioned for her to sit to his right. There the honour stopped, it seemed, for the table was not set for lunch sent round from the Criterion as last time but held two plates of sandwiches. Lettuce curled like escaping caterpillars and egg and cress seeped. The inquisition was either to be relatively civilised or a long one.

'So, how did you find our friend Waller, then?' she was asked by one of the suits.

'A good boss – and a good man,' replied Lois.

'He worked you too hard, I suppose?'

'No harder than anyone else, or, indeed, himself.'

'Nothing untoward there.'

It wasn't quite a question, but it might have been.

'No, of course not. I have a great deal of respect for him.'

'Good, good…'

The Ambassador came next under consideration. Surely an honourable man. If he had a failing, it was overwork. It was said he was the man who had stopped Philby from being appointed head of the Secret Service some five or more years earlier.

'Might be a magnificent blind, of course,' Robinson put in. 'Know him personally, believe I can vouch for him. But I could be wrong. Any of us can be wrong, and it's the refusing to accept that possibility that has brought us to where we are now.'

'Burville, too. Good man under pressure,' said one of the others. An assumption not a question.

'Rather prone to flap, actually,' said Lois. Burville deserved that.

Eyebrows raised. 'Was he indeed…' smirked a possible rival.

Vere Sinclair. John Linton. Both gaining experience still, but on course for the very top. Intellectually snobbish, perhaps socially, too. But not guilty of hating enough to be a traitor. Too much to lose, they agreed.

The young intelligence man with his nice wife, then? Hardly. Not a sliver of a doubt about them.

Bill Stoneley, a one-off, no? But what had he unearthed? Railway timetables and the price of eggs. The pleasant new housing developments and road building projects. Open source intelligence, open to interpretation.

Genial laughter.

'Open-minded about the Soviet system, though,' said Lois. 'It doesn't make him a communist. If you wanted someone to cultivate Zhigunov, the two of them could probably find common ground and a basis for trust.'

'Noted,' said Robinson.

'So,' said the man who wanted to get on with it and apparently knew the least. 'Brass tacks. There's no leak in the Moscow Embassy.'

'It's probable, is it not,' said Lois, 'that the radio receiver and transmitter found in the Ambassador's office linking to Chancery is the leak you were looking for? You do know about this? I thought the news of that discovery went straight back to London.'

'It did. It was discussed at length. The question remained: was that *it*?'

'Best to assume that it was not,' said the avuncular Robinson. Perhaps a man in his position would always err on one more layer of deception. He had dispensed with the sludge-green tweed jacket and woollen tie of his Shropshire persona and wore a dull suit, but his ruddy face, wide shoulders and large hands were still every bit the country squire down from his country estate. Now and then he gave Lois an encouraging glance.

'Very small fry,' persisted his impatient colleague, with the air of a man who had cancelled a decent lunch to be with inferior company.

Robinson took off his owl spectacles and polished them with a napkin. 'Not the point, surely.'

'Fed up with hearing about Philby, too. That business has all been dealt with, hasn't it?' drawled someone, affecting boredom.

It was the same old inertia, the same confidence in the familiar. Good *enough*, like crumpets and weak tea. For all the talk, did they *want* to find anything that might disturb their cosy world? They would get their "K"s like Sir Duncan Mountbeech and enjoy the deference for a while until they entered a distinguished retirement. That was part of the game too. You wouldn't get one if you rocked the boat, upset the wrong people.

Maybe this was the whole point of the exercise, thought Lois. Go through the motions, find nothing, and cover their backs. A depressing thought.

Which was why she was so taken aback by what came next. One of the committee, until now unobtrusive and silent, reared up and launched a spitting tirade at her.

'You talk about Zhigunov, you went to Sukhumi! Of all the irresponsible, damaging, hot-headed, idiotic pranks!' he began. He proceeded to tear her character and motivations apart, batting away Robinson's protests. She had endangered, if not outright ruined, six months work by Head of Station in Moscow, by the Office in London and select associates in Washington evaluating his bona fides, a painstaking process. How else were they to know whether Avrely Zhigunov was top-of-the-line Soviet smoke, pure-grade hokum, or whether he was the genuine article? Quite apart from the sheer stupidity of the risks she took, it was unprecedented, *unprecedented*, what she had done... and on and on.

From below came the sounds of ordinary life: a news vendor shouting on the bustling pavement, the squeal of brakes on buses, car horns blaring. Lois sat speechlessly, taking in every word, every background noise. When the rant was over, even the other men seemed stunned by it.

A terrible pause yawned. Lois waited for further recrimination from another direction, but it did not come.

'Let's talk about Zhigunov,' said a man with gravitas.

'I'm assuming you have the photographic material I sent,' said Lois, sounding distant to herself. *Don't give any of them the satisfaction of seeing you break.*

'It's being evaluated.'

'We really need to see the original material. Either the Russians were setting him up – or setting *us* up.'

'You don't have it?' asked Lois.

'We're looking into that. The images you sent weren't of the highest grade. Amateurish, frankly. Why didn't you use the Minox?'

'Let Miss Vale start at the beginning, please,' Robinson commanded.

They would hear her out. She gave her account of the intercept on the train, the Vienna trip to try to establish whether he was genuine, the concern that those responsible at the embassy were not taking the opportunity seriously.

'You and Dreschler were watched in Vienna, you know,' one of them interrupted.

She had not known.

'Led our Vienna station a merry dance, too, tying up resources better deployed elsewhere.'

No wonder Fielding had been in Burville's room when she was reprimanded on her return. They must have known everything, would have been waiting for her to incriminate herself – so why had they not pursued the matter?

Finally, they came to the meeting in Sukhumi.

'Made life bloody difficult for Fielding,' said the man who had shouted at her. 'No one thought you would take it on yourself to go that far.'

'I realise that now.'

'Nevertheless, it seems Zhigunov took to you,' broke in one of the others. 'He had no reason to think you weren't working with Fielding. He doesn't seem to have twigged you'd gone off-side trying to do Fielding's job for him.'

'It was a singular position in which we had placed Miss Vale,' added Robinson. 'She more than fulfilled her brief.'

'Indeed,' said a more reasonable voice.

'Does Zhigunov want to defect?' demanded someone else crossly. 'Why doesn't the man just defect and put us all out of our misery?'

Lois caught Robinson's eye, and he nodded. 'He says he wants to work for us in place,' she said. 'He believes that if we know more about the Russians and the true state of their military, there will be a balance between us that will hold the peace.'

'Is he genuine, though? You met him, talked to him. We have to assume you have some abilities or—'

'Dear boy, *please*,' interjected Robinson.

'I think he is genuine.' She did not want to say too much, yet it was vital to convey his most urgent message. 'He has deeply held views about parity between nations,' careful now, 'what we have in common, not what divides us. He told me,' safer ground, 'that much of what the Soviet people are told, as well as what we hear, is untrue. Khrushchev is far from winning the bomb and missile race. Though he is not, as claimed, melting down obsolete weapons to make more tractors, they are struggling to catch up using the German-trained scientists in Sukhumi. The Soviets are posturing on the world stage but are years behind the western powers. They go to world atomic conferences in the hope of gleaning any new information they can from the West.'

'Ah, yes.' Her interlocutor flicked through a report in front of him. 'Vienna. Another of your... initiatives.'

Lois dug her heels in, refusing to be cowed. Not after all she had been through.

'Let's face it, you wouldn't have sent me to Moscow if you hadn't been desperate.'

'So far, we think Zhigunov's genuine,' Robinson told the committee in a mollifying tone. 'Fielding's going through everything. Though now the Americans aren't convinced.'

'Not all Americans,' said Lois. 'There's a faction that believes in him. Coincidentally, or not, the same faction that remains convinced that Philby passed material to the KGB while he was in Washington.'

'Zhigunov, then – old warhorse or weathervane?' This question was addressed to the table at large.

They could not agree.

Fielding was a safe pair of hands in Moscow, and he would untangle the truth. Lois was a reckless young woman who had probably been fooled by this Russian. For a few minutes, they spoke about her between themselves as if she were not there.

'According to the latest from Fielding and Wachorne,' said the man with gravitas, 'the Russian does seem to know something. He's pointed the finger at a certain clerk at the Moscow Embassy, for instance. No longer in post, thank God—'

'Vassall,' cut in Lois. 'I put that in my immediate report.'

The startled looks around the table were a picture.

'Zhigunov told me. It was a classic homosexual blackmail case, information for money or the KGB releases the film. I thought that was it, at first – the answer. Vassall worked for the Naval Attaché and was lonely and unhappy his last months in Russia. Maybe he's still part of the puzzle. Does he still work at the Admiralty? Zhigunov claims he does, also that Russia isn't lacking spies in US and UK's nuclear development programmes.'

Hasty notes were made.

Lois picked up her water glass and put it down. No one had

eaten the sandwiches. They sat on the plates like monuments to ordinary life. She was not finished. She had to speak, for her own sake. She needed conformation of her conclusions, raw and painful as they were.

It was the meeting on the train, she said, that bothered her. Was bothering her still. The exact words the Russian had used. 'I know exactly who you are.' She had taken it for granted at the time that he had used his rank to check the passport records at the border crossing from Finland. She had seen him there, watching as her luggage was checked by customs. But what if that was an entirely wrong assumption? What if he knew who she was because he had been told by some person unknown on the inside of the British operation, either in Moscow or in London? Knew *exactly* who she was.

It was the devices – the brooch and the spy camera – that she had either not used or that had not worked when needed but had told her something, she explained. Each routine job, each conversation, each look had an unsettling duality. Inversions. Contortions. *Trust no one, only Johann.*

'We can't see what we don't *want* to see,' said Lois. 'That's what keeps the lie going. Why the same old mistakes are repeated.'

A subliminal force crackled across the table like static.

It was true of love, it was true of organisations, and it was true of nations. Zhigunov was incontrovertibly right about one thing. There were bad intentions lurking everywhere, hidden among the good, clothed with supposedly good intentions. Good people who could not conceive they were used for outcomes they were never supposed to understand.

'It was Johann, wasn't it?' she said. 'You wanted me to watch Johann, find out what he knew and which side he was really working on.'

Right up to this point, life could have gone on as before.

After it, there was thick silence broken only by the muffled traffic noise of Piccadilly below. A troubled shuffle of papers. A throat was cleared. No denials.

The world shifted on its axis as she had feared it might. Lois felt herself shrink. She was the size and value of a dust mote. Not even floating free in sunlight but lying spent in a grimy corner. She lowered her eyes to the silky carpet as if it might anchor her and steady the tilt. She had always known it was a dirty game, but this confirmation knocked her off balance. They had used her from start to finish. Not wanting to believe it themselves, they had requisitioned her innocent belief in him. How far would her trust lead, and what might it reveal? Johann, worldly and handsome enough to tempt her. Who knew what kind of fool she had made of herself by falling for him.

'He's not German, is he? An Austrian, I knew that from the start.'

'Austro-Hungarian,' said Robinson. 'His mother was Hungarian, he had family there, though he was born and brought up over the border, east of Vienna. He worked for us for years, ever since Berlin post-war. A perfect friend afterwards in Frankfurt and where the foreign desk sent him – or we suggested he put in for. He went rogue after the Soviets clamped down on the Hungarian uprising in '56.

'He was close to cousins – real cousins, his own – in Budapest who were part of the revolt against Soviet rule; one of them was killed. He thought he'd be in a position to influence us to help, but we were still smarting from Suez. The Hungarian rebels had always been told by us, by the CIA, by Radio Free Europe that we had their backs, but in the event… Dreschler believed he was left fighting not only communism, but those who had let all freedom-loving Hungarians down. He was going to take what he could, and leverage it, whether to the Russians or the Hungarian patriots, to get any advantage, to put on any pressure he could. He was playing both sides.'

'And I proved it,' murmured Lois.

She pictured Johann in Vienna. His flare of anger at the Prater with Sonia, the discussion about Hungarian refugees that seemed to come out of nowhere. His absent, unaccounted hours, and subsequent disappearance. The newspaper report filed from Budapest. All the oddities aligned. The execution of Nagy along with three other Hungarian revolutionaries in June must have hit him hard. He must have known what was coming, maybe even tried to make a difference.

'The question is, did Dreschler see the material from Zhigunov?' asked Robinson calmly, as if he were making plans for a day off. Kindly country uncle he may have been, he was still a hunter and a ruthless shot.

'I left it in the agreed dead drop. I have no idea if he ever collected it.'

A frisson went down the table like a light breeze. Papers were rustled again, and hair had to be smoothed.

That was why the Service had kept Zhigunov at arm's length. Of course. She was surprised to find herself relieved, even as she was being turned inside out and shaken, that at least it all made sense. If they didn't trust Johann, then naturally they would be suspicious of the Russian he was trying to bring to the table. Fielding and Moscow Station had been watching and waiting to see how the story ran.

Robinson massaged his jaw and winced as if he had toothache. 'Lois, you should know that Johann Dreschler is reported killed,' he said.

The room tilted. She failed to strangle the rawness of her protest. A horrible noise came from her throat before she regained control.

'When?' she managed to whisper.

'Conflicting reports, I'm afraid. A few months ago, it seems.'

She stared at the confident men in their suits, at the wilting sandwiches. All suddenly unreal.

'Where?'

'Some say in Budapest. But it could have been in Georgia.'

'The Russians?'

The men around the table were cold and silent as snow in darkness. Once again, in her mind's eye, Lois saw Tony Fielding come out of the chemist's shop in Sukhumi. Conflicting reports. Such a wonderful catch-all for the covering of tracks.

Did Miss Harcourt know? If so, why had she not said anything to prepare her for this? Lois felt sick.

'Neither of you found any evidence of a loose link at the Moscow Embassy, though,' reiterated one man. 'Some welcome news, at least.'

'Loose ends to tie up,' said another. 'Long game, I'm sure you appreciate that.'

A wave of fear broke over Lois, fiercer than any that had engulfed her in Moscow. Was this the best they could do? The mess and muddle and obfuscation and the vested interests and wrong horses backed, lies told and histories rewritten. She thought of the German nuclear scientists who were divided into teams for the long game, some to play for America and some for Russia. What if Zhigunov was right and the problem was too big, too far-reaching, to be resolved? '*To find truth is hard, but to discover what to do with it… that is hardest.*'

And if Zhigunov was mad, a fraud, or both, then she had been played and defeated by all sides.

The man with gravitas (who had said the least) assumed control of the meeting and formally declared that MI6 was wrapping up this irregular operation.

'We achieved our aim, and that must be counted a success. As ever, not quite to plan, but a solid effort.'

She ought to mention the one strip of negatives that would have remained out of Johann's reach even if he had collected from the cathedral dead drop; the insurance policy because, by then, she knew she could no longer trust him completely. The photographs she had taken, for the same reason, were the only remaining proof that Zhigunov had actually passed any material. *As if it would make any difference*, she thought bitterly. She so nearly told them, but...

'No, no, no! It was a farce!' burst out the irascible man. 'Why do these operations always turn into farce? And what are you planning to do with *her*? She can't go running around knowing what she knows.' He turned to Lois, fury now unrestrained. 'What in hell did you think you were doing? This is what happens when we have women—'

'Enough,' cut in Robinson.

Lois straightened her back to accept the onslaught, then realised that, like Zhigunov, she had nothing left to lose. Johann was dead. Dead and a traitor who had used her, just like all these men.

'So what would you have done with a woman like me?' she asked pertly, just about keeping control. 'What's the usual fate? Will I be sent to a nunnery? Or perhaps you could marry me to the Service and I'll take a vow of silence.'

'It shouldn't come to that, Miss Vale,' said Robinson.

'That's settled, then,' said the man with gravitas, as if his thoughts were already somewhere else.

On the familiar clattering train home, Lois sat opposite a young mother with a small girl. The child was chewing a velvet rabbit. An elderly couple by the window discussed the matinee performance they had just seen. As smoke-blackened buildings passed in the lowering dusk, she took out the letter from Johann. It was dated September 14, the day he had sent her to meet Zhigunov in Sukhumi. No doubt Miss Harcourt had read it, perhaps more than once, while it was in her possession. But in the end she had asked no questions, and for that, if only that, Lois found a grain of remaining respect for her.

Forgive me, Schatzi! The world is dark, darker than the depths of pine forests on the mountains or the spread of an eagle's wing. I send you my heart from far away. I shall remember, wherever I am, whatever I become. And I shall greet you in spirit in Zell when I am alone. Always yours, Johann.

> *I am too alone in the world, and yet not alone enough*
> *to make every moment holy.*
> *I am too tiny in this world, and not tiny enough*
> *just to lie before you like a thing.*
> *When something is coming near,*
> *I want to be with those who know secret things*
> *or else alone. Rilke*

'Lois? Lois Vale?'

The train had stopped at London Bridge. A wave of new passengers broke over their cosy compartment.

'Budge up, room for a little one!' It was Hilda Perkins. Wide face, big lips. Long-ago classmate at primary school, garrulous on her way home to Lewisham where she now lived with a husband and two children. Mother, still keeping well, thank you, was looking after the nippers. 'Remember Jean Doughty? On the way back from seeing her, lunch and a good natter. She's part-time with the Post Office now. Haven't seen you for ages, I must say! What have you been up to?'

'I've been working away –I fancied a change.'

'Where've you been, then?'

'Shropshire.'

'Didn't work out?'

It must have been showing on her face, all she'd been through. Lois clutched the folded letter tightly.

'It was all right. Rather dull, actually. Seems I'm better off in the old Smoke after all.'

'Nowhere better, eh? That's what I always say. Something in your eye, dearie?'

'Yes… speck of something, I expect.' Lois pulled out her handkerchief and dabbed at a tear that had welled quite unconsciously. 'That's better.'

Hilda prattled on – Jean had been to the Isle of Wight, the little ones grew out of their clothes so fast, don't go to that new dentist on Queen's Road, terrible puller-out, he was – until the train drew in to St John's station. Thank goodness Hilda no longer lived around the corner from Lois's mum and dad.

Lois alighted from the train, knowing for certain now that she was walking into a world forever altered. Orange lamplight glistened on the familiar homely platform, at the same time infinitely strange. Plane trees marked with faded white rings waist-high on their trunks stood sentinel either side of the roadway as she walked home from the station. Golden leaves rustled under her feet. On the main road, a sprinkling of people waited patiently for buses, secure in their own urban routines.

She left them behind, took a turning past bomb-ruined houses, still utterly desolate, claimed only by rampant weeds. Someone else turned the corner too; she heard the footsteps, firm and regular. Instinctively, she stiffened. She slackened her pace to allow the person behind to overtake her, preferring to see an anonymous fellow in front than to sense an unknown entity behind. But no figure appeared. The footsteps changed their rhythm to match hers. She crossed over the road, listening all the while. A streetlamp flung her giant shadow forward over the crown of the road.

Whoever it was hesitated a moment, then followed. Her heart raced. She began to hurry. She dared not look round as the footsteps came nearer. No one else in sight. Naked trees, dark and indifferent. From far off on the night air came the heavy gasps of shunting railway engines: expiring, echoing, too far off to be of comfort. She heard him panting, almost on her shoulder. Finally, she looked round. He lifted something towards her. She stayed perfectly still. She was caught.

'You dropped your glove down the road, Miss.'

It was already behind her, the possibility of a future that had briefly shone with promise. She felt it viscerally, as she stood trembling on the pavement, damp face, shoulders heaving. All that she had risked – it had been for nothing. She was a stone spat out of the machine, too small to stop its iron mechanism, the folly of her ambition, to have dared to offer herself only to be sacrificed and forgotten, crushed by its inner workings. To have been in the room where history was made – or was agreed, rather – was a burden not a privilege.

What now for her and those like her, who had seen into the black heart of power? Who had sight of what could not now be unseen. Who knew the intricacies of a truth that might forever be untold. She had not got out intact with her copy of the small blue document she had signed, she had lost twice over. Gone was the satisfaction of achieving something of importance. Gone was the quiet recognition from the Service and her colleagues, perhaps even the recognition in history when it emerged from secret archives. That would have been enough for her. She would forever pay the price of trying.

She went over and stood by a dark wall. Composed herself before going home. Thought of her parents waiting, the table set for tea: Mum who had been so proud of her working abroad, a credit to the family, and so much more worried about her than she had ever let on; Dad who had quietly come to terms with no longer being able to protect her. She would never be able to reveal what she had done, not even to them.

Tuesday, November 25, 1958

Read Rilke, again, all afternoon, but yet for once my mind, despite all calculation, could make no sense of it. Apart from one whole line that I really understood, it was just words on the page.

Rory came down from Lancashire and made a good impression at home.

I said "Yes".

Twelve Years Later

On a biting February evening, a woman in a fake fox-fur coat walked with purposeful strides through the anonymous residential streets of suburban south-east London. The coat was perfectly warm, still more than serviceable. At Bexleyheath railway station she caught a rattling, dust-caked train to Charing Cross, where she had arranged to meet an old friend.

Lois Kendalmoor: housewife and mother of two young daughters, on a rare night out. Just an ordinary woman, still quietly attractive in her early forties, sitting in a train carriage lost in her own thoughts. She was coming to a decision about the diploma course in psychology and sociology she had been taking at evening class for the past two years; despite consistent high marks, praise and encouragement from the lecturer, she thought she would probably not bother taking the final examination. She had enjoyed the course, but what would be the point? She wouldn't be able to use it. Sooner or later she would be abroad again, taken for granted by the Office as usual, unpaid support to her husband.

When Lois Vale returned from Moscow in late 1958, she had had to give up her job on marriage. That was the way it was for women in the Service. The story of the telegrams, the welcome command back to London and the proposal, and her reply, "tentatively yes, but many questions", had become ingrained in the version of their history they gave to family and friends, like the romance trailed by the KGB and the balmy September holiday by the Black Sea.

Two months after their January wedding, they were posted to the desert town of Kuwait. At twenty-five, Rory was the youngest vice-consul ever appointed, or so the family legend ran, and had the distinction of somehow quelling an uprising in the Persian Gulf, which gave their houseboy great status among his peers in the local marketplace, though Rory was considered too young for the official recognition mooted by London. By all reckoning, they had a happy enough time in Kuwait. Their first daughter was born while they were there, and another followed on their posting back to London. They scraped together every penny they had for a deposit on the house in Bexleyheath; not only their own home, but a sensible toehold in the property market while they would be abroad. Then they were off again to Peking and the Cultural Revolution, then duller years in Europe when more exciting things may or may not have been going on under the surface. Their little girls' main playmates were the children of a high-ranking CIA man.

Despite the cold wars that played out privately between them, the marriage had lasted somehow. But how keenly she sometimes resented being taken for granted as a wife! Not so much by her husband as by the Office for all the moves she orchestrated, all the entertaining she did, all the support she gave him with how to handle difficult personalities, and the welfare work she did helping the younger wives cope, all unpaid and almost always unrecognised.

Arguments were normally conducted at night and in barely controlled hisses, often while one of them was running a bath. The bugs in the walls had been replaced by the avid ears of two small girls.

'I saved you!' he once flung at her. 'If we hadn't got married… kept you in the fold…'

It all happened too fast. In the moment, the maelstrom of despair and disappointment, fury and, yes, excitement, she hardly had a chance to consider the decisions she was taking. Living with those choices was hard sometimes. Was it the five-year age gap between them, or were they even compatible personalities? She wished he were more finished, more cosmopolitan. She still thought sadly of Johann, his worldliness and panache, and tried not to remember his ultimate betrayal. But she kept a photograph of Rory at Sukhumi in her handbag: he stood on the beach, one of the strange Soviet piers in the background, looking relaxed and handsome as a film star in a white shirt, collar up in the breeze that lifted his hair.

The train wheezed gingerly over the river and slid into Charing Cross station. Lois alighted and moved briskly past the ticket collector and across the concourse. The big clock over the central WHSmith stall showed two minutes to seven o'clock. Bang on time. She walked out onto the Strand and immediately turned right into the station hotel. Straight past the desk and up the curving staircase to the first floor bar to look for the usual spot. She had been meeting Elsie here for years – convenient for them both.

Lois made her way over to the tables they favoured by the big front window. One had a single occupant but the other was free. She was about to claim it, when she stopped in her tracks. The woman at the other table turned and looked up.

'Nan Trusloe!' cried Lois.

So it was.

'Hello, Lois.' Nan stood up.

'What are the odds? I can't believe it!'

Beaming, Lois took in her old flatmate's appearance: the salt and pepper hair and the deeper frown lines. Still the same old Nan. Though the knee-length crimplene dress and matching jacket, all blue and purple swirls, was a startling departure from her habitual Moscow tweeds.

'How have you been?' asked Nan.

'Oh, not so bad. Home tour at the moment, a much-needed few years in London,' said Lois. She saw Nan look at her ring finger. 'The girls' schooling has been a bit hit and miss.'

'Daughters!' Nan grinned in the old complicit way.

'Two daughters, eleven and eight. What about you – still with the Office?'

'Still in harness.'

Lois assumed that meant that, like Elsie, Nan had never married. There were times when Lois wondered whether she should have stayed single and carried on working. Where might she be now? At least she would have been a person in her own right. But she loved her daughters profoundly, and if her husband got all the credit at work, she had made her decision and learnt to live with it.

'I'm meeting Elsie Glover,' said Lois. 'We were in The Hague together. Ever come across her?' They would be about the same age.

'I know Elsie. In fact—'

'Don't know where she's got to. She's usually a stickler for time.'

'Actually, Elsie's not coming,' said Nan.

'Oh? I confirmed with her only this morning – ah, I see.'

A waiter arrived. 'Two G&Ts, better make them doubles,' said Nan decisively. 'Sit down, Lois.'

Lois obeyed. 'Care to tell me what this is all about?'

'All in good time. How's Rory?'

'Fine. Hates the commute. Hates not having the allowances we get abroad, so money is always tight. He's on the interview board for new recruits at the moment, so he hates that too.'

Nan gave a short, knowing laugh. 'I always did wonder…'

We should have been ships that passed in the night, Rory and I, Lois thought but did not say. She had thought it often enough. Yet here they were, struggling on.

'It's not all bad. Rory's a decent man. He's never let me down,' said Lois loyally. She sensed without knowing quite why that she had to be careful what she said.

'I'm glad to hear it.'

'Tell me about you. Any good postings since Moscow?'

Nan spoke in vague terms about Washington and Bonn as the waiter brought their drinks.

They sipped in silence.

'Come on then, Nan, out with it. What's this about?'

'The cold place, I'm afraid.'

'I see.'

Nan looked around instinctively, hiding it in the actions of reaching for her cigarettes, offering and lighting one, surveying the room with an apparently disinterested flicker of her eyes. Lois knew the gesture well and wondered what it presaged.

'Old friends. Your Johann… and others. We might need to cover ourselves.'

Lois felt her hand tremble as she put down her glass. 'Go on.'

'I can't tell you everything. You know how it is.'

Ridiculous, Lois thought. Just because she was no longer actually on the pay roll. She knew well enough what went on through Rory. Helped him in ways no one in the Office could ever know. She said nothing.

'I think you know there were suspicions about Johann Dreschler.'

'Did you know that at the time, in Moscow?' asked Lois.

'I did not. Until a couple of weeks ago I knew nothing about what went on then, and what you did. Well played, Lois, I must say. Right under my nose, too. I take my hat off to you. Johann rotted up your Vienna operation, didn't he? Did he do it on purpose? That obvious honey trap... he probably orchestrated that himself.'

'Really?'

'So it seems. Gave him the excuse to go AWOL and set you up to receive Zhigunov's promised proofs at Sukhumi. Whose side was he on exactly?'

Lois looked around at the chattering, clattering London scene, the room emptying of theatregoers abruptly realising the imperative of making a seven-thirty curtain up, their places being filled on the tide of others meeting and taking a drink on the way to somewhere else. The sheer strangeness that had fallen over this normality.

'That's a lot of questions,' she said.

'The matter has become rather pressing.'

'After all this time?'

Nan spread her palms.

Lois reached for her drink. 'This makes a change, I must say. I'm usually either invisible in Office circles or I'm told by some pipsqueak straight out of Oxford that I wouldn't understand anything and can't possibly appreciate the pressure he's under because he has to write a report.' There, she'd said it, not that it would do her any good.

'So you have the advantage of him.' Nan raised a sardonic smile. 'You have proof the man's an immature idiot, while he knows nothing about you.'

Lois took a slow breath. 'I was let down by Johann in

Vienna and didn't know why. We were supposed to be working together. Before we went to Vienna, all was going to plan – as far as I knew, anyway. It was only when I got back to London I was told there were doubts about his true allegiance and they had given me a job to do that wasn't what I thought it was.' She found she was still angry about that, too.

'How many times did you see Johann after you returned from Vienna?'

A presumptive question. In Moscow, to Burville and Fielding, she had lied by omission and never reported their last meeting in Gorky Park where he briefed her about Sukhumi. She had to be careful now, though.

'Once,' she said truthfully.

'Where?'

'The cold place.'

'Not the Sea as well?'

'No. I only got a message from him there.'

'Tony Fielding followed you and Rory on your seaside holiday – did you know?'

'Yes.'

An appraising stare from Nan.

'I saw him.'

'When did you see him?'

Lois frowned. 'The morning after I met Zhigunov. Why is this suddenly important now?'

'On the night you went to meet Zhigunov, Fielding trailed you.'

'He must have been bloody good!' Lois burst out, then felt silly. Fielding was Head of Station. Why wouldn't he be good? Better, and far more experienced, than she was.

'Just as well he did,' said Nan. 'A trap had been set. We think Dreschler recruited – bribed – a band of Azkhabian thugs to pose as KGB, wanting to muddy the waters with Zhigunov.

Seems his aim was to make our operations look foolish and misguided. Luckily for you, Zhigunov was military intelligence with no squeamishness about killing.'

Lois acknowledged this.

'Now,' went on Nan. She leant forward and spoke so softly that Lois was lip-reading. 'And I shouldn't tell you this, but in the circumstances I am going to... we believe that Fielding dealt with Dreschler.'

'Johann died that night?'

'Yes.'

Lois raised a hand to her mouth, not trusting herself to say anything. The shock of hearing it, even all these years later, was acute.

'Fielding... killed him?'

'Highly irregular, of course, not to say illegal. Kept off the record ever since, but... these things have a nasty habit of surfacing.'

'You mean that's what's just happened...? How?'

'That, I can't tell you. But I do need to check with you how exactly it was that Johann Dreschler got involved with Zhigunov in the first place.'

Lois thought hard. 'I'm not sure I ever knew, exactly. Most likely Zhigunov approached him. He had tried every other avenue and been dismissed as bait. A journalist would be a less obvious conduit to the major powers but still effective.'

'How did Johann verify him?'

'Probably through an FBI man who was a contact of Johann's. I only ever knew him as Pal.'

'James Ingssen, FBI veteran. He'd been on the team that traced Donald Maclean's tracks in Washington. He spent years pointing the finger at British traitors while being ignored by their protective chums in MI6 and the CIA.'

The two women exchanged a glance. Kim Philby, for one,

was still a sore point. The spy who had done so much damage had not been definitively cornered until January 1963, when he defected to the Soviet Union and was welcomed as a hero.

Nan continued: 'Ingssen was in Russia to see what he could pick up about Zhigunov. For personal reasons, he also had a point to make about the British situation. But his job got harder when he was joined by a CIA "occasional" called Nayland, a nuclear physicist who was supposedly evaluating the Zhigunov situation from a scientific perspective. Nayland got himself murdered for his trouble.'

'This is all a matter of record now?'

'With the right security clearance.'

Lois was unsure where this was leading and how it involved her. Nan seemed already to know more than she did.

She trusted her instincts and asked: 'Tony Fielding. What happened to him?'

'Well, that's rather what this is about,' said Nan. 'He had a fine career. Went from strength to strength.'

'Went?'

'He died in a plane crash about a month ago. Small private plane over Cambodia.'

The rising conversational hubbub around them only seemed to intensify the silence that settled across their table.

'I'm sorry to hear that,' said Lois at last.

'I'm not sure you should be.'

Again, Lois waited. It was all coming back now, the underlying fear that never faded, the ever-present threat – but of what? What could be a threat to her now, sitting over gin and tonic with an old colleague in her home city? The unexpected conversation had unsettled her for no reason, she decided.

'Tony Fielding was an adventurer with a reckless streak,' stated Nan. 'We don't run black operations, not officially, at least. We certainly don't turn a blind eye to maverick officers seeking to act for personal gain in the course of their duties. But we will cover up for them if their nefarious activities come to light. We have to, obviously.'

'What are you saying?'

'Tony had lucrative side deals wherever he went. Not traitorous ones, never that. He was Establishment through and through, in his way. But he got in deep to every situation, let's put it that way. The flight that came down in Phnom Penh was – somewhat predictably given Fielding's involvement – carrying gold for the opium trade. Most likely he would have had a personal stake in some of it. But he would also have been gathering exceptional intelligence. No doubt he would have said there was no other way, and he may have been right.'

'Go on.'

A sigh. 'He had a knack of getting lucky, knowing the right people at any given time. Not always a good thing, especially if big money and valuable information are involved. Word is, maybe he knew too much, had done too much.'

Lois allowed the silence to curl in the air to the point of discomfort between them before she spoke.

'So the question is, why did he kill Johann – did Johann have something on him?'

'*Did* Johann?' Nan asked.

'I have no idea. If he did, he never said.' A pause. 'And Fielding knew more than I did about Johann all along?'

'Oh, I would have thought so, wouldn't you? Johann ever mention a Swiss banker in Moscow? Ever say that Fielding knew him?'

'Not that I remember. Look, Nan, play straight with me. What's this really all about?'

Nan picked up her cigarette case, turned it around but did not open it. She did not look up.

'The Johann Dreschler story is seeping out. The usual way. Ingssen decides to let a ghostwriter loose on his Cold War memoirs, journalists both sides of the Atlantic pick up on the stray bullets and throw everything at finding out who fired them. Then suddenly there's a nice current angle with Tony Fielding's demise. The Dreschler business is going to be embarrassing enough – I assume you knew the gist of it – and we'll do our best to downplay it. Keep you out of it, obviously.

'So far, it seems the Fleet Street defence correspondent taking the most interest here has proved susceptible to a certain pressure, shall we say, to ignore the connection with Tony Fielding, and we'll do our level best to keep it that way. But the Zhigunov angle is a different matter. There's so much re-evaluation of those frozen years going on. Was your Sukhumi drop of Zhigunov's material collected by Fielding? What became of it? That's the question. The Office only ever had your account and photographic evidence. You're the vital link, Lois.'

'There's nothing I can tell you. I simply don't know. Anything I did know, I put in my report to London after the fact.' And faithfully reiterated to the anonymous Peter Committee before she had been so carelessly discarded.

'We need to see your diary, just to check,' said Nan. 'I'm sorry to have to ask.'

Lois shivered. It seemed extraordinary, but was it possible they were suspicious of her?

'Miss Harcourt's diary,' she said evenly. 'For just such an eventuality.'

'Standard procedure, I'm afraid.'

A few weeks later, a lead feature appeared in the *Sunday Telegraph*. Window dressed with a black-and-white composite illustration of Cold War thriller clichés, it exposed Johann

Dreschler, journalist and sometime MI6 agent, as a Hungarian spy. Son of an Austrian postmaster, a committed anti-fascist, and a Hungarian mother, Dreschler was born in the Austrian countryside east of Vienna, close to the border with Hungary. During the Second World War, father and son had helped the Allies' secret communication network in Hungary.

The British intelligence services had made use of Johann Dreschler after the war in Berlin and maintained a connection with him as he advanced in his newspaper career. He was a trusted and highly effective operator, especially in the political sphere. When he was given a posting to the Budapest bureau of the *Frankfurter Allgemeiner Zeitung* in 1955, Dreschler also went with a brief from MI6. He was close to his mother's relatives and shared their horror of the authoritarian regime imposed by the Soviets post-war, considering it as bad as the fascism that had been defeated.

All went well until the failed Hungarian Uprising in 1956 and its brutal crushing by Soviet forces. The Hungarian revolutionaries had been assured that the Western powers would support them but in the end, the West looked the other way and did nothing. After that, it seemed, Johann Dreschler felt let down by the West.

Ostensibly, he continued to work for MI6, but he was a man on his own mission. He seemed to be using the contacts MI6 provided to uncover information for his own unknown purposes. Some claimed Dreschler was a secret communist, though this seemed highly unlikely. Given the doubts being raised, a special operation was mounted in 1958 to ascertain his true allegiance. This took place in Moscow, where he was Russia Correspondent for a leading German newspaper; he was also, as so often, in the pay of a special branch of MI6 under his journalistic cover. In May of that year, he stopped taking orders from London and went rogue. Some claimed he was associated with money and influence brokers who operated between the great powers, a man who gathered inside information from both East and West to use as personal currency. But whether this was indeed the case, or he was simply an adventurer, was unclear.

Whatever the truth, Dreschler was a dubious character in a complex puzzle, though conspiracy theorists had it that he had received from a mysterious GRU Colonel Avrely Zhigunov evidence that the Soviet military was far less advanced in nuclear technology than supposed in the West, information that Colonel Oleg Penkovsky later passed to the West, just in time to save the world from annihilation over the Cuban Missile Crisis in 1962. Zhigunov himself was prone to make wild claims about an all-powerful international syndicate that manipulated world events from the shadows and would kill to keep their secrets and control, which may or may not have been why he disappeared sometime in 1959, having been first incarcerated in a mental asylum. He was believed executed by the Soviets after a summary trial, foreshadowing the fate of Penkovsky in 1963.

Dreschler's end was equally uncertain. According to the article, he left Moscow in mid-1958 and was last seen in the Black Sea resort of Sukhumi in September of that year. It was probably no coincidence that Zhigunov was also there, attending a national conference on nuclear power. Either Dreschler went to ground, or, more likely, he was quietly dealt with by the Russians who had been watching Zhigunov.

There was no mention of Tony Fielding. If he did know too much, as Nan inferred, then the Establishment were interested not so much in protecting his reputation as their own.

The story was buried after a day or two. The book the piece was based on was badly reviewed across the board and, according to the woman who ran Lois's local bookshop, had subsequent distribution problems. Evidently, some truths were only true when the right people decided they were, no matter what other facts might show.

Lois's 1958 diary arrived back in the post the next day like an expired passport, with the same blank compliments slip.

It was Monday morning. Rory was at work, the girls at school.

Lois went upstairs and made the beds. At her dressing table, she picked up her tin-framed photograph of Zell-am-Ziller. The pressed edelweiss in the corner, still velvety and pale yellow, was the one Johann gave her. She contemplated the mountain valley with its lovely village and the flower for a few minutes before she carefully opened up the back of the frame. The hair she had stuck over a join was undisturbed.

Under a layer of thin card behind the photo was a strip of negative camera film. Between further layers of flimsy paper were a single negative and a homemade print, also from Johann Dreschler: the snatched shot he had taken at the Hotel Ukraina of the man whose name she should never know. She had fretted how she would ever keep this evidence safe from discovery in Moscow. In the end, she had put it in a letter home, not to Miss Elsie Glover in Heathview Court but to her mother in Brockley, asking her to keep the enclosure unopened for her return; she had cautiously waited until the very last moment to slip it into the diplomatic bag as it was closing.

In the light of the bedroom window, overlooking her safe suburban back garden, Lois held up the strip of negatives. Two frames seemed to show documents, and two frames were group photos showing water and hills behind. She set this cache down carefully on the bedspread and went to her sewing table on the landing. She slid open the lid and lifted out a tray containing needles, cotton reels in all colours and spare bobbins, and another of scissors and other tools. Under this was a collection of paper dressmaking patterns, from one of which she pulled a small clipping from a newspaper.

Picking up a magnifying glass from the sewing table, she returned to the bedroom. Now she opened the travel trunk under the window and quickly found a package of old photographs rejected as not good enough for a place in an album. Among these was a print she had made herself in Peking during a crash course in photographic techniques and developing given by one of the other wives; there was always a need to stave off boredom during the day and have a new interest and topic to talk about at the endless, mindless parties in another closed community.

Lois sat down on the trunk and examined these relics of another life carefully: the negatives she took from the Zhigunov package in Sukhumi; Johann's shot of the Swiss banker; the tightly folded photo cut from a German newspaper that showed the same man in a group at Chartwell with Churchill and President Truman, dated 1952; the enlarged print she made from the Zhigunov negatives. Stalin, still supreme, was instantly recognisable. In 1951, Stalin had spent five months at his Black Sea dacha in Abkhazia, not far from Sukhumi. It seemed to Lois highly likely that the group photograph was taken there. The nameless Swiss deal broker struck the same powerful pose as he did with the Western leaders.

She stared at the ceiling. Thought of Zhigunov, his courage and his words about the human condition. '*We make mistakes not because we cannot see the truth but because we do not want to believe it.*' She thought of Nan and Elsie, both still career women in a man's world. Their subterfuge and the engineered meeting at Charing Cross had opened a wound. *Et tu, Elsie.* Why set her up like that – what had made them suspect her? Lois's memory was sharp as ever – no, sharper. It snagged too often on all the stupid, disdainful men who had used her and cast her aside. The Peter Committee. The arrogant young second secretaries at embassy parties who could barely bring themselves to notice the wives, let alone converse with them. She was as invisible as ever.

More fool them, thought Lois as she gathered up her own small fragments of history, this inconvenient, unwanted history. She remained still for a few seconds, then crumpled them in one fist. Down in the kitchen, she took out scissors and a small rusting tin that once contained tobacco and snipped the negatives into shards over it. They caught the sun as they fell, flickers of dirty lightning. She did the same with the prints, then struck a match and used the newspaper clipping as a taper.

The fire wouldn't catch. Down the hall the letterbox on the front door rattled. Something fell on the mat below. Another match, trembling fingers. All was raw again: the sulphur scent of danger, the terror of discovery, of knowing she was on her own with this and had been since the beginning.

At last, flames licked the tiny pyre. It was just like old times.

AUTHOR'S AFTERWORD

Joy, in the mid-1950s

This novel is based on my mother Joy's experiences in Moscow in 1958 and the diary she wrote that year. Some of the words used as Lois's diary entries are only lightly edited from the original. The dropped glove passage at the end was also written by my mother, taken from pages of creative writing she kept for decades. I never knew until I found this cache after she died that as a young woman she had harboured hopes of writing a book. It was typical that she never told me, even as I began to be published.

Apart from the obvious dramatic fiction – there was no personal quest for proof about a traitor or a Russian spy; the imaginary Zhigunov is a precursor of Oleg Penkovsky a few years later – most of the contemporary details are authentic. The brief mention of John Vassall, the Admiralty clerk who had been at the Moscow Embassy in the 1950s, is true (he was not arrested until 1962). It was a jittery time for MI6 in 1958. Despite so many suspicions about him, Kim Philby, the "Third Man" in the traitorous Cambridge spy ring with Guy Burgess and Donald Maclean, was living in Beirut, ostensibly working as a journalist for the *Observer* and the *Economist*, but covertly being paid both by MI6 and the KGB. He would not be forced to defect to Moscow until January 1963.

My mother worked nominally as the personal assistant to the Minister at the British Embassy in Moscow and was previously in The Hague for two and a half years. At the embassy in Moscow, she met my father, Stan, who was nearly six years younger, a bright but unassuming young man from Lancashire who set out to win her away from her cultured, older German boyfriend and eventually succeeded. He sent an unexpected proposal by telegram from London after he had left Moscow, which she recklessly accepted. They married six weeks later on her return, and my sister and I grew up with their stories of bugged apartments and stormy romance trailed by the KGB.

The oblique conversations I had with my mother about her career were a thread that ran through our close relationship, though it was only after an intriguing event when she visited me at Cambridge that I began to make imaginative connections. It would be many decades before she took me over to one of the overflowing bookshelves in her upstairs sitting room in Chislehurst and pulled out Keith Jeffery's *The Secret History of MI6, 1909–1949* saying, 'This one's interesting, though it doesn't go up quite far enough. Of course, we never talked about what we did.'

She had always been generous with her past, quick to derive pleasure from recounting her traveller's tales and stories of her old romances, and happy to answer questions about her experiences. I realised then how selective she had been under the guise of complete openness.

The past was never very far from the present. It resonated throughout my childhood, imbued in the England that was often far away: the war my parents experienced as children; the fateful meeting in Moscow; Kuwait, at that time little more than a desert frontier town with oil wells and dust roads, where they were posted after their marriage in March 1959. By odd coincidence, Joy and Stan were living there when Kim Philby visited Kuwait on a fact-finding mission in 1960. I was born while they were living there. Then came Peking, as it then still was, exciting and full of friendly, smiling people until the clamp-down of Mao's Cultural Revolution in late 1966. When it became too dangerous for Westerners to remain in China, my mother bravely brought me and my younger sister out on a train full of Red Guards, revolutionary music playing loudly on the Tannoy system. We returned to London via Hong Kong, while my father stayed.

When my parents entertained, which was often when we were abroad, the talk was all of foreign postings and people and upheavals, political and personal. The cold grey atmosphere and underlying threat of Soviet Russia loomed large. It was a lot for an observant child to take in. I would sit quietly, lest I be told to go out of the room, absorbing it all, as the tales rolled out of people who had disappeared, what had been tried to save them, or find them, or help them across a border, like the European nuns who had taught me and other international children at the Convent of the Sacred Heart, the last Catholic school in China. Ludicrously accused of being foreign spies, the nuns were publicly humiliated, and the building sacked by

Red Guards, a scene we children had witnessed as we arrived for school one morning. We had wanted to jump out and save them, but the driver of the embassy bus wisely put his foot on the accelerator and drove us swiftly back to the diplomatic compound.

As we were growing up, my mother made sure my sister Helen and I knew that she thought satisfying careers for girls were far more important than finding husbands. Though in the long run, husbands and families were to be encouraged, they shouldn't be considered until we had plenty of life experience. When I left school after taking Oxbridge entrance examinations in December, I found she had booked me a secretarial course in Brussels, where we were living at the time, starting in January. Her reasoning was simple: with typing and shorthand skills, I would be able to earn good money in the university holidays and would always have something to fall back on. I did wonder, even then, whether there was a subtext. She wanted me to understand that clever girls could forge interesting careers by careful choice of which typewriters to bash. 'I was a lot more than a secretary,' she used to tell me, though that was decades before I understood what she meant.

Your relationship with your parents changes for the last time after they die. Their story becomes clearer, from diaries and letters that had remained private during their lifetime. It becomes a family history, and on the way, it recalibrates your own.

Joy would have had a natural aptitude for intelligence work. Despite her beauty, she was self-effacing almost to a fault. She did not court attention and was irritated by those who did. She was analytical and patient, interested in psychology and sociology; her nature was self-sufficient, and she was extremely hard-working and reliable. She was often underestimated which, while useful in such work, left an abiding distaste for being taken for granted. The casual arrogance of men, especially the young Foreign Office high-flyers who dismissed her as just another wife, would infuriate her and she, of course, could reveal nothing to put them right.

A long-time friend of my mother's, who also worked in British intelligence, has confirmed to me several key assumptions: that young people who did not have the social and university connections that had led to the misplaced trust that had proved so fatal to the services were indeed recruited in the 1950s after the Burgess and Maclean debacle; that contrary to many public accounts implying stalemate under heavy surveillance, agent-running was extremely active at the British Embassy in Moscow at this time; and, most importantly, that it was entirely plausible that an MI6 service member might be infiltrated unobtrusively under deep cover in order to observe any possible weak links or suspicious activity within the ranks of a crucial diplomatic mission at this most sensitive time.

I must make it clear that my mother never discussed any specific work she did, but I came to her diary for 1958 knowing what she had finally admitted, that she had worked for MI6 and that 'there were four of us who knew all the secrets' at the embassy in Moscow. Realistically, I think she must have meant there were four secretaries who took the secret work, rather than only four people in the whole embassy, but as my father once said, 'You never know, with your mother.' As in the novel, my father remained all his life a closed book regarding the specifics of his own career.

One name in the diary particularly sparked my interest: Harry Rigby, for whom Joy typed lengthy reports. Rigby, I discovered, was an Australian academic who specialised in the Soviet Union and was an advisor to MI6 at the Moscow embassy. He went on to become one of the West's most respected Sovietologists. It ought to go without saying, but just to be clear: the character of Bill Stoneley is completely fictional and owes only his nationality and embassy status to the eminent Professor T H Rigby, in tribute to him and the fascination with which I read his posthumously published *Memoirs of a Bourgeois Falsifier*.

Even had they wanted to, my parents could not have returned to Sukhumi, scene of their memorable first holiday together on the shores of the Black Sea. The pleasure piers of Sukhumi are still there, rusting and suspended in time. The grand old Intourist hotel and Soviet government buildings are pitted with bullet holes. The airport and fine railway station have been abandoned to romantic decay. Scarred by battle, the city remains a chimera of the Stalinist era.

These days, Sukhumi is the capital of the breakaway Georgian republic of Abkhazia and as off-grid to foreign tourists now as it was in the 1950s. It has had a complicated history since the collapse of the Soviet Union and war between Georgian government forces and Abkhazian separatists. Only Russia and a handful of other countries recognise Abkhazia as an independent nation despite its declaration in 1994. Abkhazia has a gritty population of about two hundred and fifty thousand – they drove out the last of Georgia's troops in 2008. Meanwhile, Moscow has tightened its control over this lush coastal area and a second breakaway Georgian region, South Ossetia. When the Russian holidaymakers began to trickle back, for many it was with nostalgia for bygone times, to a ghost nation defended by a ragtag Abkhazian army and a Russian military base, its Stalinist architecture preserved by dereliction.

As in any novel, there are small parts that are true and large parts that are not, small details that are invented and a big picture that may or may not be true. A novel of uncertainties, then – and the question of where that leaves those of us in real life who caught clues and glimpses of history and could only wonder what it really meant.

Some people – perhaps most people – want to seem more than they are. Very few people are content being more than they seem, but my mother was one of them. She seized her chance to have an exciting career, having spotted what she described as 'an intriguing and beautifully worded' advertisement in the *Times*, then married and had children while travelling and experiencing life in other countries. 'Don't be sad for me,' she told me during her final weeks. 'I've had a long and interesting life.' She was very nearly eighty-seven, a woman of her time, and for most of her generation that was about as close as it came to having it all.

Finally, and very importantly, I want to thank my wonderful sister Helen, whose support for the writing of this book has been unwavering and whose input and memories have been invaluable.